D1349613

The Ugly Truth

The Ugly Truth

L. C. NORTH

BANTAM PRESS

TRANSWORLD PUBLISHERS
Penguin Random House, One Embassy Gardens,
8 Viaduct Gardens, London SW11 7BW
www.penguin.co.uk

Transworld is part of the Penguin Random House group of companies
whose addresses can be found at global.penguinrandomhouse.com

First published in Great Britain in 2023 by Bantam Press
an imprint of Transworld Publishers

A CIP catalogue record for this book
is available from the British Library.

ISBNs 9781787636378 (hb)
9781787636385 (tpb)

Typeset in 12/16 pt Dante MT Std by Jouve (UK), Milton Keynes
Printed and bound in Great Britain by Clays Ltd, Elcograf S.p.A.

The authorized representative in the EEA is Penguin Random House Ireland,
Morrison Chambers, 32 Nassau Street, Dublin D02 YH68.

Penguin Random House is committed to a sustainable
future for our business, our readers and our planet. This book
is made from Forest Stewardship Council® certified paper.

PART I

Melanie Lange video 1/9
Published on Melanie Lange YouTube channel on 2 August 2022

I'm Melanie Lange. Today's date is the seventeenth of June 2022. I can't give you any proof because I have no access to the news. The only reason I have a phone is because it was smuggled to me earlier this week.

I'm recording this video from the bathroom of the house I've been locked in for the last four months. I've got the shower running and I'm whispering but I need to be quick. There's a guard in the next room. No lock. This is the only room in the house with a door. This is the only time I'm ever alone.

[Pause]

[Crying] I'm a prisoner. I'm not allowed to leave. There is someone watching me every minute of the day.

[Gasping] I don't know where I am but I believe it's somewhere in England. It's a private estate with no escape and no other houses anywhere nearby. The house is modern, newly built and on the coast somewhere. There's a cliff that leads down to a small private beach. I'm trapped. I can't leave. I've not seen or spoken to my . . . [crying] . . . my beautiful, precious boys for four months. I miss them so much. All I want is to hold them in my arms.

My father, Peter Lange, brought me here on the fourteenth of February. He tricked me into recording a video for my YouTube channel, telling people that I was taking some time away from the public eye. I thought it was for a few days. Not this . . . this hell. Please help me!

MELANIE LANGE: MY FATHER IS KEEPING ME PRISONER

Former model and businesswoman Melanie Lange (34) has appeared in secret video recordings claiming she is being held prisoner by her father, billionaire business tycoon Sir Peter Lange, in a 'private estate with no escape'.

The two videos, which have now been released, show a distressed Melanie begging for help. 'I've not seen or spoken to my beautiful, precious boys for four months.' Her two sons, Sebastian (6) and William (5), currently live with their father, entrepreneur Finn Parker.

The first video was allegedly recorded on 17 June of this year and sent to close friend and personal assistant Nell Stevens, who kept the videos private following Melanie's instructions. Posting her own video to Melanie Lange's YouTube channel, Nell said: 'Melanie wanted to find a way to free herself that didn't involve the media. These videos were her safety net should all else fail. She asked me to keep them safe and only publish them if contact between us stopped. And it has. I'm deeply concerned for her safety.'

Melanie has not been seen publicly since her birthday celebrations ended in chaos in February.

Sir Peter Lange, who made his money in a global hotel chain (Lange Hotels) in the nineties, was not available for comment.

Statement from Sir Peter Lange, 6 August 2022
Read by a spokesperson for Lange Hotels

Following a breakdown earlier this year, my daughter, Melanie Lange, is currently being treated at a private mental health facility supported by medical professionals. She is safe and healthy and grows stronger every day. She will return to public life as soon as she is able.

The media reports released this week are not reflective of the actual situation, but we would like to thank everyone who has raised concerns for her safety and reassure all of her fans that Melanie is being well cared for by people who have her best interests at heart.

Extract from National Newspaper, 18 August 2022

NETFLIX COMMISSIONS DOCUMENTARY ON MELANIE LANGE STORY

Netflix has announced today that it has commissioned a documentary on Melanie Lange's disappearance which will start filming next month and be aired in October. This tell-all three-part documentary series, titled *The Ugly Truth*, will delve into Melanie's rise to fame and promises to uncover the truth behind Melanie Lange's reported imprisonment by her father. No one from the Lange family is thought to be taking part.

Twitter
18 August 2022

Connie Rose @Wannabeawritergirl
#SaveMelanie I love ya girl!

James Hilton @James_T_Hilton
Who actually cares about #TheUglyTruth?? This is just another stunt by an attention-seeking woman! #MelanieLangeHoax

> **Tahlia J @TahliaJenkins55**
> YES!!! Next week they'll be launching a new product for sure! #MelanieLangeHoax

Kaitlyn M Davids @Mummyrulestheroost
OMFG how is this woman still a prisoner? Let's finally get #TheUglyTruth #SaveMelanie

Jane Godfellow @WorldofCats2002
I knew there was something off about Melanie's last YouTube video! It had a really bad vibe. She's been imprisoned by her father for 6 MONTHS!!!!! #SaveMelanie

Lucie Bolton @LucieBoltonOfficial
Is it any wonder #MelanieLange went totally off the rails with the way the British media have hounded her her whole life? Her dad is clearly looking out for her #HelpPeter

Richard T Maloney @Richard&LesleyM
This is a private family matter surrounding a woman's mental health problems. Why can't everyone just leave this family alone? #HelpPeter

Jessie W @Jessiebakescakes4U
This would never have happened to a man! #SaveMelanie

Amy B @GirlAboutTownBlog
Guys!!!!! Who else is excited about #TheUglyTruth???? I'm #SaveMelanie
ALL THE WAY!

Kaitlyn M Davids @Mummyrulestheroost
You are such a hypocrite @GirlAboutTownBlog! How can you be
#SaveMelanie after everything you've said about her?

Netflix Original Documentary:
Melanie Lange – The Ugly Truth

INTERVIEWS RECORDED 19–22 SEPTEMBER 2022
(220 DAYS SINCE MELANIE'S DISAPPEARANCE)

Narrator

In 2003 fifteen-year-old Melanie Lange stepped into the limelight as one of Britain's most famous models. By the summer of 2005 her modelling career would be over and yet for nineteen years, Melanie Lange has been one of the country's most recognized celebrities, facing intense media scrutiny and nearly two decades of public fascination with her private life.

But on the fourteenth of February 2022, after posting an emotional video on her YouTube channel, Melanie Lange disappeared from the public eye, from her role as CEO of Lange Cosmetics and Baby Lange, and from her life.

VIDEO FOOTAGE. SOURCE:
YOUTUBE, MELANIE LANGE CHANNEL

Date posted: 14 February 2022

Hey folks, this is a super-quick video I wanted to post as I know a lot of you are worried about me after seeing the news over the weekend. The last few months have been the hardest of my life and . . . Well, the truth is, I haven't been coping well. I'm sorry for the distress I've caused my family and my fans. I'll . . . I'll be OK.

[Pause]

I'm going to take some time out now to get some help and work on my mental health.

I love you all!

Narrator

It looked to the world as though Melanie had stepped out of the limelight and all public appearances to recuperate from a public breakdown widely thought to be due to her divorce and losing custody of her two children.

No one close to Melanie has seen her since this video was posted. Not her best friend. Not her ex-husband. And most notably, not her children. Only Melanie's father, Sir Peter Lange, claims to have seen Melanie after the fourteenth of February. And now, in a shocking revelation, secret videos released on the second of August this year tell a different story.

VIDEO FOOTAGE. SOURCE:
YOUTUBE, MELANIE LANGE CHANNEL

Date posted: 2 August 2022

I'm a prisoner. I'm not allowed to leave.

Narrator

In nine emotional videos, Melanie describes in detail her imprisonment at the hands of her father. While those closest to Melanie fear for her safety, Sir Peter Lange has released his own statement, urging Melanie's fans not to believe these claims.

Are these videos the desperate actions of a deeply troubled woman driven to a breakdown by a life lived in the harsh glare of the tabloid media, or are they the result of a controlling father who'll do anything to protect his daughter and his business?

This is the story of what happened to Melanie Lange: her rise to fame, her fall from grace, and her troubled relationship with her father – one of the wealthiest and most powerful businessmen in the world. This is the ugly truth of Melanie Lange.

Nell

I'm Nell Stevens. I'm Melanie Lange's personal assistant and her best friend. I first met Melanie in 2003 when we were both signed with First Models, a modelling agency in Soho. I was sixteen at the time, nearly seventeen. Melanie was fifteen, not that you'd have known that from looking at her. We were both sent to this god-awful casting in some warehouse in East London. The photographer was late and we were sat around for hours. I noticed Melanie straight away because she had her nose in a book. Some business manual or something. It was unusual, you know? The rest of us had magazines or were just chatting. It was 2003 and iPhones weren't a thing then. God, that makes me feel old.

Vic Watson, tabloid editor

Melanie captured the eye of the photographers and the public straight away. She was a gorgeous young woman. The big brown Bambi eyes, a smattering of freckles across her nose. Lips that looked like they were drawn on, they were so perfect. Slim, but with hips and tits and this long shiny brown hair. Melanie Lange radiated health and wealth.

Nell

Just looking at Melanie I knew there was no way I was getting the job, but we got talking and something just clicked with us. People talk about soulmates when it comes to relationships, but I think your soulmate can be a friend, and I certainly felt like that with Melanie. We had such different backgrounds. Melanie grew up in a mansion. She went to private school. Her family had a chauffeur, for God's sake, that's how rich they were. I grew up on spaghetti hoops and Birds Eye Crispy Pancakes. I went to the kind of school where there was one maths book for four of us and it usually had dicks drawn over the pages.

But something between me and Melanie clicked, and we saw each other every day after that first meeting – if her dad would let us, that was. I think sometimes I'm the only one who really knows her. Not this party-girl screw-up the British press always want her to be, or the innocent little girl her dad sees her as, but the real her. The real Melanie. One of the things I wish people knew about Melanie is how generous she is. She has this almost sixth sense when it comes to understanding people. Like she can see a step ahead of someone and be there for them with whatever they need.

The last seven months without Melanie have been the hardest of my life. I miss her so much. My life feels empty without her in it, but worse than that feeling is this constant weight in the pit of my stomach, this fear. I'm so worried about Mel right now. This whole situation is insane. I can't believe the police haven't arrested Sir Peter.

Brian Bent, modelling agent
Melanie and Nell were both stunning girls. From the moment they met, they were inseparable. We called them the twins at the agency. 'Where are the twins today?'

[Laughs]

It wasn't really a fair assessment though. Don't get me wrong, Nell was beautiful, but it was manufactured. She had the extensions, the brows, a nose job in her teens. For Melanie it was effortless. There was never a bad photo or a wrong angle for Melanie. She could have gone all the way if she'd wanted to, but she treated modelling like a Saturday job. Nell was the one who was focused and worked hard. I think she could have done well for herself as a model. She certainly had the right attitude, but she stuck with Melanie and got dragged into her dramas and missed her shot.

Vic Watson, tabloid editor
When Melanie first came on the scene, she was the quintessential girl next door. Girls wanted to be her; boys wanted to sleep with her. From the moment she stepped on to that red carpet at the launch of the Lange London in 2003, she was destined to be a star.

SIR PETER LANGE —
MY SIDE OF THE STORY (UNPUBLISHED)

*Interviews between ghost writer Ryan Morris
and Peter Lange, 3 October 2022*

Ryan: Sir Peter, first of all, thank you for clearing so much of your diary to speak to me this week.

Peter: Not a problem. Do you want a coffee? I can buzz my secretary.

Ryan: The water is fine, thanks. As I'm sure you know from the publisher, the publication date for your autobiography has been brought forward to capitalize on recent media attention surrounding your family. For obvious reasons, the focus of the biography is now going to be on your relationship with your daughter, Melanie Lange.

Peter: So it would seem. Please remember that I have full approval of all copy. The last thing my family needs is more lies being told about them. It's important to me that people – Melanie's fans – hear the actual truth.

Ryan: Absolutely, of course. We're on the same team, Sir Peter. I'm recording these sessions so there can be no mixing of words. I'll be filling in the gaps with the puff about the whens and wheres, but the personal stuff is all you.

Peter: Let's get on with it then.

Ryan: Right, yes. I'm sorry for diving in with this one: You lost your wife, Linda Lange, to aggressive breast cancer in the summer of 2002. Can you tell me about the immediate aftermath for you and your daughters, Zara and Melanie, and how you coped with this tragic loss?

Peter: You don't mess about, do you? I like that.

There are no words to truly describe the grief I felt at losing Linda. It was the worst time of my life. Linda supported me, inspired me, she made me laugh, she told me off when I did things wrong. And let me tell you – there comes a point in life for those who reach a certain level of success, like I've done, when the people around them become too scared to say when that person is doing things wrong, but not Linda. She saved me from making some terrible business decisions. Anytime I had an idea, it was always Linda I went to first. She was every bit as business-minded as I was, but the moment she fell pregnant with Zara she was adamant she wanted to stay home.

Linda's death hit me hard and broke my heart, but it hit the girls a lot harder. Linda was a fantastic mother. She was there at every assembly, every bake sale, every party; everything those girls did or wanted to do, Linda was there, cheering them on. She was their world. I'm ashamed to say that I missed most of their childhoods building up Lange Hotels. When Linda died, Zara was eighteen and studying for her A Levels, Mellie was fourteen, and I remember when the dust was settling that summer, there was this feeling of a huge void in our family.

Ryan: How did you cope on a practical level after Linda's death?

Peter: At first we tried Zara looking out for Mellie in between studying, but that didn't work out too well. Those girls are chalk and cheese. Linda was the bridge between the girls. I had hoped that the shared grief of losing their mother would create a bond between them, but it didn't.

Zara and Mellie didn't hate each other. They never have, despite what the media would have you believe. They're sisters and they love each other. They got on fine. They hung out in front of the TV – you know, normal sister stuff.

I shouldn't have asked Zara to look out for Mellie. Zara had enough to cope with, and as with everything Zara does, she took the role seriously, nagging Mellie to do her homework and tidy up. That kind of thing. But Mellie has never been the type to take orders, and it caused friction between the girls.

So I asked my neighbour at the time – a woman called Sunny – if she could help out. I thought of her as a housekeeper, I suppose – an ageing matriarch type who could cook the meals and do the washing while the girls were at school. Sunny was a widow too and her children had grown up and left home. I thought Sunny's care would give the girls someone to come home to. But Mellie was having none of it. She did everything she could to avoid coming home. She'd stay at friends' houses overnight whenever she could, or she'd linger at school or at the park as long as possible. I got the message loud and clear that no one was going to fill Linda's shoes.

It was a worrying time. Even more than the devastation I felt at losing Linda was the fear I felt for the girls, especially Mellie.

Ryan: What were you scared of?

Peter: I was scared I'd lose them as well if I didn't do something drastic. So I did the only thing I could think of. I cut back my hours at the office. I worked from home whenever I could, and I made sure I was there for the girls every day after school and college, in the evenings and at the weekends.

It almost cost me my business. The board weren't thrilled with the prospect of me spending time away from the office. They couldn't see the vision I had for Lange Hotels. Of course it all worked out, but it wasn't perfect by any means. I was being pulled in a lot of directions, but first and foremost I started to realize that I knew nothing about my daughters' lives. I took the time to get to know them better and spent some proper time with them.

I once read that people think we lived in a palace with servants and gold-plated teacups, but it was total bullshit. It was just me and the girls.

Ryan: You mentioned Zara and Melanie were chalk and cheese. In what ways were they different?

Peter: In every way. Zara is tall like me. Pretty in her own way, not that she's ever cared about her appearance beyond looking presentable. Back then, she was focused on her studies and was set on joining the business straight after her A Levels. She'd been helping out answering phones and doing admin in the holidays for years. It was a very natural step for Zara to join Lange Hotels. I felt, rightly or wrongly, that she was on track. She's always had her head screwed on right.

Mellie was the opposite in a lot of ways. She was smart but didn't apply herself back then. She has always been beautiful, but it was never just about her looks. People are drawn to Mellie. This was the case even before the fame. I can't tell you the rage a father feels when they witness their twelve-year-old girl getting cat-called from a passing van.

Everything came easy for Mellie. Maths, English, P.E. There was no subject she didn't excel at. It was that, in part, that caused tension between Zara and Mellie. Zara got the grades, but she worked for them, and it was frustrating for her to see Mellie achieve the same results with none of the effort. Like I said, they bickered sometimes. Show me two sisters who haven't at some point in their lives.

Ryan: When you say bicker—

Peter: Stupid stuff. Mellie would goad Zara about not having to study, and Zara would respond by calling Mellie an airhead. For Mellie's part, she couldn't understand what all the fuss was about. She thought everyone was like her. She didn't feel like she had to try and that's not a great attitude to have. Linda got the best out of Mellie in a way that I never could. I still can't.

Netflix Original Documentary:
Melanie Lange – The Ugly Truth

INTERVIEWS RECORDED 19–22 SEPTEMBER 2022
(220 DAYS SINCE MELANIE'S DISAPPEARANCE)

Narrator

Melanie Lange may have stolen the heart of the nation when she first stepped on to the red carpet in 2003, but just one year earlier at the tender age of fourteen, she experienced her own devastating heartbreak when her mother, Linda Lange, died following a short battle with breast cancer.

Nell

I wish I'd known Melanie when her mum died. I wish I could have been there for her, that she'd had someone she could lean on. She didn't speak about her mum much, or her grief, but it was always there with her, like an extra shadow. When she did talk about it, it was clear that on top of the grief there was a deep loneliness too. Mel told me once that she'd always felt like Zara belonged to her dad and she belonged to her mum, so losing her mum hit her like a freight train. It affected her whole life, especially when Mel became a mum herself. I think it hit home all over again how much she'd lost.

From everything Mel has told me, it seemed like her mum's death was when Sir Peter first started trying to take control of her life. He didn't have much to do with her before that.

Bruno Kowalski, former Chief Operating Officer for Lange Hotels Limited

I was working real close with Peter back in 2002 when his wife died. It was a hard time for him, everyone could see that, but I don't think anyone expected what happened next. I certainly didn't. You don't

16

build a global empire from scratch without working hard – really damn hard. Peter put in the hours. Long days. Weekends. He was always in the office. He and Linda had a real typical marriage. He went to work and Linda stayed at home and raised the kids. It didn't work for everyone. Hell, it didn't work for me and my ex, but it seemed to work for them.

I remember Sir Peter coming into my office not long after Linda's death and agonizing over what to do with Melanie. Zara was all set – she had a role on the graduate scheme lined up for that summer – but Sir Peter thought that Melanie was too young to live on her own. I suggested a boarding school. I gave him the details of the one my kids went to in Berkshire, and when he left my office I thought that was the end of it. The next thing I know, he sends a company-wide email announcing a change in the business. He said, 'I want to be at home for my girls after school, and if I'm going to change my hours so I can raise my family, then it's only fair that everyone else working for Lange Hotels should have that chance too.'

You have to remember that this was before flexible working was even a thing. Companies at the top like we were didn't do different working hours or part-time. And it wasn't just those in the business side of things. The email went out to everyone, in every hotel, right the way down to the hotel cleaners.

As soon as I read the email, I thought that was it for the business. I phoned up the Chief Financial Officer at the time and I said, 'If everyone goes part-time, then Lange is going under. We'd better start updating our CVs.' I wasn't alone in that thinking, but it didn't matter. Nothing anyone said was going to change things. We all knew that when Sir Peter wanted something, he got it.

By the end of the following week, Sir Peter had hired an entire HR team to roll out flexible working. And hey, I'm the first to put my hands up and admit when I'm wrong. And I was wrong then. Within three months of launching flexible working, productivity went through the roof. Employee satisfaction was at an all-time high. We were paying people for four days' work and they were so grateful to get that time off that they were squeezing in five or six days' worth. We were voted best employer seven years in a row. Sir Peter was proud of that, but he did it for the very real reason that he wanted to raise those girls himself.

It was a good example of Sir Peter deciding something and pushing it through. He had a hand in everything that went on at Lange. I wouldn't say he *liked* to be in control. It was more of a need for him. From what I saw, Sir Peter treated his girls a lot like his business. Only he knew what was best. In the same way that he'd do anything to keep his business on track, I truly believe he'd do anything to keep Zara and Melanie safe and make them happy.

I don't have the first clue what's going on inside Lange Hotels any more. I left years ago, but my take on it is this: if Sir Peter has got Melanie locked up somewhere, and I'm not saying he has, but if there's any truth to it, then it's because Sir Peter is protecting what he loves – his business, the girls, whichever one.

Sunny Bhatt, family friend

I lived next door to the Langes for nearly fifteen years. It was me that Zara called the day her mumma died. The poor thing. Sir Peter had only popped out for one meeting and that's when it happened. It broke his heart that he wasn't with her at the end. I'm sure that's why he made sure he was there for the girls afterwards. He put them before his business every single day, which I'm sure wasn't easy for him. You could tell how important those hotels were to him, but the girls meant more, and he did everything he could to make sure they knew that. Wherever Melanie is right now, if Sir Peter says she's safe then she's safe.

From: Zara.Lange@LangeHotels.com
To: Peter.Lange@LangeHotels.com
Date: 12 September 2022
Subject: Media silence

Dad,

Are you sure media silence is the best way to go here?

I know you want to protect Melanie and the businesses, but the statement last month has done nothing to calm the situation.

That Netflix producer has been calling again! Every incoming call is a journalist wanting an interview with anyone who'll talk.

Z x

SIR PETER LANGE —
MY SIDE OF THE STORY (UNPUBLISHED)

*Interviews between ghost writer Ryan Morris
and Peter Lange, 3 October 2022*

Ryan: I'd like to talk about your business for a moment. Back in the early 2000s everyone knew Lange Hotels and most people of a certain income will have stayed in one at some point in their life.

Peter: I have always striven for affordable luxury.

Ryan: In March 2003 you launched your flagship hotel – Lange London. It's at this time that things seemed to change for you and for Melanie. You went from being an unknown businessman to being perhaps not a celebrity, but a recognized face. That must have been very strange.

Peter: Strange doesn't begin to describe it. One of the directors at the time, a man by the name of Thomas Gordan, was a bit of a maverick. One of those hotshot types who wore jeans when the rest of us were in suits. He wanted to make his mark. He felt that our branding wasn't sexy enough. I wasn't convinced hotels needed to be sexy, but he was quite persuasive and so I didn't object when he hired an outside publicity team to organize the Lange London launch. It was the most expensive party we had ever held but it certainly put the hotel on the map in a way that we'd never had in any of our hotels before. The Lange London was designed to be our most prestigious hotel. Something that would rival The Ritz in glamour but wasn't just for the elite. I've always been incredibly proud of its creation.

The launch party was months in the planning. I remember it felt at times as though the party took more organizing than the building of the hotel. But yes, I guess you'd say it paid off in putting Lange Hotels on the map. It also put me front and centre, and of course Melanie.

Ryan: Tell me about the launch party.

Peter: About a week before the party, Thomas Gordan announced at a meeting that the publicity firm had confirmed that several Premier League footballers and two of the members of Girls Aloud had RSVP'd. Thomas was ecstatic. He felt it was a guaranteed way to get Lange London mentioned in all the tabloids and gossip magazines.

Ryan: And did they show up?

Peter: If there were celebrities there that night then I didn't see them. The fact that the only photo from the launch party that made it into any newspaper was one of Mellie says a lot.

Ryan: Tell me about that photo of Melanie. You were overheard once saying that you hate it.

Peter: [Sighs] Mellie had only just turned fifteen when that photo was taken. It exposed her to a completely different way of life. It changed the trajectory of all of our lives and so I think it's only natural I have strong feelings about it.

Ryan: Do you regret taking Melanie to the Lange London launch party?

Peter: Yes. It's one of the very few regrets I have in my life. As I said, it changed everything. Mellie wasn't supposed to be going to the launch party in the first place. Zara had been working in the business for about nine months at that point. She'd been doing a block in HR and had busted a gut getting the staff we needed for the flagship. I wanted to take her to the launch party and show her what she'd been part of creating. But it was a school night for Mellie and I felt she was too young. She was disappointed at first and annoyed that Zara was going, but I spoke to her about it and we agreed our neighbour, Sunny, would come over and sit with Mellie. I promised Mellie a dinner out somewhere the following week and a tour of the hotel.

Ryan: Isn't fifteen old enough to be left alone for one evening?

Peter: I think . . . it depends on the child.

Ryan: Teenager, you mean?

Peter: On the person, then. Mellie had lost her mum the year before and was very up and down emotionally, which was completely understandable. I tried to give her space to grieve in her own way. I tried to be sympathetic, but there were things she did . . . Well, she tested me, I suppose.

Ryan: In what way?

Peter: She'd sneak wine out of the cellar when she thought I wouldn't notice. She'd come home from seeing friends a few times quite late and it seemed obvious to me that she'd been drinking. It was normal teenager stuff, but without Linda I really didn't know how to handle it.

It's not easy to talk about this, to admit the mistakes I made with Mellie. I feel a lot of guilt for all the times I didn't see . . . I didn't protect her.

[Pause]

Ryan: Sir Peter, would you like to take a break?

Peter: [Coughs] No, I'm fine. Where were we? The launch party. As I was saying, Mellie wasn't supposed to go. The week before the party, Mellie was over at Sunny's house having ice cream and somehow sneaked vodka into her drinks. She came back steaming drunk. I blamed Mellie rather than Sunny, but the trust had gone from both sides and I didn't know who else I could leave Mellie with on short notice who would watch out for her in the way I wanted them to. So in a moment of madness, I told her she could come to the launch, but that she would be by my side the entire time and I was making damn sure she'd find it as boring as hell.

And I know what's coming next. You want to ask about her outfit. Mellie pulled a fast one on me there. I'd been very clear that she needed to wear something sensible, and when she came downstairs an hour before the car was due to arrive wearing a black knee-length dress with a silver wrap cardigan tied at the top, I was relieved to be honest. I'd been expecting ten rounds of our usual 'you're not wearing that'.

We pull up outside the hotel and I climb out first to open the car door for the girls. There's a roped-off area where a dozen or so cameras are flashing in my face and all I'm thinking about is getting the girls inside, so I'm not paying attention to Mellie when she steps out of the car without the cardigan, and her sensible black dress is now an off-the-shoulder number that's five inches shorter on the thigh. Mellie steps away from me and turns to the cameras like a pro and smiles, one hand on her hip, like she's been posing for cameras her whole life. And that photo, my grinning fifteen-year-old daughter who got one over on her old man, was the one that landed in all the tabloids.

[Sighs]

So you can see why I hate that photo. Every time I see it, it reminds me of all that came next for Mellie. It's the first time I truly felt like I was losing control.

Ryan: Losing control of what?

Peter: I think you have to be a parent to understand the answer to that question.

Girl About Town

Gossip Blog

14 March 2003

GUYS!!! I know you all want me to be talking about the new (or should that be ongoing?) rumours of a certain London footballer and his famous wife splitting up, but let's take a moment to chat about the photo in today's *Metro* of fifteen-year-old Melanie Lange..

How cute is she????

Daughter of hotelier Sir Peter Lange – you know those Lange Hotels in every town? What am I asking? Of course you do! Well, he owns them all and Melanie is the little hotel princess we didn't know we needed in our lives.

I've got an *Amy Said It First prediction* for you today . . . Melanie Lange is on a one-way ticket to stardom! And I can't wait. I'm already a little bit obsessed. That hair! That cheeky smile!

Comments

Melanie Lange is so beautiful! I love her hair. I wish mine would look like that.

You can totally tell she's got what it takes.

That dress is way too slutty for fifteen! My daughter is sixteen and I'd never let her wear that. She's a walking advert for a spoilt child and bad parenting if you ask me.

Love her already (but not as much as you, Amy!!)

Of course she's going to be a star. Her dad is a billionaire. He probably paid for that photo to be in the papers.

Netflix Original Documentary:
Melanie Lange – The Ugly Truth

INTERVIEWS RECORDED 19–22 SEPTEMBER 2022
(220 DAYS SINCE MELANIE'S DISAPPEARANCE)

Narrator

Despite the tragic loss of her mother, Melanie continued to excel in her schoolwork under the watchful eye of her father.

Terri Byford, retired teacher

I'm Terri Byford. I was a teacher at St Augustine's, a private school in South London. I taught both Melanie and Zara for the duration of their time at school.

Zara was head prefect and head of the school council. Very studious, very polite to all the teachers. But some girls, for whatever reason, aren't well liked, and sadly Zara was one of them. It was nothing in particular that she did or didn't do. She wasn't teased or bullied as far as I could see. She just didn't have many friends.

Melanie on the other hand was very popular. She grew up in what I like to call the 'dumb girls' era, when it was popular for girls to be these blonde airheads without a brain cell between them. Melanie wasn't like that. She was certainly popular, but she was down to earth too. She always looked out for the younger kids. Most of the girls as they moved up the school either ignored the younger students or were outright nasty to them. I can't tell you the trouble we had, but not Melanie. She made it her business to learn the names of almost every girl and would remember little details about them, like if they enjoyed horse riding, she'd always ask them how it was going. It sounds like a simple thing, and I think to Melanie it was, but as a teacher looking in on the situation, it made her stand out even before the fame.

Sunny Bhatt, family friend

Zara was a lovely, lovely girl growing up and she's a wonderful young woman now. We still have lunch together now and again. Of course, she's very busy running things at Lange and clearing up Melanie's mess. She'd never say as much of course, too classy to ever badmouth her sister to anyone, even me. But I see those headlines and I feel sorry, very sorry, for Zara and Sir Peter.

I was brought up to believe a leopard never changes its spots. Some people might call me old-fashioned, but I've always stood by it. And Melanie Lange was nothing but trouble for her father growing up. I'm sure she's nothing but trouble for him now.

I honestly thought she'd give Peter a stomach ulcer the way she carried on with the drinking and sneaking out. I once saw her kissing a boy on her driveway. It looked like she was wanting to take him inside, but I banged on the window and he soon cleared off. Once when she was fifteen, she even stole some alcohol from my kitchen when I wasn't looking. After that, it was hard to be around Melanie.

Terri Byford, retired teacher

In my thirty-five years of teaching, I saw every kind of parent imaginable. The wrap them in cotton wool types, the sun shines out their kids' rear end types, the don't care types – now they're the worst – and the pushy types. And my impression of Sir Peter Lange was that he was the latter. From our talks at the parent–teacher evenings, it was made clear to me that anything below an A for either Zara or Melanie was unacceptable. It's not unusual for parents to have these expectations at such an elite school, but it wasn't a view shared by Mrs Lange when she was alive. She was much more focused on Zara and Melanie's wellbeing than their grades. I seem to remember her worrying a lot more about Zara than she ever did about Melanie. I suppose I felt rather sorry for those girls losing their mother and only having Sir Peter at home with them.

Twitter
23 September 2022

James Hilton @James_T_Hilton
I swear I just saw #MelanieLange shopping in Waitrose on Kensington High Street! She had a baseball cap and sunglasses on but it was totally her. #MelanieLangeHoax

> **Kaitlyn M Davids @Mummyrulestheroost**
> Yeah right! Where's the photo? She's been missing 7 months!!! This is not a stunt! #SaveMelanie

> **Dom Pereyra @Dom_the_man_can**
> I thought I saw her last week too! South London too. #MelanieLangeHoax

> **Lizzie Folly @DreamChaser543**
> My housemate works for Lange Cosmetics and it's not a hoax! They are in full freak-out mode. #SaveMelanie is real!

Amy B @GirlAboutTownBlog
Join me at Trafalgar Square next Saturday (1 October) 10 a.m.! #MarchforMelanie #SaveMelanie

From: Zara.Lange@LangeHotels.com
To: Lange Hotel Employees (all); Lange Cosmetics Employees (all);
Baby Lange Employees (all)
Date: 24 September 2022
Subject: URGENT: Media Blackout

This is a reminder that all Lange businesses are currently in a media blackout. If anyone from the press contacts you directly, please report it to the press office using the email: Mediarelations@LangeHotels.com

Any employee found to be communicating with the media, either directly or via social media, will have their contract immediately terminated.

Regards

Zara Lange

VP Lange Hotels

CEO of Lange Cosmetics (acting)

SIR PETER LANGE —
MY SIDE OF THE STORY (UNPUBLISHED)

*Interviews between ghost writer Ryan Morris
and Peter Lange, 3 October 2022*

Ryan: So after the flagship Lange London hotel launch, what was life like? Did it change overnight for you and Melanie?

Peter: To be honest, yes. We woke up the next day and Mellie went to school and I went into the office with Zara. My secretary was waiting for me as I came out of the lift, which is never a good sign. Since she was holding a newspaper in her hands, I assumed we'd had a bad write-up for Lange London.

Then she showed me a section in the *Metro* called Celeb Spot and right in the middle of the page is Mellie in her black dress, grinning back at me. I couldn't believe it. My first thought was of Mellie and whether she knew yet. I wondered about taking her out of school, but that seemed pretty extreme. I reasoned with myself that it was one photo on a slow news day.

But an hour later I'd had half a dozen phone calls from model agents wanting to talk about Mellie's career. Bear in mind that this was happening the day after the biggest hotel launch we'd ever held. The party had been a huge success and we were trying to capitalize on that as much as we could. What I'm trying to say is that I was busy.

I don't think I stopped until lunchtime when Zara came into my office. She handed me a cup of coffee and a sandwich and sat down. I think she was one of the only people in the office who wasn't struggling with a hangover. Everyone else I'd seen that day had a sheen of alcohol sweats to them, but not Zara. She's never been much of a drinker. Something else she and Mellie don't have in common.

I told her about the calls from the modelling agencies and Zara looked me straight in the eye and asked me if I was going to tell Mellie, which I think was the first point I realized that I had a choice to make. Zara suggested that it might be better not to tell Mellie about the modelling interest, and I could see her point. Mellie was a year away from her GCSEs and didn't need any distractions, but in the end I thought about Linda and I knew she would've wanted Mellie to have the choice.

I even wondered if modelling might do Mellie good. Linda had modelled as a young woman and she'd always told me how tough it was. Long hours and doing as you're told. Look this way, look that. I thought Mellie would do a few shoots and it would teach her the value of hard work.

I often wonder how different all our lives would have turned out if I'd followed Zara's advice.

Melanie Lange video 2/9
Published on Melanie Lange YouTube channel on 2 August 2022

I'm Melanie Lange. Today's date is the twentieth of June 2022. I want to tell you more about my life right now. The part of the house open to me has one bedroom, an en-suite and a living room-dining room area. I don't have access to a kitchen. My food is brought out to me at 7.30 a.m., noon and 6 p.m. My diet is vegan and healthy. Lots of fruit and vegetables. I'm given no choice whatsoever. I either eat what's on the plate or I go hungry. The only drink I'm given is water.

There's a door that leads into a kitchen and the rest of the house. It's always locked.

There is a guard watching me all the time.

There's a woman who calls herself a doctor who visits me every day to talk for an hour, but none of the guards talk to me beyond giving me basic commands. When I talk to them, it's like I don't exist.

I . . . I'm so lonely. So alone. I can't describe how much I miss Sebastian and William. It's so painful to think about them, and yet they are all I think about.

[Crying]

Netflix Original Documentary:
Melanie Lange – The Ugly Truth

INTERVIEWS RECORDED 19–22 SEPTEMBER 2022
(220 DAYS SINCE MELANIE'S DISAPPEARANCE)

Narrator

In March 2003, at the age of fifteen, Melanie was photographed by paparazzi at the launch of Lange Hotels' flagship hotel in Knightsbridge – Lange London. A fortnight later Melanie signed with London modelling agency First Models, and quickly became a recognized face, modelling for Dior, H&M and L'Oréal. Just six months after her first modelling job, Melanie made her debut on the catwalk at the prestigious Paris Fashion Show.

Brian Bent, modelling agent

The minute I saw the photo of Melanie from the hotel launch, I knew I had to sign her. Before the ink was dry on the contract I had three jobs lined up for her.

Vic Watson, tabloid editor

Melanie was catapulted into the spotlight overnight. Every other advert in the magazines was her face. She was cutting ribbons at store openings, appearing on catwalks, and then Lacoste signed her as the face of their teen sportswear brand. It was a huge campaign. She was on the sides of buses, she was in TV adverts, and she was on a giant fucking billboard on Oxford Street.

Melanie might only have been fifteen, but that attention brought with it a massive buzz. People wanted to know what she was doing and we wanted to be the one to tell them.

Nell

The early days when we were both modelling were a lot of fun. We got invited to a lot of places. We only did the fun stuff though. Even back then, the paparazzi were following Mel around like a pack of stray dogs. We were both busy modelling and Melanie was also studying for her GCSE exams, don't forget, so she couldn't do everything she wanted, especially when her dad took away her phone while she was sleeping and locked her in her room.

There were times when I'd think to myself, like OK, what Sir Peter is doing is really bad and really wrong, but it can't get any worse. I thought that more than once, you know? And every time, he found something worse. Right now, I'm terrified about what he's going to do next.

Vic Watson, tabloid editor
By the time Melanie was sixteen, we had photos of her coming out of restaurants and events. Even if it was innocent to start with, the rumours started that Melanie was underage drinking and doing all sorts. It was a ticking time bomb. We were all waiting for the money shot of Melanie falling drunk out of a club. And we didn't have to wait long.

SIR PETER LANGE —
MY SIDE OF THE STORY (UNPUBLISHED)

Interviews between ghost writer Ryan Morris
and Peter Lange, 3 October 2022

Ryan: Melanie's modelling career started in 2003 and ended abruptly in the summer of 2005. Let's talk about that time period. What was it like?

Peter: To start with, it all seemed to go well. Mellie and I met with about four agents and signed with Brian Bent, who I felt had the right approach when it came to work ethic and looking after the models.

Ryan: So modelling was something Melanie was interested in?

Peter: Absolutely. It was one of the first things I'd seen her excited about in a long time. We had an agreement that Melanie would keep her grades up at school or she'd have to stop. For a while, she really applied herself to both school and modelling. It was clear immediately to me and to Brian Bent that Mellie had a long and successful career in modelling ahead of her.

Very quickly, she started getting work. I went with her the first few times and felt happy with how Mellie was being treated. Brian was there a lot too. After that, our driver started taking her and collecting her from the auditions and then the shoots themselves, acting as her chaperone. It was all going well. Mellie was happy and growing up a bit. And then a few months in, Mellie met Nell.

Ryan: This is Nell Stevens? Melanie's best friend and personal assistant?

Peter: [Laughs] Personal assistant is a bit of a stretch. She was on the payroll with Lange Cosmetics for a long time, but her exact role for the past twenty years has been to drag Mellie into as much trouble as possible. From the moment they met, Mellie started lying to me. She would pretend she had an audition when in actual fact she was shopping on Bond Street with Nell. Or she'd tell me she was sleeping over at Nell's house and the next day I'd see a photo of Mellie in the papers on a night out.

It's impossible to know how all our lives would've turned out if Mellie hadn't met Nell, but one thing I know with absolute certainty is that Nell has always been trouble, and all the problems Mellie has had in her life, including her most recent ones, are in no small part down to Nell.

Back then, I'm not sure who I was angrier at – Mellie and Nell for lying and sneaking around behind my back, or the tabloids for publicizing every move Mellie made.

I . . . I found it hard. And that in itself was hard. With my business, I could always see the right path. With Mellie, I found I was second-guessing myself and my judgement. One minute I'd feel like I was being too soft with her and the next I felt like I was being too harsh. I struggled, really struggled to find a balance between the two. It's not an excuse, but that side of parenting was completely new to me. Linda had always dealt with Mellie's temperamental side.

The more I tried to get it right, the worse it got. Mellie was growing in confidence and it felt like it was my job to keep reining her in, which she didn't like. Despite how well she was doing, her schooling still had to come first and she had her GCSEs to focus on. Mellie was smart, and if she needed her exam results to fall back on, then I wanted them to be good.

Ryan: So Melanie stopped studying? Did her grades suffer?

Peter: Not as such, but Mellie stopped prioritizing her studying. Every time I turned my back, she was sneaking out somewhere with Nell. Remember, Mellie was only fifteen or sixteen at this point. The stricter I became, the sneakier Mellie got. It was a constant battle. I tried to be at home as much as I could. I even had a gym installed at home and got myself a personal trainer who'd come to the house most mornings, so I could be at home when I was working out.

I'm not saying it was easy for Mellie. She couldn't go anywhere without a story and photo popping up about her in the tabloids or the weekly magazines. To this day, I don't understand the media interest in my daughter. They'd pick at everything. Her clothes, her hair, her face. One week there would be a headline about Mellie having an eating disorder. So Mellie would make a point of being seen eating a burger. The very next week the same magazine was suggesting she needed to diet.

Ryan: How did Melanie handle that level of attention? As you say, she was only sixteen.

Peter: On the surface, she seemed to take it in her stride, but underneath I think she found it very difficult. It became a lot harder for her to leave the house. She put a lot of thought into her outfits. Sometimes I'd catch her crying over stories about herself. The stories were never nice, never kind, and I think they started to chip away at Mellie's self-confidence. Then there were these gossip blogs, they called themselves, which seemed to take whatever the tabloids said to an extreme, and people commented on them. The attention Mellie got was constant. It only got worse when social media became a thing. Then it wasn't just one comment from a nasty journalist, it was hundreds of comments from all sorts of people. It felt like I was watching someone I love step into the firing line and take bullet after bullet every damn day.

And for my part, I felt my control over the situation begin to slip even further, and it happened so slowly that it took me a while to notice.

Girl About Town

Gossip Blog

15 May 2004

Who spotted those sexy red Louboutin heels Melanie Lange was
wearing to lunch yesterday? She is rocking that little black dress
but the heels are to die for! I would literally kill Melanie for
those shoes! Ha ha, just kidding.

I know you're after some super-HOT gossip today so listen to this – hotel
princess Melanie Lange has a new personal trainer and he is FIT
(and I don't just mean in the athletic way). He's been seen visiting the
house every morning before little Melanie skips off to school.
Take it from me, guys, those training sessions are X-rated!
No wonder she's smiling all the time.

Comments

OMG I saw a pic of her personal trainer last week and he is soooo sexy!
Lucky bitch!

Is this true?

She needs to start actually working out if she wants to continue
modelling.

I love Melanie's outfit. She's so pretty and down to earth. We have the
same birthday! Aquarius twins!!

Melanie Lange video 3/9
Published on Melanie Lange YouTube channel on 3 August 2022

I'm Melanie Lange. This is a short video. I'm really scared today. I think they're getting suspicious, but I really want to tell you all some of the rules I have here.

No TV. No music. I miss music a lot.

No leaving the grounds. I used to be allowed on to the private beach but they stopped that.

I'm not allowed to see what's behind the door in the kitchen. I'm not allowed through the door.

I can't choose anything for myself. Even these clothes are like a prison uniform.

The worst thing is . . . they're drugging me. Sometimes I lose whole days with whatever they give me.

I have to go now. I just wanted to tell you what my life is like here.

Please, you have to save me!

Netflix Original Documentary:
Melanie Lange – The Ugly Truth

INTERVIEWS RECORDED 19–22 SEPTEMBER 2022
(220 DAYS SINCE MELANIE'S DISAPPEARANCE)

Narrator

As Melanie's modelling career took off, her popularity with the tabloid media and the weekly gossip magazines grew. For a six-month period between November 2004 and May 2005 every weekly gossip magazine featured photographs of Melanie on the front cover. By the summer of 2005, Melanie Lange was one of Britain's most recognized celebrities. She was seventeen years old.

Ellen Armstrong, Professor of Finance at the London School of Economics

Were the shareholders of Lange Hotels Limited nervous about Melanie Lange and the negative press she was receiving on a weekly basis? I'm sure they were. I'd love to have been a fly on the wall during those meetings. But if you analyse the share prices towards the end of 2003 and the summer of 2005, what you actually see is a significant rise. One highly feasible theory is that this rise could be attributed to the addition of their flagship hotel in London. However, if you look at the day-to-day figures and compare them with press coverage for Melanie, what you notice is that as her presence in the pages of the tabloids increased, so did the share price, and this is regardless of how negative the stories were. So I'm certain the shareholders would have been nervous about Melanie Lange, but at the same time the old adage 'there's no such thing as bad press' is absolutely right here. Of course, it all changed later when Melanie got involved in Lange Hotels, but between 2003 and 2005 Melanie Lange was good for business.

Terri Byford, retired teacher

I think all the teachers waited for the modelling to go to Melanie's head. It was certainly discussed many times in the staff room. But she was always the same Melanie when she was in my class.

I don't know when she did her homework, but she did it. It was never late or below her usual standard. I'd walk past a shop and see Melanie's face on the front page of a newspaper, showing her coming out of a restaurant at 3 a.m., and then I'd walk into my classroom at 9 a.m. and she'd be sat in her usual chair looking her usual bright and cheery self. I really started to question at that point how true the stories about her were.

She did very well in her GCSE exams. A*s and As across the board. I'm sure her father was pleased. I expected the results to make it to the front pages, but I don't think they were even mentioned.

Nell

2005 was when things started to change for me and Melanie. In June of that year, one of my brother's girlfriends moved into our family home – a three-bed terrace with one bathroom which already had five of us living in it. There just wasn't room. So I took the plunge and rented a studio flat in Soho. It was nothing fancy. In fact, it was a total dive.

[Laughs]

It didn't even have its own bathroom. If you needed the loo, you had to take toilet roll and a hand towel down the hall to this godawful bathroom shared with three other flats. It didn't have a kitchen either. Just a sink and a fridge and a plug-in single hob. Not that I ever cooked. There was a restaurant next door and the whole place reeked of garlic most of the time. I'd practically shower in perfume before I went out. And don't get me started on the cockroaches. Those little bastards were all over that restaurant. Makes me shiver just thinking about it.

Despite all that, I loved it. I loved the freedom it gave us. I didn't even care that this one shitty room with no bathroom cost the absolute earth. I moved there for Mel as much as for myself. She needed somewhere she could have some headspace away from her dad. I thought with her GCSEs done the previous year he'd cut her some slack, but if anything his controlling got worse. It was like he could see her growing up and making her own decisions and he hated it.

She couldn't go to the supermarket without him wanting an update. Is it any wonder that he's locked her up now? He's a massive control freak.

The best example I can give you is my eighteenth birthday, a month before I moved into my own place. Melanie knew my parents wouldn't be doing much to celebrate and so she laid on this whole day of surprises. First I get this text at 10 a.m. telling me to get dressed and be ready to leave the house in twenty minutes. Her driver pulls up and Mel jumps out with a big Happy Birthday balloon and gives me this massive hug, before whisking me away to her favourite salon. We sat side by side and had our hair and nails done. It sounds like a Hollywood movie, and to be honest that's what it felt like. The summer was starting, it was warm – there was this feeling of change in the air, you know? Like things were just going to get better and better.

By the time we leave the salon we've got the proper giggles. Just looking at each other set us off. The next place we go to is a boutique off Bond Street where a private shopper comes in with all these outfits and Mel tells me to choose whatever I want. When we finally get back in the car, there are so many bags we can barely see out the windows.

The car takes us back to Mel's and we get dressed up before she takes me to The Ivy. It was the night Robbie Williams came over to say hello. I mean, I knew Mel was popular, but I didn't know she knew Robbie Williams. ROBBIE WILLIAMS! I've only loved him since I was like seven years old. Melanie tells him it's my birthday and he leans down and kisses my cheek and wishes me a happy birthday. Then he sends over a bottle of Cristal for us. It was one of the most exciting moments of my life.

The second he walks away, I drag Mel to the toilets so I can freak out and ask her how the hell she knows Robbie Williams. Then casual as anything she replies, 'Oh, we've known each other for ages. My dad hired him to sing at my thirteenth birthday party and since then we've been invited to his place for a garden party every summer. It's no big deal.'

No big deal? I was like, 'Mel, we tell each other everything. How could you not have mentioned this?'

It was about ten thirty by the time the desserts were finished, and I could tell Mel was getting twitchy about the time. I thought she had another surprise arranged and so I asked if we were going dancing, but Melanie said she had this cheesy sleepover film fest planned back at hers.

She didn't say as much, but it seemed pretty obvious to me that Sir Peter had given her a curfew. Don't get me wrong, I didn't mind at all. It had been an awesome day and I was happy to hang out at hers.

But when we get outside the driver isn't there. Mel phones him and he tells her he's stuck in traffic. Melanie calls her dad like twenty times to tell him she's running late, but he doesn't pick up. By the time we make it back to Melanie's house it's twenty past eleven, and Sir Peter starts yelling at us the moment we walk through the front door. All this stuff about respect and boundaries. Mel was twenty minutes late because her driver was late. It wasn't her fault and she tried to call him, but Sir Peter wouldn't listen.

Mel completely exploded. It was the first time I ever saw her angry. She's normally so chilled, but she went off the rails at her dad that night, screaming at him that he's ruining her life, at which point he tells me to leave and I'm taken home by his driver. On the car ride home, I ask him why he was late picking us up and get this – he says Sir Peter asked him to run an errand, and he told Sir Peter where he was and Sir Peter said it was fine. Sir Peter totally set us up to be late. If you ask me, he just wanted a reason to punish Melanie.

After that, all me and Mel talked about was moving in together. I got the impression that even when she turned eighteen, she thought she'd only be able to do it when Sir Peter said she could. There were so many times I wanted to talk to her about her dad and how controlling he was, but Mel didn't like to talk about it so I never pushed her on it. I really wish I had done now. Maybe if I had, things would be different.

Rick Glen, former press officer for Lange Hotels Limited

I was on Lange's graduate scheme from 2002 to 2005 and I was doing a stint in the PR department when Sir Peter's daughter, Melanie, was modelling and getting a lot of attention in the media. Somehow I got lumbered with the job of checking the tabloid newspapers every morning and phoning Sir Peter directly if his daughter was mentioned. God, those phone calls were hard. Sir Peter is not a man you want to cross. I got told once – and this is second-hand information so I'm not sure how true it is – that a few years before I started, Sir Peter fired the entire graduate intake because he caught them stood in the kitchen having a laugh together during a coffee break.

Maybe it was just a stupid story we got told to make sure we were working hard, but you can imagine how nervous I was making those calls. Every morning, I had to go out to my local corner shop at five thirty and buy the papers. I'd go through them and call Sir Peter by 6 a.m. if Melanie was mentioned, and she was mentioned a lot. Most of the time Sir Peter would say thanks and hang up, but then the photo of Melanie at that party hit the front pages and I swear he actually roared down the phone at me. I quit later that morning. To this day, it was still the most stressful job I've had, and I'm in politics now.

Girl About Town

Gossip Blog

19 September 2004

GUYSS!!!! I have just seen Melanie Lange shopping on Bond Street! Like face-to-face seen, like reaching for the same top and smiling at each other seen!

Obviously, once I spotted her I kept a close eye, and I know you're dying to find out what she bought. Melanie bought a cream cashmere jumper and a knee-length faux-leather black skirt.

Did I follow her into the changing rooms to see her show her mate the outfit? You bet I did! She looked amazing.

I've got an *Amy Said It First prediction* for you – faux-leather skirts are going to be big this autumn!

Comments

Buying one right now!

Wish you'd taken a photo.

I'm dying to know if she's as chubby as the photos in the magazines made her look last week! I don't know how she can model for a sports brand.

Anyone else desperate to hear from Melanie? She never does interviews! Amy, you have to get her to come on your blog!!

What's going on with her hair? I love Melanie but that girl needs Frizz Ease ASAP!

How about a threesome, Amy? I bet Melanie is a right filthy bitch!

Twitter
3 October 2022

Amy B @GirlAboutTownBlog
Guys, check out this photo of Peter Lange in today's papers . . . He has guilt written all over him! #SaveMelanie

> **Curtis Oliver @MelanieL_BiggestFan**
> No wonder he looks stressed. We are on to him now! #TheUglyTruth is going to destroy him. #SaveMelanie

> **Jane Godfellow @WorldofCats2002**
> Did you see the sneak peek trailer for #TheUglyTruth? That Nell looked so gaunt!

> **Ashton Becker @ProudStayAtHomeDad**
> You have all been brainwashed! Has it not occurred to you that Peter Lange looks stressed because he has a camera in his face when he's trying to look after his poor daughter? Shame on you! #HelpPeter

Amy B @GirlAboutTownBlog
Thank you to the AMAZING #MelanieLange fans who marched across London on Saturday!!!! There were so many of us #MarchforMelanie #Proud #SaveMelanie

Leah Hurst @FantasyFictionFan101
Am I the only one wondering if Zara is behind all this? She has a face like a cat's arse and has clearly been jealous of #MelanieLange her whole life.

SIR PETER LANGE –
MY SIDE OF THE STORY (UNPUBLISHED)

*Interviews between ghost writer Ryan Morris
and Peter Lange, 3 October 2022*

Ryan: How did you balance your commitments to the business with your commitments at home during this time?

Peter: Not well, my critics would tell you. In early 2005 we were having difficulties with the management of one of our European hotels. Foolishly, I didn't take an active role in the resolution process. Communications broke down, things were missed, and the staff went on strike for two weeks. We lost a lot of money and our reputation took a big dent. By the time I stepped in, the damage was already done and we ended up selling the hotel. I should have handled everything myself. It was a mistake I've tried very hard not to repeat.

Ryan: It must have put a strain on your home life as well.

Peter: Between the business and Mellie, yes. It was a difficult time. Zara was a rock both at the business and at home, especially when Mellie was being challenging. Zara could've moved out and got her own place. She certainly had the means, but she stayed at home because she knew I needed her support. If I had late meetings, she'd make sure she left on time and cooked dinner for all of us. She took over making sure we had food in the house too.

In hindsight, I can see that the situation caused resentment on both sides. Mellie didn't want another mother figure in her life, especially not Zara. And even though Zara never said anything, I wondered a few years later when Mellie got her own apartment if Zara felt that she'd put her life on hold for Mellie.

[Sighs]

Ryan: Nell Stevens has been quite vocal in the media that on multiple occasions during this period, you locked Melanie in her room and forced her to study for her exams. Is that true?

Peter: [Laughs] That woman wouldn't know what the truth looked like if it jumped out of her mouth and smacked her in the face. Mellie had a maths exam on a Monday morning at 8 a.m. On the Saturday evening before, I caught her dolled up and sneaking out of the house without my permission. I did what any parent would do in that situation. I took away her phone and I banned her from watching TV, and I made sure her focus was on her exam. It worked too because she got an A* in Maths.

Ryan: And the locked room?

Peter: For God's sake, are you not listening to me?
[Sighs]
Sorry. Can we take a break? I'm going to need a stiff drink if we're going to keep going. Do you want one?

Ryan: No, thank you.

[Knock at door]

Peter: Denise, could I get a whisky, please?

Female voice: Yes, Sir Peter. You also wanted me to remind you at seven about your call.

Peter: Thank you, Denise. And you should go home to your family. I'm sorry for keeping you late. Ryan, can you wait outside for a few minutes?

Ryan: No problem.

[Pause]

Peter: Hi, it's me. How's it been today?

[Pause]

Peter: For God's sake. Do whatever is necessary. Shit . . . hang on.

Peter: I'm sorry about that.

Ryan: No problem, Sir Peter. I appreciate you're a busy man. If it's too late, we can pick it up tomorrow. You seem a little . . . flustered. Is everything all right?

Peter: Fine. Now, where were we?

Ryan: I mentioned Nell's claim that you locked Melanie in her room.

Peter: Right. I think it's time I told this next story then. Not many people know this about me, but I had an older sister. Her name was Janet, and she died when she was seventeen. As far as Zara and Mellie knew growing up, Janet died at home from falling down the stairs. This is the story my parents told people and it's the story Linda and I decided to continue to protect the girls. The truth is, Janet . . . she killed herself.

Ryan: I'm so sorry to hear that.

Peter: Thank you. She killed herself on a Tuesday afternoon in November. I remember because I normally stayed at school on Tuesdays and did my homework in the library, and my mum would collect me on the way back from her shift at the local supermarket. But that day I had a headache and decided to get the bus home straight after classes. It was one of those blustery damp days when you can't wait to be home and warm, and when I walked through my front door on that particular day, I was thinking about nothing more than having a hot chocolate and watching TV. I knew the minute I was inside that something was wrong. It felt like a storm cloud was hanging in the air. At first I wondered if we'd been burgled – it was that kind of feeling.

I started moving through the house, checking all the rooms and calling Janet's name. She was in the first year of her A Levels and was normally home on Tuesday afternoons doing her coursework. She was planning to go to university and study to be a pharmacist.

I couldn't find her anywhere and assumed she'd gone out. Then I check the bathroom and find the door locked. I knock and call Janet's name again. Then I bang and shout. The silence on the other side of that door still haunts me to this day.

I race downstairs to the landline and call my dad. He tells me he'll come straight home and then, just as I'm about to say goodbye, he says, 'Call 999, Peter.' So I did. I didn't even know if I needed the police or an ambulance or what, but I just kept saying, 'The bathroom door is locked and my sister isn't answering. I think she's fallen and hit her head.'

I hang up and run back upstairs and start throwing myself at the door. I broke my collarbone trying to break through the lock, but it was one of those sliding metal bolts and I was a pretty puny lad. I just couldn't get it open.

A fire engine arrives pretty quick. I let them in and stand to one side while they use a battering ram on the door. It flies open in seconds and there's my sister, floating in a bath of blood. She waited until the house was empty. She ran herself a bath and she slit her wrists. We found out later that a group of girls on her course were bullying her pretty badly. She never said a word about it to anyone.

If it wasn't for that lock, then maybe I'd have got to my sister in time, maybe she'd still be alive today, maybe Zara and Melanie would have an aunt who dotes on them. So to answer your question, there have never been any locks on any internal doors in any of my properties. I didn't lock Melanie in her room and force her to study. I baked her favourite blueberry muffins and cooked big plates of pasta. I'm sure Nell conveniently forgot to mention that.

Ryan: That's a very tragic story. I'm so sorry for your loss.

Peter: It was a long time ago but it still haunts me. I see a lot of Janet in Mellie. The same hair and mannerisms.

Ryan: Have you told Zara and Melanie the truth about your sister?

Peter: Zara, no. But I told Mellie when she was nineteen. I felt that she needed to know. We only talked about it once. It's not something I find easy to speak about.

Ryan: Do you think it's fair to say that the tragedy you suffered as a boy, being unable to save your sister, affected how you treated the girls?

Peter: Without a doubt. I would, and still do, lie awake some nights, my heart pounding in my chest, worrying about my girls and that it will be them and I won't be there for them like I couldn't be there for Janet.

[Heavy breathing]

Ryan: Are you OK, Sir Peter? You've gone very red.

Peter: I think I'm done for today. Can we pick this up tomorrow?

Ryan: Sure. Of course.

RECORDING STOPPED

Melanie Lange video 4/9
Published on Melanie Lange YouTube channel on 4 August 2022

I'm Melanie Lange. My father is keeping me prisoner. I don't think I'll ever be free again. I feel like I'm lost in the sea I can hear crashing against the cliff outside. I'm so cold. I can't warm up.

The woman who comes to talk to me, she calls herself Dr Sam. She's in her early fifties with short blonde hair and she likes to wear pale suits. She says she's a psychiatrist. Someone must know who this woman is.

I think I'm on the east coast. The sun rises out at sea and disappears over the house in the evenings.

There must be a beach nearby that people go to. I saw kayaks once when I was still allowed on the beach.

Sebastian, William, please know that I love you with every piece of my heart. You are everything to me. I love you. I won't give up, I promise.

Netflix Original Documentary:
Melanie Lange – The Ugly Truth

Narrator

By the summer of 2005, seventeen-year-old Melanie had twelve A*
and A GCSEs and was a year into her A Levels in Business, English
and History. The Lacoste youth sportswear campaign had been a
huge success for Melanie. She was voted World's Sexiest Woman by
readers of men's magazine *Loaded*. She was also a familiar face on
the London nightlife scene. But her growing fame came at a price.
On the second of August 2005, she was days away from signing a
second contract with Lacoste when a photograph emerged which
changed the trajectory of Melanie's life for ever.

Vic Watson, tabloid editor

I got a call pretty late in the evening telling me about a photograph
of Melanie at a house party. Someone snapped this photo on a digital
camera and within ten minutes of taking it they'd called the news
desk. I've been asked a lot over the years if that photo was a set-up.
The answer is, probably yes. Someone saw Melanie at a party and
decided to make some money. I didn't even haggle. It was front-page
material. It was exactly what we'd been waiting for, except better,
and we had it in time for the morning papers.

Nell

I'm not saying Melanie was innocent all of the time, but that
photo was totally staged, and it wasn't some stranger trying to
make a few quid either. Here's what none of the papers reported
about that party – it was Zara's boyfriend's party. Yes, that's right,
Miss Perfect had a boyfriend. Albeit briefly. I'm sorry, I know I'm

sounding like a bitch, but you have to understand that Zara ruined Melanie's life that night.

Mel and Zara didn't see eye to eye on much, but they didn't hate each other back then either. In fact, they got on all right. Zara used to boss Mel around a lot with school stuff, but when Mel got her GCSEs, Zara took a step back which helped improve their relationship, I think. Zara even came shopping with us once. I mean, me and Mel were always shopping, strolling up and down Oxford Street on Saturdays. We didn't buy loads of stuff, we just liked seeing what was there and chatting.

When Zara came with us, Mel was really sweet to her, buying her clothes and showing her styles that would suit Zara's figure. Zara has always loved grey, but it completely washes her out. Anyway, you could tell Zara felt pretty uncomfortable on the shopping trip – fish out of water kind of thing – but she gave it a go and we all had a laugh. And so when Zara invited Mel to go with her to this party, Mel said, 'Sure.'

I assumed at the time that Zara invited Mel because it looked good to arrive at a party with a famous sister, but afterwards I wondered if she'd planned it all from the start.

The party was in Hackney, on the ground floor of a converted warehouse. It was a cool place. Open plan, funky colours on the wall. The kind of place where you imagine there's a party every night. Certainly not the kind of place I'd have expected a boyfriend of Zara's to live.

We get there about ten, and straightaway Zara starts popping bottles of champagne and taking photos of everyone on a digital camera like it's New Year's Eve. The party picks up and I get talking in the garden to this guy I knew from school, and so I lose Mel for a while. Next time I see her, she's up against a wall being chatted up by Zara's boyfriend, and Zara has a look on her face like she's going to go Glenn Close on his arse. You know, proper dagger eyes.

I head over there and drag Mel away to dance, and then Zara

comes up to us and she's like, 'Mel, hold my drink. I wanna get a photo of the two of you.'

So Mel takes the drink and Zara takes the photo. Neither of us think anything of it and carry on dancing for ages. Mel loves dancing. She always has. She doesn't need a bottle of wine in her like I do to get my arse moving. If the tunes are right, then she can be stone cold sober and hitting the dance floor like it's the last party on earth.

You know she's not allowed to listen to music in that place? I get that it's not even close to the worst injustice in all of this, but it cuts me up to think of Mel trapped in that house right now with only silence. She always had music on, even in the office.

Brian Bent, modelling agent

It was the worst thing that could've happened to Melanie. She was on a one-way trajectory to stardom. Lacoste were paying a shitload and had all these plans for her. Then this photo appears on the front pages of Melanie and Nell at a house party somewhere. Melanie has a glass of champagne in one hand and a cigarette in the other. It doesn't sound too bad, does it? But bear in mind that she was seventeen and the face of a sports brand, so underage drinking alongside the smoking didn't look great. Maybe if that had been it, we could've smoothed things over and done some image work, but right behind Melanie there was this glass coffee table with lines of white powder on it and someone bent over snorting. And that was it. Game over.

Nell

I didn't even know there were drugs at that party until the next day when we woke up in Mel's bedroom to Sir Peter going ballistic at us, waving a newspaper in Mel's face. I got kicked out of the house pretty quick that morning.

So here's the thing, right – Mel never would've been at that party if Zara hadn't begged her to go with her, and the photo that made it to the papers, that ruined Mel's entire modelling career and mine, was taken on Zara's camera.

Of course, Zara immediately said she put the camera down and someone stole it, but I don't buy that for a single second. She wanted Mel at that party so she could get a photo of her that would damage her career. It's that simple.

The question I've always wondered is, why did Zara do it? The obvious answer is jealousy, and of course Zara was jealous of Mel. But Zara has the personality of a potato. Like, she's smart and everything, but she's not the type of person to break rules or think outside the box. It seems pretty clear to me that someone put Zara up to selling Mel out like that, and the only person Zara would do something like that for was her dad.

I keep asking myself – is Zara involved? Does she know where Mel is right now? I honestly don't know the answer, but her silence speaks volumes.

Brian Bent, modelling agent
I felt sorry for Melanie when Lacoste dropped her. Overnight she went from the face everyone wanted to the face no one would touch. For contracts anyway. The media were still lapping her up, more so than before even. We even had paparazzi waiting outside the offices for days on end hoping to get a shot of Melanie.

I'm not saying I approved of what happened, but all the models were drinking and smoking, going to parties. It was the lifestyle. We had some problem girls but Melanie wasn't one of them. It was me who had to sit Melanie down and tell her that her career was over. She was only seventeen years old. I think I was more upset than she was. Such a waste. We could've made so much money from her. But Melanie just shrugged and thanked me for all I'd done for her. That was the last time I saw her in person.

Nell stayed at the agency for another year. She had a few shoots but never anything big and then people wanted newer faces, fresher looks, and we ended up letting her go too. She was devastated. Nell wasn't some rich kid like Melanie. Her family had spent a lot of money making her dreams come true and she needed to work.

Nell

It was total overkill for First Models to drop Mel. If you ask me, her dad had a hand in that too.

From: Zara.Lange@LangeHotels.com
To: Peter.Lange@LangeHotels.com
Date: 4 October 2022
Subject: Where are you?

Dad,

I've been trying to get hold of you. Denise said you've cleared your calendar for today. You're not answering your phone! Where are you?

This is not a time to be out of reach! Are you OK?

Staff are getting anxious. It's the bloody press constantly harassing everyone. Two of the designers for Baby Lange handed in their notice yesterday and one of the finance team was a no-show this morning.

We need another press statement ASAP. Shall I talk to legal about drafting something?

Z x

SIR PETER LANGE —
MY SIDE OF THE STORY (UNPUBLISHED)

*Interviews between ghost writer Ryan Morris
and Peter Lange, 5 October 2022*

Peter: My apologies for cancelling our meeting yesterday, Ryan. I had urgent business away from the office.

Ryan: Did you see Melanie?

Peter: [Sighs] I didn't see Melanie, no. I regularly visit the medical facility where she's staying and speak to staff regarding her recovery. It's not always best for her health to see me on these occasions.

Ryan: Will you tell me where she is?

Peter: No. Let's get back to the questions.

Ryan: All right then. There is a rather famous photograph of Melanie which was taken when she was seventeen. It's—

Peter: I know the one you're referring to.

Ryan: What happened there?

Peter: I'll tell you what happened – Mellie set fire to her entire modelling career in one night.

Ryan: You still sound angry about it.

Peter: Is that surprising?

Ryan: Considering what Melanie went on to achieve, some might say yes.

Peter: I presume you mean Lange Cosmetics and Baby Lange. She'd have launched her business either way, but she'd have come at it from a better position. I can't tell you how hard she had to work to be taken seriously after that photo and all the stories that came later.

You have to understand that on the one hand Mellie finished her exams with good results and her modelling was taking off. She was studying business at A Level and had ideas – good ideas – for what she was going to do. On the other hand, Mellie and I were arguing a lot. It didn't matter how flexible I tried to be with her, she would always break the rules. If I said be home by eleven because she had college the next day, she'd stumble in at midnight. If I said midnight, she'd turn up at 2 a.m.

The minute Mellie turned seventeen she started talking about moving out. It was all she talked about, especially when we were arguing. She was making good money too, so it wasn't as though she needed my financial support.

Her desire to move out worried me a lot. While Mellie was under my roof, I could keep an eye on her. I could support her when she got upset about the papers ripping her apart. When she needed a night off – a break – I could make sure she took it. Mellie had grown up a lot, but emotionally she could still be very up and down, and I obviously wanted to keep an eye on that after what happened to Janet.

It didn't help that Nell had recently moved to a flat in Soho and was whispering in Mellie's ear about getting a place together.

Ryan: You said you argued a lot. Was it just about Melanie wanting to move out? Did you argue about other things?

Peter: What didn't we argue about? It felt like weeks would go by when all we'd do is argue. About her desperation to get her own place, about modelling too. I wanted her to slow down a little, study more, have a normal teenager's life.

Ryan: So Melanie's abrupt end to modelling wasn't all bad then? Presumably, without her own income any more, she was stuck at home and would have more time to study.

Peter: It was a hard time for Mellie. She was devastated when First Models dropped her. She was upset with herself more than anyone else, I think. One minute she'd be closed up and wouldn't say a word at dinner times with me and Zara, the next she'd be angry and screaming at us both about never having any privacy. Zara got a lot of blame from Melanie over the photo, I think because it was Zara who invited Melanie to the party. They'd been getting on better. It seemed like both of them were making more effort with each other and were growing up a bit. But after the party, they could barely say a civil word to each other for weeks. Melanie blamed Zara for ending her modelling career, and Zara blamed Melanie for causing the bad press and the effects it had on me and the business. Every mention of Melanie included a mention of Lange Hotels. Zara knew the business was everything to me. It still is. First the girls and then the business. Always that order.

After that photo hit the papers, it felt like I was in the middle of this constant battle between the girls and between myself and Mellie. And I didn't feel like I was winning either.

I really felt like I was failing as a father. I was at the end of my tether. I didn't know how to help Mellie make the best decisions. I didn't know how to control her behaviour. All I knew was that I couldn't stand there and watch her struggle so much emotionally while swearing blind that she was fine.

I don't consider myself a naive person, but I genuinely thought that the photo of Melanie at that party, and the end of her modelling, also meant the end of all the parties, the trouble, the tabloid interest in her. I thought Mellie would come back to earth with a bit of a bump, but she'd brush herself off, throw herself into studying, and be my Mellie again. But it turns out that photo was like a catalyst. Everything just got worse from—

[Knock at door]

Female voice: Sir Peter?

Peter: What is it?

Female voice: I've got an urgent call from Sea—

Peter: Thank you. Ryan, please step outside for a moment. And turn that damn recorder off. Take it with you.

RECORDING STOPPED

Girl About Town

Gossip Blog

8 August 2005

SUPER-HOT GOSSIP ALERT!!!! You know the photo of Melanie Lange last week? Who am I kidding? OF COURSE you know the photo. Naughty Melanie at a party with drugs. Well, it turns out that Lacoste Sports aren't too happy with her and they've dropped her.

Is this the end of Melanie's modelling days? I think so! A little bird told me her modelling agency have also kicked her to the kerb.

Is Melanie going to disappear into thin air like a 90s one-hit wonder? Or is there more to come from the hotel princess? My money is on more! In fact, I've invited Melanie on to my blog to tell her side of that party photo!!

Comments

She was a shit model anyway. Only had one pose and that made her look like a constipated duck.

I'm sooooo gutted! I love Melanie. I hope she does something else. It's so unfair what's happened to her. She wasn't taking the drugs.

She'll probably bring out a music album next. I'd buy it.

I can't wait for the interview! You're the best, Amy!!

Melanie Lange is such a spoilt rich girl. Being dropped by her modelling agency is the best thing that could've happened. People like her need to think about how they're role models for so many young girls.

Netflix Original Documentary:
Melanie Lange – The Ugly Truth

INTERVIEWS RECORDED 19–22 SEPTEMBER 2022
(220 DAYS SINCE MELANIE'S DISAPPEARANCE)

Nell

Obviously Mel was cut up about her modelling career ending, and sure she had a few tearful days, mostly because the press she got and some online comments were pretty harsh. Even though she did nothing wrong and she wasn't taking drugs at that party, she felt really bad for her younger fans. She knew she was a role model, and she felt she'd let people down.

But modelling was never what Mel was going to spend her life doing. She knew that better than anyone. And the fact that Mel stopped modelling made zero difference to our lives. We just had more free time to hang out.

Vic Watson, tabloid editor

The tide really turned on Melanie Lange after the party photo. She was a slow-motion train wreck and everyone wanted to see it happening. Every weekly magazine ran photos of Melanie on the cover. Weight gain, cellulite, split ends, acne, boozing, spendaholic. The stories were endless and none of them were kind or particularly true, but that's the price you pay for living in the public eye. And all that negativity was before we even got to the boyfriends. And there were quite a few of them.

Nell

There were always photographers hanging around outside my place, waiting for Mel. It was annoying sometimes but we knew they were just trying to make a living, and for the most part we pretended they weren't there. Sometimes they'd try to antagonize us. They'd bunch around us, pushing the cameras right in our faces.

They'd shout Mel's name and ask her really personal questions about who she was sleeping with. But if Melanie showed even a drop of annoyance, then they'd get their photo of Melanie looking pissy and we'd see a headline about some completely made-up problem. One time, *NOW* magazine even suggested a rift between me and Melanie because they had this photo of Melanie walking ahead of me and we both look miserable. I mean, the reason we weren't walking side by side was because there were twenty photographers crowding around us, and the reason we looked miserable was because there were twenty photographers crowding around us.

There were times when the paparazzi would get Mel down, but it was the stories that were printed that had the biggest impact. It wasn't something I really paid attention to or noticed at the time, but the stories and lies were relentless and some of the stuff they said was really hurtful. Like, imagine you leave the house in a new outfit, feeling good about yourself, and the next week a magazine posts a photo of you suggesting you've put on weight, or you're pregnant. Like I said, it was harsh. Melanie started wearing these massive sunglasses anytime she was outside. Day or night. I think it made her feel like she could hide a part of herself behind them. I look back at that time now and wish I'd been . . . I don't know. I was there for Mel, always, but I guess I never really asked her how it felt to be ripped apart in the press like that week after week, and I wish now that I had done.

Bill Cutting, former paparazzi photographer
I'm Bill Cutting. I was a freelance photographer for almost two decades. It was my job to stand outside a club or a restaurant or a celebrity's home and wait for them to come out. I'd take a thousand photos and sell one or two to the papers and the magazines whenever I could. We're a pretty hated bunch of people, I get that. But the public still want to see the photos we take, don't they? Most celebrities use us as much as we use them. There is a value in having your photo splashed about.

It was a pretty cut-throat profession. It still is. Except now it's a lot harder, because as well as us, you've got Mr Joe Public with his iPhone posting the same shot on social media for free that we've just taken, and he's got video too, which devalues our work. I'm not expecting any bleeding hearts, I'm just explaining how it is.

Nell

Oh my god, I swear if Melanie stood within a metre of a guy, then it was splashed about that they were dating. It made her a target. All these idiot boys who wanted to be the next big thing saw Mel as their ticket.

Bill Cutting, former paparazzi photographer

To make a living, you needed patience. You needed to be in the right place at the right time and you needed to know what was going to sell. And it was a damn sight easier if you had contacts, both on the papers and in the inner circle of the celebrities – someone close to the celebrity who'd keep you updated on their whereabouts.

Officially, I was told that photos of Melanie Lange were hot property. Unofficially, I was told that photos of Melanie Lange drinking, looking a mess, looking angry, upset, with a bloke, that kind of thing, would be worth a lot more. So from the back end of 2005 I got to know Melanie Lange and Nell Stevens pretty well. I knew where they were going to be and what time, and I made a lot of money.

You've got to imagine, I'm out on the street, cold, hungry, probably in desperate need of a piss, but knowing full well that I can't leave my spot. I could be in the same place for four, five hours just waiting for a twenty-second glimpse. I'll take dozens of shots in that time and then I'm going to pick the one that gets me the most money. Is that the one where Melanie is smiling, or is it the one a split-second later when she's stopped smiling and is blinking, so her eyes are almost closed making her look drunk? It was a no-brainer.

Of course, the real money came when Melanie got herself a proper boyfriend. The public could not get enough of them.

Vic Watson, tabloid editor

As soon as Jonnie Welbourn-Jones became a fixture in Melanie's life, things went from bad to worse for her.

Jonnie Welbourn-Jones, owner of Jonnie Jones Microbrewery

I met Mel and Nell in the VIP area of a nightclub in 2006. Don't ask me which one because I can't remember. We were all smashed off our faces. I was living in Camden at the time and everyone came back to mine with a boatload of other stragglers to carry on partying. At some point in the early hours of the morning, Mel and I sobered up and got talking and we quickly realized we had a lot in common – namely that we both had issues with our dads.

Nell

Jonnie was shit to Mel and anyone else who crossed his path.

Jonnie Welbourn-Jones, owner of Jonnie Jones Microbrewery

Nell was jealous as fu— sorry. She was jealous of me and Mel and the time we spent together.

Anyway, my relationship with Melanie lasted about six months, give or take. I was twenty-one and Mel was eighteen. I had this grungy thing going on back then. The long hair, the baggy jeans and black clothes. I was pretty skinny and smoked these disgusting roll-ups that took me an absolute age to roll because I was so crap at it, but I thought it made me look edgy. I cringe when I see the photos now.

I was trying to make it as a singer and doing gigs in these absolute dives for no money, not even a free drink. I think meeting Mel and spending time with her opened my eyes a bit. The thing about Mel is that despite all the crazy shit that was going on around her, she was very level-headed and pragmatic most of the time.

I basically thought I was God's gift to music before I met Melanie, but then I reckon her way of thinking about the world rubbed off on me. I was able to take a step back and realize that maybe I was OK talent-wise, but I was never going to make it. It sounds like a painful realization and maybe it was at the time, but it also meant I could grow up and get on with my life.

Nell

I wasn't jealous. I just didn't like Jonnie. I thought he was nothing but trouble and it turns out I was right.

Jonnie Welbourn-Jones, owner of Jonnie Jones Microbrewery

The relationship I had with Melanie was special to both of us. We were both living this weird double life. It was like we were two people. Three actually. There was Mel and Jonnie out on the town, smiling for the paps, going to all these club and restaurant openings Mel got invited to, and me doing my gigs. Then we'd wake up the next day and we'd get our books out and spend all day studying. I was trying to finish a business degree that I'd been delaying for a few years, and Mel was finishing her A Levels. She was so smart. I think she wrote half my dissertation for me. I probably shouldn't say that, should I? Hell, it doesn't matter now. I work for myself! And then there were the times when it was just us and the studying was done, and we'd turn off our phones and veg out on the sofa with a massive bag of crisps and watch Bruce Willis movies. She loved Bruce Willis. I think they were my favourite times. We'd stay up late and just talk and talk. She had this idea for a natural skincare range, no chemicals, totally eco-friendly. It sounded like a pipe dream to me, but even back then Mel was excited about it.

Nell

Jonnie was the kind of bloke who could make any conversation about him. Like when Steve Irwin died and it was absolutely hor-rific how it was caught on camera – Mel and I were having this big discussion with a couple of friends about what right the public had to see it and whether it was fair on his children, and Jonnie jumped right in and started banging on about a time a photo of him naked at his eighteenth birthday party got posted online – because that's the same thing. And just like that, we're talking about Jonnie.

Bill Cutting, former paparazzi photographer

Jonnie had this image he wanted to portray to the world of a tortured rock star, but growing his hair and wearing tatty clothes couldn't wash the stink of money and privilege off him, which meant that sometimes you'd get nice Jonnie – a smile and wave for the cameras, a protective arm around Melanie – and other times, like when we'd camp outside his house in Camden, he'd be royally pissed off. He didn't want his fans to see that he had Daddy's money and lived in Daddy's house and was as far from a struggling artist as it was possible to be. Not that I think for a single moment Jonnie had any fans. He was only of interest to us when Melanie was with him. Photos of them together were great, but what we really wanted were shots of Mel leaving his flat alone, looking tired or upset. The weeklies loved those shots.

Vic Watson, tabloid editor

Jonnie Welbourn-Jones was a rich-boy nobody. If he'd been twenty-something in today's world, he's the kind of bloke who'd have gone on *Love Island* and been hated by every female viewer. His relationship with Melanie lasted around five months. It seemed completely obvious to everyone that they weren't serious, but we really milked their story. We had young love, lovers' tiff, pregnancy rumours, engagement ring shopping, secret wedding. Is Jonnie cheating on Mel with mystery blonde? Is Mel cheating on Jonnie with her personal trainer? Half of London must have heard our screams of joy from the office when their relationship actually did blow up.

Twitter
5 October 2022

Jonnie @JJMicrobreweryltd

I just wanna say that there's no truth to the #Jonnie&Melanie rumours going around that #MelanieLange and I were an item before she disappeared. I love Mel to bits but we're just mates.

> **Meg Hillis @MegHillis88**
>
> Rumours you started no doubt!

> **T. S. Wesley @WesleyWezzlar**
>
> Dude! I'm gutted. Thought you guys were so good together!

> **Jessie W @Jessiebakescakes4U**
>
> So typical of a man to make a woman being held prisoner all about him!!!!!
> #SaveMelanie

> **Kaitlyn M Davids @Mummyrulestheroost**
>
> Exactly this! #MelanieLange has been missing 8 months. All we want is for her to be free!!!!! #SaveMelanie

From: Zara.Lange@LangeHotels.com
To: Peter.Lange@LangeHotels.com
Date: 5 October 2022
Subject: Press outside! Urgent!

Dad,

Now you're back in the office, we need to reconsider our media silence ASAP!! The press are everywhere. I'm being hounded for a comment day and night. It's unbearable! We can't wait for your autobiography to come out. We have to consider a new statement that explains what's going on with Melanie. Piers Morgan's people called about an interview. Maybe that's the way to go?

I'm in the office until late. Call me when you've finished today and we'll head home together.

Z x

SIR PETER LANGE –
MY SIDE OF THE STORY (UNPUBLISHED)

Interviews between ghost writer Ryan Morris
and Peter Lange, 5 October 2022

Ryan: In 2006 a lot was made of Melanie's relationship with Jonnie Welbourn-Jones. How did you feel about Melanie dating?

Peter: I was always happy for both Zara and Mellie to date. I wanted them to find the same happiness I'd shared with Linda. I can't say I was thrilled with Melanie's choice of boyfriend. For a smart, beautiful and confident young woman, Mellie seemed to like dating idiots and losers. Jonnie was no different, except he seemed to hang around a bit longer. In the end I had to have a word with his father and get him to back off.

Ryan: This was after Melanie's arrest on the twentieth of August 2006, I presume?

[Silence]

Ryan: Sir Peter?

Peter: Sorry, what was the question?

Ryan: I asked about Melanie's arrest in 2006?

Peter: That's what's next, is it?

Ryan: Yes, but only if you're up for it. Can I get you a glass of water?

Peter: No, I'm fine, but let's take that break.

Ryan: Sure. No problem.

RECORDING STOPPED

Netflix Original Documentary:
Melanie Lange – The Ugly Truth

INTERVIEWS RECORDED 19–22 SEPTEMBER 2022
(220 DAYS SINCE MELANIE'S DISAPPEARANCE)

Narrator

In the early hours of Sunday morning, the twentieth of August 2006, little more than a year after her modelling career ended, Melanie was arrested by the Metropolitan Police for car theft, driving without a licence, driving without insurance, and driving while over the legal alcohol limit. The charge of car theft was later dropped.

Nell

The night Mel got arrested was awful. Even thinking about it now, I get really hot and my pulse starts racing. I could've killed Jonnie after that. It was all his fault.

Jonnie Welbourn-Jones, owner of Jonnie Jones Microbrewery

I was wasted that night, otherwise there was no way I'd have let Melanie get behind the wheel. I still can't believe Nell did, to be honest.

Nell

Jonnie was on something that night. It was obvious to me that it was more than just alcohol. The weather was hot and not in a good way. The kind of sticky heat that makes you feel grubby. We'd all been drinking in the garden of Jonnie's local pub in Camden. It was me, Jonnie, Mel and this guy I'd been seeing. It was fun at first, but by closing time I was ready to go home. So was Mel. She'd taken it easy. She had maybe three glasses of wine over the space of the whole day. She was having lunch with her dad and sister the following day and the last thing she needed was to turn up hungover.

Jonnie was supposed to go to the lunch as well, but the more he drank, the more obvious it was that he wouldn't be going. Mel was furious, but Jonnie was beyond caring.

Personally, I thought it was self-sabotage on Jonnie's part and I didn't blame him for that. I'd sat through enough lunches with Sir Peter to know how painful they could be. No one was good enough for Melanie in his eyes, especially not me, but Mel liked support at the lunches. She wanted someone else to talk to so she didn't have to talk to Zara any more than she needed to. By that point, they were barely speaking, and that was only when Sir Peter was in the room with them.

I got the impression that having a wingman at these lunches meant Sir Peter couldn't grill Mel on her life choices. Sir Peter was always hard on her, always wanting more.

Mel had been working at a boutique in South Kensington after finishing her A Levels while she figured out what she wanted to do, and Sir Peter was on a mission for her to go to university. She's always loved fashion and she got to choose some of the lines they stocked. She was happy, but that didn't seem to matter to Sir Peter.

I suggested to Mel that she crash at mine that night. Jonnie could be a really fun drunk, but he had a tendency to turn a bit nasty and I could see the fight brewing between them. The guy I was seeing left at some point and then Jonnie wanted to carry on drinking back at his place. The plan was that we'd walk him home and then Mel would grab her bag and we'd find a taxi.

Except the minute we turn on to Jonnie's street, we see about ten paparazzi. It's clear they've been waiting for a while and are all pretty restless. Those guys . . . I knew most of them by name at that point, and individually they were all pretty OK blokes. Normal guys, you know? A lot of them were married with kids. It was weird sometimes to think about them that way, especially those times when they were together like they were that night. Mel calls it pack mentality or something. It was like they stopped being themselves. They were just this faceless group.

The minute they see us, their cameras start going off and one of them says something and then they're all shouting. Melanie puts on her sunglasses and we pick up the pace. We're moving closer and they're moving closer, and then all of a sudden they surround us and we can't move. I remember feeling really freaked out.

Jonnie being Jonnie decides to make a big show of affection towards Mel. He throws his arm around her and starts kissing her neck and her lips. He keeps saying, 'Let's just give the shits what they want.'

Mel keeps smiling the whole time and tries to laugh it off, but I can tell she's getting upset. People don't realize how scary it is to have a group of people surrounding you like that, flashing a camera in your face and shouting at you. They wouldn't get out of the way and very quickly, Jonnie goes from Mr Affectionate Nice Guy to wanting to kill them all. He starts shoving at the group and then grabs Mel and drags her down the street and into the house so fast she can barely stand up. Obviously that's all caught on camera as well.

The minute we're through the front door, Jonnie goes mental and rushes into the living room. He's throwing stuff about and looking for something. We follow him in and stand in the doorway and Mel tells him to calm down, but of course he doesn't. And then he pulls out an old cricket bat from behind the sofa and starts yelling about how he's going to smash up the cameras.

Melanie and I are stone-cold sober by this point and just want to leave, but on Mel's part, she's also trying to calm Jonnie down because she knows that if he does go outside, it's going to reflect badly on her in the press.

Mel blocks the doorway and Jonnie gets this crazy look in his eyes, and I take a step between them, trying to get Jonnie to put the bat down. We're all screaming and swearing at each other to shut up, which doesn't help.

Then Jonnie starts swinging the bat and yelling at us to move. He takes a step forward and that's when the bat smashes into a vase on the coffee table. Glass flies everywhere and there's this weird moment where we all just stand there, looking at the broken glass, and I think, 'Great, it's shaken some sense into him,' but then he starts moving towards the door again.

Mel can be stubborn. Especially if she knows she's right about something, then she's going to dig her heels in. But Jonnie wouldn't listen to a word she was saying and it didn't look like either of them were going to back down. Then Jonnie swings the bat again and I jump back and that's when I step on a shard of glass from the vase. I'm only wearing a pair of cheap sandals and the glass just cuts straight through the sole and right into my foot.

Instantly, there's blood everywhere and the pain – God, it was awful. I'm hopping around trying to get away from the other pieces of glass. Jonnie drops the bat, forgets all about going outside, and starts freaking out about the blood staining his dad's carpets. Mel grabs a towel and makes me sit down on the sofa, and it's completely obvious that I need to go to hospital. But there's all these photographers outside the front door and there's no way we can get past them to grab a taxi.

Jonnie becomes convinced that I've stepped on the glass on purpose because I want Mel's attention. Mel tells him to shut up and he flounces off to bed in a major sulk, which was the only useful thing he did that night.

So there I am, bleeding like crazy, and Mel starts crying and keeps saying she's sorry, like any of it is her fault. Then Mel gets this idea that we can go out the back and down the alley that runs along the back of the houses. Jonnie's car is parked a little way down the street and we reckon we can sneak around the photographers to get it. Mel is like a week away from passing her driving test so it's going to be me that's driving, except I'm feeling pretty woozy from the shock of seeing all the blood, but we make it down the alley and around the side of the house. Mel props me up and we hobble as fast as we can to Jonnie's car. Then just as we get there, Mel grabs the keys from me and pushes me into the passenger seat. I try to tell her not to drive, but she's so upset, she won't hear of me driving.

I have no idea why it didn't occur to either of us to call an ambulance. It just didn't. I think it was the knowledge that my foot needed medical attention but I wasn't dying or anything. Obviously, if I could go back now I would call an ambulance in a heartbeat. But on that night, we were both tired, slightly drunk, plus Mel was upset, and we weren't thinking straight. You have to remember that we'd just been boxed in by the pack of paparazzi. We were freaking out and no one made the right decision.

Jonnie Welbourn-Jones, owner of Jonnie Jones Microbrewery
We got home from the pub. I passed out. The next day I woke up to a million messages and the police at my door telling me they'd recovered my car and asking me who else drives it. I was like, 'Just me, man, so it must have been stolen.' It was only when I sobered up a bit and realized it was Mel who'd taken it that I said I'd lent it to her. I hadn't, but it wasn't stealing. She just borrowed it.

From: Zara.Lange@LangeHotels.com
To: Lange Hotel Employees (all); Lange Cosmetics Employees (all);
Baby Lange Employees (all)
Date: 6 October 2022
Subject: Revision to Working From Home Policy

You'll be aware that recently there has been an increase in the number of press outside the office. We understand how difficult this has been and would like to thank all of you for your continued patience. We are working with the building security team to resolve this situation, but in the meantime please speak to your line manager if you would prefer to work from home on a short-term basis.

Regards

Zara Lange

VP Lange Hotels

CEO of Lange Cosmetics (acting)

From: Zara.Lange@LangeHotels.com
To: Security@LangeHotels.com
Date: 6 October 2022
Subject: FW: Revision to Working From Home Policy

IT'S A FUCKING CIRCUS OUT THERE!!!!! There must be something you can do!!

SIR PETER LANGE –
MY SIDE OF THE STORY (UNPUBLISHED)

*Interviews between ghost writer Ryan Morris
and Peter Lange, 6 October 2022*

Ryan: Are you feeling better this morning, Sir Peter?

Peter: Yes, I'm fine. Apologies again. I got called into several urgent meetings yesterday regarding a hotel issue, which is why we couldn't continue. I hope my secretary explained all that.

Ryan: Yes, she did. It was no problem.

Peter: Let's carry on then. You wanted to talk about Mellie's first arrest?

Ryan: Yes. That's where we got to yesterday.

Peter: [Sighs] Mellie had finished her A Levels and was working in a clothes shop, which was quite frankly beneath her, but I was trying very hard during that time to give her more freedom. She'd asked if she could sleep over at Jonnie's house on that particular Saturday and I'd reluctantly, stupidly, agreed.

I'm not a great sleeper at the best of times, but knowing Mellie wasn't home made it doubly hard. I was still awake in the early hours of Sunday morning when my phone rang and it was Mellie in absolute hysterics. I could barely make out a word she was saying. It took five attempts before I understood she'd been arrested and was being held at Kentish Town police station. The first thing I did was call my lawyer, Frank Jacobs, and then I jumped in my car and drove over there. Frank was waiting for me, suited and booted, and the first thing we saw was a photographer outside the station. To this day I don't know how he found out so quickly that Mellie had been arrested.

Frank and I quickly established that Mellie was driving that stupid friend of hers, Nell, to the hospital. She was breathalysed at the scene and found to be over the limit by one point. There was also some question over whether she'd stolen the car, but that was later dropped because quite frankly it was ludicrous. Things were bad enough.

Ryan: There were reports at the time that your intervention got Melanie a lighter sentence, considering your political connections and friends in high places.

Peter: Melanie was charged with driving without a licence, driving without insurance, and driving over the legal limit of alcohol. She pleaded guilty to all three and received three hundred hours of community service and a one-year driving ban. The average number of community service hours given at that time for similar offences was closer to a hundred hours. Melanie didn't receive a light sentence. If anything she received a harsher sentence because the CPS were desperate not to be seen as lenient under the scrutiny of the media. I did not step in at any point. I did not call in any favours, regardless of whether they were owed to me. I felt it was important for Mellie to learn from the experience.

Ryan: And do you feel she did?

Peter: It was very hard to watch her go through that period of her life. It broke my heart to see her struggle, but yes, I did feel she learned from it. Until her second arrest.

Netflix Original Documentary:
Melanie Lange – The Ugly Truth

INTERVIEWS RECORDED 19–22 SEPTEMBER 2022
(220 DAYS SINCE MELANIE'S DISAPPEARANCE)

Narrator

After pleading guilty, Melanie received a one-year driving ban and three hundred hours of community service cleaning the streets of East London. Despite countless offers from TV chat shows and reporters, Melanie never commented publicly or apologized.

Nell

Like everything with Melanie, the tabloids are going to say whatever they want to say to sell their papers. The actual story is completely ignored or twisted into something unrecognizable.

For starters, Melanie was a week away from taking her driving test. She could drive fine. Hell, she was a better driver than me. I used to get so nervous about all the one-way systems, constantly changing lanes at the last minute.

Melanie took the keys that night because obviously I couldn't drive with a bleeding foot. I was sat beside her and had a full driver's licence, and she was only one point over the legal driving limit too. No one ever picks up on that. I'm not saying what we did was right. It wasn't, but it wasn't as bad as the papers made out. It wasn't some drunken joyride. She was trying to get me to hospital.

So anyway, she drives off and we get away from the photographers. A&E is ten minutes down the road. But of course we get stopped by a police car.

The police immediately call an ambulance for me, breathalyse Melanie, and before we've had a chance to explain, she's in the back of a police car and I'm being strapped on to a stretcher.

I didn't see her for a month after that. Her dad took her phone and she was forbidden to leave the house for anything but the community service.

Jonnie Welbourn-Jones, owner of Jonnie Jones Microbrewery

What is going on right now? Where do I think Melanie is? Honestly – I think she's hiding.

I was an outsider in the whole Melanie and Nell, Melanie and Sir Peter thing, and I haven't spoken to Melanie for years, but the only person I ever saw with their claws in Melanie was Nell. Mel was her cash machine. Where else was Nell getting her money from? The times I knew Nell, she didn't have a job or rich parents, and yet she had a studio flat in Soho, all the designer gear, and was out every night.

Bill Cutting, former paparazzi photographer

I was the only paparazzo to get the shot of Melanie leaving the police station. She had her head down and a hood up, but I was at the bottom of the steps and got a great shot of her face. Her dad had his arm around Melanie and was hurrying her towards a car. I got out of the way sharpish. You don't survive in the industry as long as I did without knowing when someone is going to lamp you, or worse, snatch your camera and smash it up.

I sold two photos that night. The first was Melanie stumbling along the road with Jonnie, the second was her walking out of the police station. Everyone always wants to know how I got to the police station so fast that night after Melanie's arrest.

The assumption has always been that I had a contact inside the police, but that wasn't it at all. The truth is, and I can say this now as I'm well out of all that, I had this super-sweet deal with Melanie's mate, Nell.

Nell

Oh God, Bill said that?

[Pause]

Look, I hate myself for it, OK? All I can say is that at the time I was young, immature, and I needed money.

[Crying]

I know I betrayed Mel. I was a massive idiot. I would do anything to go back and change it now. At the time I reasoned that the paps were always around us, like every day. We couldn't go anywhere without someone calling someone and then they'd turn up. At least with me feeding information to Bill, it meant it was just one photographer and I could control what he saw. I never called him if Mel was in a really bad way after a night out.

Bill Cutting, former paparazzi photographer

Nell would text me when they were going to be somewhere, and I'd be there with my camera to get some shots of them coming out of the back door of a nightclub or popping to Starbucks. I'd give Nell 20 per cent of whatever I got from selling the photos. It was the easiest money I ever made, working with Nell.

Nell

The thing is, the more money a person has, the less they think about it. It never occurred to Melanie that my modelling work had dried up and I didn't have an income. Money just never crossed her mind. Someone had to pay for the taxis and the bar bill at the end of the night when she was out of it, and that someone was me, and I was happy to do it, but I needed money.

I should have just said something about it. We were so close. But there were still things we didn't talk about. One of them was Sir Peter and another was how much money she had, and how little I had.

The paparazzi were going to take their photos one way or another. At least this way I could afford my own place, which, like I said, I did for Mel as much as for me. Mel told me every day how much she needed me. We were a team. I couldn't exactly get a nine-to-five job and still be there for her. Who'd have hired me any-way? That's what I thought. I'm not smart like Mel is, and I didn't have parents telling me to work hard in school because I might need good results one day. I thought I'd be a model and that was it.

Bill Cutting, former paparazzi photographer
So the reason I was the only one outside that police station to get a shot of Melanie leaving was because Nell phoned me from the back of an ambulance. She made close to six figures for that photo.

Jonnie Welbourn-Jones, owner of Jonnie Jones Microbrewery
I totally called that one. Boom! It's just like I said – Melanie was Nell's cash machine. She always has been. No Melanie, no cash cow for Nell. Is it any wonder then that Nell is so desperate to get her friend back? Even this documentary – I've got to ask, where is the money going? Nell's pocket, I bet.

Nell
[Crying]
I know it's easy to say, but I completely regret it now, especially the night of Melanie's arrest. Bill phoned me when I was on my way to hospital because he'd been outside Jonnie's house and spotted us driving away. I should've just hung up but I was drunk and panick-ing, and I stupidly mentioned that I couldn't talk because I was on my way to hospital. Bill asked if Mel was with me and I said, 'No, she's been arrested,' and he took it from there.

The arrest devastated Mel. It would have been in the news the next day regardless, but having those two photos side by side of Melanie stumbling along the pavement with Jonnie and walking out of the police station with Sir Peter made it so much bigger. That night was a real wake-up call for me. It made me realize that not everyone sees and feels things the way I do.

I'm super thick-skinned, which comes from growing up in a small house with three older brothers who'll give you a dead arm if you look at them the wrong way and tease you mercilessly if you so much as mention a weakness of any kind. I once had a spider in my room and made the mistake of screaming. After that, all three of them would catch spiders and put them above my bed and sometimes in my bed, and then they'd tell me that spiders crawl into ears and lay eggs inside brains while people sleep. So obviously, I didn't sleep for about a year.

Anyway, what I'm saying is, when I saw the emotion – the anguish on Mel's face – in the photo Bill took of her leaving the police station, it was the first time I stopped and properly wondered if Melanie was as tough as I first thought.

That photo ran on every front page. Even one of the broadsheets took the story. I got seven stitches in my foot that night and I was told not to put any weight on it. But I hobbled to the nearest shop the day after and bought a couple of the papers, and I just sat in bed staring at the total devastation that was written all over Melanie's face.

Like I said, I didn't speak to Melanie for a while after that. I think having that space gave me time to realize that I needed to get on with my own life. It was hard to accept that modelling wasn't going to happen for me. It had been my dream for as long as I could remember, but I'd been kidding myself. No one wanted me to model for them any more.

I probably could've made some decent money writing a gossip column for one of the weekly magazines, but all they really wanted was to know about Melanie and what she was doing, and there was no way I could do that. I was already feeling so guilty about working with Bill.

That's when I really opened my eyes and realized that Melanie was actually a super-private person. She never did any interviews or made anything out of her fame. When she was first in the weeklies, we'd have a laugh about it. She thought it was odd but she didn't mind. And I never really thought about how her feelings might have changed over the years because by that point in 2006, 2007 when Twitter really took off and every little thing she did or wore or was overheard saying was twisted and scrutinized into something nasty, I'm pretty sure she hated it all. It's why it took her so long to agree to release her videos publicly and show the world what her father is doing to her. I can't believe I'm still using the present tense on this. The videos of Melanie begging for freedom are out there and nothing is being done. As we're sitting here recording this documentary, Mel is trapped in a house somewhere, shut off from her whole life.

It's one of the reasons I agreed to be part of this documentary – to tell the truth with no spin, to tell Melanie's story. All I want is to save Melanie.

Girl About Town

Gossip Blog

8 January 2007

Guys!!! I know you're all desperate to hear from Melanie but she said no AGAIN!! I've asked her so many times now and every time I get this boring email from the Lange Hotels PR team saying Melanie is a private person and doesn't do interviews. I'm so pissed off!

She might not 'do' interviews but she's certainly 'doing' the men of London right now. I was thinking about it the other day, and I couldn't even remember what she was famous for anyway. Other than getting arrested! Ha ha!

But I do have some news for you today – about me! I'm now on Twitter!!! It's going to be massive, guys! You have to get on it!! Follow me for all the latest London gossip @GirlAboutTownBlog

Comments

LOL

Finally someone speaks the truth. What is she famous for? NOTHING!

Melanie has never given an interview. She actually is a private person. She doesn't ask for all the attention she gets.

Her job is to literally stand in front of a camera and say 'look at me'. She loves the attention!

She's not even that pretty any more.

PART II

Melanie Lange video 5/9
Published on Melanie Lange YouTube channel on 4 August 2022

I'm Melanie Lange. I'm a prisoner.

[Sighing]

I'm just saying hi. I miss my life so much. Of course I miss the boys the most, but I miss Nell too. I miss everyone at Lange Cosmetics and Baby Lange. You guys are the best.

I even miss Zara, which is pretty stupid because we barely saw each other and when we did, we didn't talk, not properly. Zara – if you ever watch these videos, please help. You of all people can help me!

Don't believe what Dad is telling you.

Twitter
10 January 2007

Amy B @GirlAboutTownBlog

Guys!!!! I'm on Twitter!!! So excited to be here! Follow me for all the latest all about town gossip! #LondonBaby #CelebrityGossip

Amy B @GirlAboutTownBlog

Been wondering – what do we think about Melanie appearing in the @JerboaMusic vid? Desperate if you ask me #MelanieLange #CelebrityGossip

> **Shannon Grant @CoffeeLova1000**
>
> The song was literally about her! Why shouldn't she be in the video?

> **Tammy S @TammySunflowers**
>
> I didn't care she was in it, but she could've made an effort! She looked really skinny and washed out.

> **Patsy Hanson @LeicesterWeddingPhotography**
>
> I love Melanie Lange! She should be in all their videos.

> **Trisha Aitken @TrishaVAitken**
>
> I used to look up to Melanie. I spent like a year wearing only Lacoste, LOL! But she's fucking minging now. How is she even still famous?

SIR PETER LANGE —
MY SIDE OF THE STORY (UNPUBLISHED)

*Interviews between ghost writer Ryan Morris
and Peter Lange, 6 October 2022*

Ryan: The second arrest for Melanie happened six months after the first, the day after her nineteenth birthday celebrations – the fifteenth of February 2007. Before we talk about the arrest, can you tell me what that time period was like for you and Melanie? From the outside, looking only at the media coverage of that time, Melanie seemed quite out of control. She'd been arrested and charged. She'd been sentenced to three hundred hours of community service. And there were regular stories about her drinking and partying antics. And yet, she completed her community service during that period and was working in a high-end clothing store, so my question is, was Melanie as out of control at it seemed?

Peter: Not at all. The media have always had an agenda when it comes to my daughter and very rarely does that agenda tally with any semblance of truth.

Despite her fame and the constant press attention, things calmed down a lot during those months, and that was for the obvious reason that Mellie landed herself in a whole load of trouble with the police and with me. I confiscated her phone for a month and grounded her for a total of three months. She was allowed out of the house for her community service and to work. There was a spell in those months when we stopped arguing and I wasn't the enemy any more. The arrest dented Mellie's confidence in herself, which in the long run did her good. The tabloids and magazine stories about her had been growing progressively nastier. I know the photograph of her coming out of the police station and the stories that followed were particularly hard on Mellie.

She broke up with Jonnie the day after the arrest. I'm the last person she'd have confided in about the break-up, but it was obvious she blamed him in some part for what happened. I always felt it was a shame that Nell didn't get the same treatment, but then at least without the opportunity for Nell to drag her to parties, Mellie settled down.

Ryan: One question I think the readers will want to know the answer to is: why didn't either you or Melanie give an interview after her arrest? The tabloids made quite a thing about it, calling Mel a spoilt rich girl on numerous occasions, painting her as the villain. Surely you had ample opportunities to explain the full story and gain some sympathy?

Peter: It was certainly discussed with Lange's PR manager at the time. We thought a breakfast TV interview on *This Morning* would give the best chance to explain things. I felt that a public apology, an admission of her mistakes, would calm the flames. But Mellie was completely against it. She was convinced that the media would twist whatever she said. You have to remember that Mellie has never given a single personal interview in any magazine or tabloid.

Ryan: Why is that?

Peter: Melanie may have modelled as a teenager, but she never asked for or craved the public attention she received. She took every single story told about her to heart. I can't tell you how many times I've found her crying over some ridiculous story about her weight or her life choices. She told me once, 'An interview would be poking the hornets' nest.' She felt very strongly that the media had given her the label of a trouble-maker, and nothing she did or said would ever change that. I can't say I agreed at the time, but I respected her decision.

Ryan: Did the change in your relationship with Mellie have anything to do with Miriam Short?

Peter: Perhaps. I worried at the time about introducing Miriam to the girls. A big part of me still felt it was too soon after Linda's death. But the three of them got on like a house on fire.

Ryan: How long did you and Miriam date?

Peter: Around six months before I introduced her to the girls, and then I think it was another six months before we ended the relationship.

Ryan: Why did it end?

Peter: Miriam wanted more from me and our relationship than I could give her. She didn't have a family of her own and she wanted to be part of one. On my more pessimistic days, I think the reality of us didn't live up to her expectations of family life. She asked me once if I'd ever put her before the girls. It was the kind of question only a person without children would ask. I was very fond of Miriam and I didn't want our relationship to end. I sometimes wonder what would've happened if I'd answered that question differently, but I have always been one for brutal honesty, and so I said, 'No,' when perhaps what I should have said is, 'Not right now.' She ended things soon after that. It was all very amicable and we remain friends.

Ryan: It was during this period that Melanie completed her community service. How did she handle that?

Peter: I have always instilled in both girls the understanding that hard work of any kind is never something to shy away from, and Mellie did her hours without complaint. Mellie, more than anyone, knew she'd made a huge mistake getting behind the wheel of that car and wanted to make amends. She might not have apologized publicly for her behaviour but she was most certainly sorry.

Ryan: And the events surrounding her second arrest? What happened there?

[Silence]

Are you OK, Sir Peter?

Peter: Melanie's nineteenth birthday was one of the worst times of my life. I've never spoken about it before.

[Silence]

Can we take a break?

Ryan: Of course.

RECORDING STOPPED

Netflix Original Documentary: Melanie Lange – The Ugly Truth

INTERVIEWS RECORDED 19–22 SEPTEMBER 2022
(220 DAYS SINCE MELANIE'S DISAPPEARANCE)

Narrator

Between the late summer of 2006 and February 2007 Melanie kept a low profile. Photos taken of Melanie during that period showed her out shopping or completing her community service. She remained front page news and was once again voted World's Sexiest Woman by *Loaded*.

Miriam Short, family friend

My name is Miriam Short. I guess you'd say I was a family friend to the Langes. I dated Sir Peter and got to know both Melanie and Zara very well when Melanie was around eighteen.

I met Peter at one of those hideously stuffy business networking events. It was a warm-white-wine-in-plastic-cups kind of event, and not something I usually attended. However, the organizer was a dear friend of mine and I had my arm twisted into being one of the two keynote speakers. Peter was the other. I can't remember a jot about that speech, but I gave a lot of talks back then about smashing the glass ceiling. I remember Peter's speech though. Ha! That man knows how to command a room. He talked about the importance of supporting colleagues. He specifically talked about women in business being pitted against each other to the detriment of both parties and the business. I still remember it today. 'Support and collaboration are at the heart of a thriving company.' It was inspiring, and a darn sight more important to the feminist movement than my speech. But of course the irony is that no one wants to hear a women talk about feminism, least of all a Black woman. Far better to have it 'mansplained', as my goddaughter likes to say.

After our speeches, Peter asked me if I wanted to get a proper drink, and I did. I thought he'd take me to some fancy members' club, not the dusty-floored wine bar near Blackfriars that we ended up in. It was nothing fancy, but it was intimate. I still love that wine bar.

We dated for around a year. Peter is a very funny and charismatic man. So many men I dated back then couldn't stand how successful I was in business. Oh, they'd say they didn't mind, but then it wasn't long before they'd try to belittle me. Little things at first. Picking at my age or my clothes. Like living with a horrible little bird. Peck, peck, peck. I kicked them to the kerb sharpish. You don't rise to the top by listening to the opinions of men.

Peter, for all his faults, wasn't like that. He saw me as an equal. There was a time when I'd hoped we would go the distance. But it soon became clear that Peter only had time for two things in this life – his business and Melanie.

I don't know how Zara coped with it. I'm sure that's why she joined the business. I'm not sure Peter would've noticed her other-wise. I offered her a chance to jump ship and come work with me, even offered to double her salary, but she turned it down. I always thought that was a shame. You can't make someone notice you, not even your own father.

My take on it, for what it's worth, was that Peter loved Zara every bit as much as he loved Melanie, he just didn't have room in his life to show it the way he did with Melanie, and it caused a lot of tension between the girls. Family dinners around that table were more toxic than a boardroom takeover.

I spoke to Peter about it once, but he brushed it aside.

I got on very well with both girls, but in the end there just wasn't room for me in Peter's life. I wanted to be part of a family. I'd never had my own children. Rightly or wrongly, I didn't believe women could have it all and I wanted my business over children back then. But there was something very wrong beneath the surface of that family. Peter was far too obsessed with Melanie to be a normal father to either of the girls, and so with a heavy heart I walked away.

I won't pretend to have any insight into what's happening right now, but I would like to say this: Peter was a good father during the time I spent with him. His only crime perhaps was caring too much. From one control freak to another, I understood completely.

Where is Melanie right now? If Peter is behind it, then I'm absolutely certain that she's safe and being well cared for.

Vic Watson, tabloid editor
Melanie kept her head down for a while after the first arrest in 2006, especially when it came to boyfriends. I remember one of my colleagues at the time saying that Melanie Lange's star was fading and that the public were losing interest in her. I wasn't so sure. We even had a bet over it, and obviously I won.

Jonnie Welbourn-Jones, owner of Jonnie Jones Microbrewery
We broke up. It was a joint decision. We both knew it wasn't going anywhere.

Nell
Mel dumped Jonnie. He took it badly, and as soon as Mel was allowed out again he kept turning up everywhere we went, begging her for a second chance. I think Sir Peter spoke to his dad in the end and then he backed off.

Palomi Lawal, community service coordinator
I met Melanie when she was eighteen. She'd been sent to me for community service. I was expecting an absolute brat, to be honest. We get them all the time, but that wasn't Melanie. She was polite for one thing, always listening when I was talking, always pleases and thank yous. I swear some kids think I get up every morning with a mission to ruin their lives. I'm just doing my job.

Melanie pitched up ten minutes early on day one. It was cleaning graffiti from walls and litter picking in the East London area. There was an urbanization project of some kind underway. She kept her head down and did the work. Lord knows how she did it with those cameras in her face and all up in her business. I remember one of the days she couldn't even move, they were all around her. It's enough to send anyone crazy. Not that I'm saying for one moment that Melanie is crazy, you understand, just that there is no way that girl could have any kind of normal life with the way they treated her. Like she belonged to them.

I caught her crying in the toilets once. She was so apologetic and promised to make up the time, but I told her not to worry. Now, there have to be boundaries in my kind of job. These kids and adults need to know that I'm the boss. I'm the one who can report back to the courts that they aren't doing their work. But all that went out the window when I saw Melanie crying. I don't think I've ever seen someone in so much need of a hug. I opened my arms and she half threw herself at me. I hugged her tight, none of this pat on the back rubbish. I hugged her for a long while and eventually she stopped crying.

I told her, 'I don't know how you do it.'

And she just smiled and wiped her eyes and said something like, 'You get used to it. Most of the time I don't even notice them. It's just when they get really close to me that I get scared. They're just trying to do their jobs. It's not their fault that newspapers and magazines will pay so much money for a photo of me.'

Of course I couldn't resist asking, 'How much?'

She laughed and said, 'Up to a million for a money shot.'

I asked, 'What's a money shot?'

And she said, 'It's a photo of me doing something wrong or stupid or looking a mess.'

Well, that got me thinking, didn't it. 'So,' I said, 'if they get all up in your business and scare you and make you angry and you lash out, then they get more money?'

She looked kinda sad then and nodded. It makes you think, doesn't it?

I offered to lie on her sheet, you know? Say she'd done more hours than she had. First and only time in my whole career I offered that. But Melanie said no and went back out there like nothing had happened. We got pretty friendly after that and she found out I volunteered at a food bank on Tuesday mornings. One day she just rocked up with a load of food and scurried into the back and helped sort everything into piles. She kept out of sight from anyone coming in. She did it for weeks and we had a right laugh. But then I was short-staffed and so she helped hand out the parcels. The following week the place was surrounded by photographers. No one could come in and get food. I didn't see her after that.

She sent me a card saying how sorry she was for the trouble she had caused. I know those papers made out like it was a stunt to improve her public image, but it wasn't. She still sends me a Christmas hamper every year, and once a month we get a Tesco van arrive at the food bank with hundreds of pounds' worth of food. I don't know for sure it's her, but I like to think I got to know Melanie pretty well during that time, and I think it is.

I never looked at the headlines the same after meeting Melanie. Seeing how those paparazzi treated her. It was disgusting.

Vic Watson, tabloid editor
Melanie Lange may not have been selling her story to every magazine and newspaper going, but do not mistake this for someone who did not want the limelight shone on her.

Four months after her arrest, she appears in a music video for Jerboa. One of the biggest bands of the moment writes a song about Melanie. They even name it after her, and does she shy away and say she doesn't want that attention? No. Of course she doesn't. She does the complete opposite. She even posed on the cover of *NME* with them.

Nell

Oh my god, that song. It still doesn't seem real that it even happened. I remember Mel getting a call from Jerboa's agent telling her that they'd written this song about her. Mel is obviously worried at first but then we listen to it and it's . . . it's magic. It captures something about that time, about Melanie and the tabloids.

'Just keep dancing, sweet Melanie.'

Sorry, my voice is screeching-cat terrible, I know, but that line always chokes me up. Mel loved it. The second she hears it, she starts dancing around and laughing. It was the first time I'd seen her properly happy since the arrest.

Then the agent tells her that they're filming the video and does she want to be in it? There was only one answer to that.

I'm in the video too. If you look really closely at one minute twenty-two seconds in, you'll see a blonde walking down the street. That's me.

The following summer we went to see Jerboa play at Reading Festival. Someone recognized Mel in the crowd and then Chris, the lead singer, spots her too and is like, 'Hey guys, how about we get Miss Melanie Lange up on stage for her song?'

The noise of the crowd was deafening. Despite all the negativity she got in the press, there were a lot of people that loved her. There still are.

Going to that festival and seeing the attention Melanie got was a huge wake-up call for me on just how famous Mel was at that point. It didn't seem to faze Melanie at all. People would come up to her and ask for a photo and she'd pose for every single one. She made every single person who spoke to her feel special.

SIR PETER LANGE —
MY SIDE OF THE STORY (UNPUBLISHED)

*Interviews between ghost writer Ryan Morris
and Peter Lange, 6 October 2022*

Peter: You were asking about Mellie's birthday.

Ryan: Yes I was, but if you want to skip this for now and come back to it at the end, that's no problem.

Peter: It won't be any easier then. I'd rather get it over with. [Sighs] I don't know where to start.

Ryan: What did you get Melanie for her birthday?

Peter: Melanie's eighteenth the year before had been a quiet affair. She never outwardly showed much upset about losing her modelling career, but I felt that perhaps, inside at least, she was still licking her wounds. I seem to remember she also had mock exams the week of her birthday and that was the focus. She'd stopped talking about moving out, but as her nineteenth birthday approached it became a sticking point again.

There were two things Mellie wanted for her birthday that year. The first was her own place, the second was her own car. But seeing as she still had another six months on her ban before she could take her driving test, moving out was all she talked about. And while I didn't feel ready, or think Mellie was ready, it was increasingly clear to me that she might move out whether I supported the decision or not. My concern was that she'd decide to sell her story to a magazine to make some money and regret it afterwards. Or move in with Nell, which I didn't feel would be a good atmosphere for her.

But no matter how I looked at it, Mellie had no desire to live under my roof. Our relationship was often strained. I could do no right in my daughter's eyes and I knew there wasn't much I could do to convince her to stay. I felt incredibly sad about this and guilty too. If I'd been around for Mellie more in her earlier years, I'm sure our relationship would have been stronger.

There was a part of me – a big part – that hoped that Mellie getting the space she craved might improve our relationship as well as her relationship with Zara, who as I said was still at home and taking care of much of the home life. The way I saw it, I had two choices. I could give Mellie my blessing and keep control of the situation, or I could put my foot down and watch Mellie pack her bags and leave anyway.

I found a nice third-floor apartment ten minutes' walk away from the house so she could pop back for dinner anytime she liked. It had a concierge and an entry system, which I felt would offer the privacy she needed away from the press.

I purposely chose a one-bedroom apartment. I didn't want Nell moving in the second Mellie got the keys. There was nothing I could do to stop the friendship between Nell and Mellie, but I certainly wasn't going to encourage it.

The entire place was only a fraction bigger than her room at home, but I hoped she'd love it.

Ryan: Did she?

Peter: Yes, she did. I'll never forget her reaction. On the morning of her birthday, Mellie wakes up and comes running down the stairs in her PJs. She hasn't brushed her hair and it's a thick brown mess. She's not wearing any make-up either. I remember because seeing her rush into the kitchen with a big smile on her face, looking all of ten years old, was like a knife to my heart. So young and also so grown-up. I imagine it's something all parents experience, but more so with the knowledge that every year that passes is another year Linda hasn't been here. Another year Mellie and Zara have had without a mother.

Anyway, that morning Mellie comes into the kitchen, hopping from foot to foot, eyeing the pile of presents and cards on the counter. She opens everything and I make her favourite blueberry pancakes. It's nice. Special. Just the two of us. When breakfast is finished she looks up at me, eyes wide and expectant, the smile twitching on her mouth, and I laugh and slide the keys across the counter.

Ryan: Was Zara there?

Peter: She had an early meeting so she wasn't there. Zara had finished the graduate scheme at that point, and when I wasn't sending her to meetings on my behalf, she was working her way up the finance team. She didn't have any staff of her own, but she was certainly not junior either. She was working hard and building a name for herself as someone who got things done. The plan was for Zara to join us for dinner that night, but Nell ruined that.

Ryan: How did Zara feel about Melanie getting her own place?

Peter: I don't think Zara felt anything about it. She expressed concerns to me that Mellie was too young, which I shared. There were no bad feelings from Zara about Mellie moving out. Or if there were, she didn't express them to me, and Zara has always been the type to speak her mind.

She told me the night of Mellie's birthday that she might start looking for her own place too, and I offered to help her in the same way I'd helped Mellie. But Zara never did look, as far as I know. The house is big enough that we're not tripping over each other and I know Zara likes to keep an eye on me, make sure I'm not working too hard.

Ryan: And what did Melanie say about the apartment?

Peter: She snatches up the keys and just screams. Then she hugs me. It reminded me of when she was very little. Maybe five or six.

I'd come home from work late and exhausted. Linda would be in the kitchen heating up a plate of whatever dinner I'd missed. I'd be in the hall untying my shoelaces, pulling off my tie, and then a little face would appear from the top of the stairs. Two big green eyes and a gap-toothed grin looking at me from between the spindles of the banister. I'd smile, and Mellie would shoot down the stairs like a little ninja and throw herself into my arms. She'd whisper in my ear, 'I wanted to see you. Don't tell Mummy I'm still awake.' Those were the best moments of my day. That's what that hug reminded me of.

It was bitterly cold for February, but no rain so we walked over to the apartment as soon as Mellie was dressed. I wanted her to see just how close she was to home. I opened the door to her apartment and we got that fresh-paint smell wafting out. I'd had all the walls painted white because I knew Mellie would want to add lots of colour herself. The place was completely empty of furniture, and Mellie spent about ten minutes just dancing around it and beaming. It was a smile I hadn't seen on Mellie for a long time.

Then I gave her a budget to furnish it and took her shopping. It was a perfect day. We laughed a lot looking at furniture. It felt like I'd finally done something right, like maybe my relationship with Mellie was stronger than I thought.

Ryan: And later? You mentioned Nell ruined your dinner plans.

Peter: Yes. I really wanted to organize a party for Mellie and keep control of what I could see was going to be another circus. After her arrest the year before, I was very anxious anytime Mellie went out. I couldn't sleep, I couldn't concentrate on anything. It felt like I was constantly waiting for my mobile to ring. It was exhausting.

I offered her a no-expense-spared, any band she wanted, any location party. But she said she was fine having a takeaway at home with me. 'Nothing mad or over the top, Daddy,' she said, and I really thought she'd grown up. Birthdays were always tricky in our house. It was Linda's thing. She would go all out. Filling entire rooms with balloons so the girls had to pop them all to find their presents. That kind of thing. After she died, it was hard to recreate that and I think we all felt her loss more on birthdays, especially Melanie.

Ryan: And what happened that night?

Peter: By about six o clock, most of Mellie's things were in her apartment. She had a bed and some furniture. Enough to get her started.

I was just about to pop open a bottle of vintage Dom Pérignon I'd been saving for her birthday, when a stretch limo turned up and Nell knocked on the door to whisk Mellie away for a night of dancing. Nell had left me a garbled voicemail the week before and said something about stopping by. I'd assumed she'd meant to give Mellie a present. I certainly never expected that she'd make plans.

Mellie was horrified at the surprise and so apologetic about our dinner plans, but what could I do? Nell was there in the doorway grinning like the sodding Cheshire Cat, and Mellie didn't have the heart to tell Nell that she didn't want to go. So I smiled and told Mellie to go and have a good time and that we'd have our dinner the following night.

It's one of the biggest regrets of my life. Mellie was never the same after that night and what followed. I would do anything, give anything, to go back and tell Mellie she couldn't go out.

I've been trying to make up for that mistake ever since. [Coughs] Get me some water, will you, Ryan?

Ryan: Yes, of course. [Pause] Here. Should I call someone?

Peter: No. Give me a minute.

RECORDING STOPPED

Netflix Original Documentary:
Melanie Lange – The Ugly Truth

INTERVIEWS RECORDED 19–22 SEPTEMBER 2022
(220 DAYS SINCE MELANIE'S DISAPPEARANCE)

Narrator

On the fourteenth of February 2007, Melanie celebrated her nineteenth birthday in Mayfair nightclub Funky Buddha. But in the early hours of the following morning, celebrations ended in chaos when Melanie was arrested for assaulting a bathroom attendant and taken to West End Central Police Station, where she was held for several hours.

Nell

Oh God, Mel's birthday was horrendous. It was so unfair. We were having an amazing night. Literally, one of the best nights ever.

After a tough few years I wanted to make Mel's birthday extra special. I wanted her to be surrounded by friends and to dance until her feet hurt. She always gets a bit blue around her birthday and I always try to make her feel loved and give her a boost.

I hired a white limo for the night. It was a total monstrosity. Mel burst out laughing when she saw it. She's always been one for understated, but that's because of the attention she gets. I think sometimes she feels like she can't let her light shine in public. But it was her birthday and I wanted to spoil her.

The first thing we do is head over to Mel's new place. It's smaller than I was expecting but still perfect for Mel. I've got to say though, Sir Peter buying Melanie that apartment down the road from the house is just another example of how controlling he is. People ask why – why would Sir Peter lock up his daughter in a house for seven months? This is the reason. He is a control freak. He has to have complete control over his business and control over Mel, and locking Mel away is killing two birds with one stone.

Like, back when she was nineteen, he couldn't just give her his blessing to move out and do it herself. Which means that straight away he's got leverage. He gave it to her and he could take it away anytime he liked. I swear it wouldn't have surprised me if he'd hidden cameras in there. Just look what happened on her nineteenth birthday. She moves out for one day. One!

Anyway, we're at Mel's new place and we start getting her ready. I'm wearing a green halterneck dress and she's pulling out this black top that she always wears and I'm like, 'Mel, you buy all these amazing clothes but you always wear that top. Why? You can wear that stuff when you're old.'

She looks a bit panicked for a moment. I was worried I'd hit a nerve, but then she shrugs and pulls out these sexy hot-pants and a silver sequin top. I was glad I said something. It was like she needed permission to go all out. I can't tell you how gorgeous she looked that night. She'd had these honey highlights put in her hair that really caught the light. Nobody could take their eyes off her.

We had a group of friends we saw at bars and clubs and the occasional lunch who I invited along. It was me, Mel, Lola and Jessie, Orlando and Ashlee. They weren't close friends but they were a laugh on a night out.

It wasn't like I could hire Robbie Williams, but I arranged a VIP area in one of Mel's favourite clubs, tracked down the DJ beforehand and asked him very nicely to play all the songs Mel loved. I never told her I did that. There were a few on the list that the DJ straight up refused to play. Blondie's 'Call Me' was one of them. God, Mel loves that song.

[Crying]

I'm sorry. This is hard, you know? Remembering how it was and knowing all the time that Mel is still a prisoner. Sorry.

So I wanted the entire night to be a big surprise, but I told Sir Peter the plan so he knew not to arrange anything. Of course, when I arrive in the limo, he acts like he has no idea what's going on. He was a total bastard about it, acting like Melanie had plans for a quiet family dinner with him and Zara.

A dinner? It was her birthday, for God's sake. He knew she'd choose going out but he wanted to make it as hard as possible for her.

Lola
I'm Lola Yang.

Jessie
And I'm Jessie Yang.

Lola
We're twins.

Jessie
Like that isn't obvious.

Lola
We run a personal shopping business called Lola & Jessie. We met Melanie and Nell in 2006 and spent about two years going out with them places. Mostly clubs and bars.

Jessie
And we're still friends now. Well, with Melanie anyway.

Lola
Sorry, did I make it sound like we weren't still friends? Of course we are.

Jessie
We fell out with Nell, but we still meet up with Melanie. We saw her for post-Christmas drinks, didn't we, Lols?

Lola

Yep. About a month before she went underground. Now stop inter-rupting. I'm trying to tell a story here.

Jessie

It's my story too.

Lola

So we got to know Melanie and Nell in the toilets at a club. We bonded over a mutual love of Yves Saint Laurent lipstick.

Jessie

Oh my god. I remember that. It was Dial R.E.D. I still love that lip-stick. It looked better on Mel than us though.

Lola

Everything looked better on Mel. She could've worn a bin bag for a dress and she'd still have looked better than anyone else in the room.

Jessie

So true. How do we not hate her?

Lola

Because she's so lovely. It would be like hating a kitten. So anyway, me and Jessie met Mel and Nell in the toilets at a club, and Mel invites us to join them for champagne and so we did. After that we'd bump into them regularly at bars, and at some point we swapped numbers and started meeting up. We weren't super close to Mel or Nell back then, but we were mates.

Jessie

Nell was such a laugh. She would crack me up. Do you remember the time she started dancing on that table like she was in Ibiza? Sud-denly everyone was dancing on tables.

Lola

Until one of the tables collapsed and the bouncers stopped it.

Jessie

Nell loved Melanie to pieces, didn't she? If anyone so much as looked at Mel the wrong way, Nell would be straight in their face.

Lola

True. And she did a great job organizing Mel's nineteenth birthday. It was such a brilliant night to start with. It was us two, Mel and Nell obviously, another girl and a gay guy. I can't remember their names.

Jessie

Wasn't one of them named after a city? Not Paris, but like Paris.

Lola

Orlando.

Jessie

Yes. Orlando and Ashling, Ashlee, something like that.

Lola

So there were six of us in the limo that night and it was epic. We made our way through the bars, dashing between the limo and the bar because it was absolutely freezing and none of us were wearing coats.

We all got pretty drunk pretty quickly, and by the time we stumbled into Funky Buddha it was already late and the place was heaving. We were there for maybe an hour when Nell gets annoyed that Mel's ex, Jonnie, is chatting up Mel on the dance floor. So we decide to intervene and drag Mel off to the toilets. She's pretty drunk. We all are. Nell and Mel start bickering about Jonnie. Nell wants Mel to tell him to sod off, but Mel doesn't want to. She's like, 'We're just chatting and having a dance.'

The attendant starts getting annoyed that we're taking up space in the toilets so she starts talking to us about trying her perfumes.

We're all, 'No way,' but she starts spraying them at us just as these two girls walk in. One of them gets perfume right in her face. It was pretty funny actually, but boy was she pissed off. She and her friend turn on the attendant and they both start screaming at her. It was totally time to get out of the way, so I grab Mel and Nell and we're trying to shuffle past when Mel tries to get the girls to calm down.

Jessie
Typical Mel. She hated seeing people upset. She invited the two girls to join us in the VIP area. She's like, 'We're getting champagne.'

Lola
But the girls are clearly off their heads on coke and think Mel is taking the piss. I don't really know how it goes from zero to something so fast, but the next thing, one of the girls is saying some really racist stuff to us and starts pushing us, while the other one clocks the attendant right in the eye. She falls against the wall and starts shouting for help. Then the bouncers come flying in and the girls start pointing at Mel, screaming about how she hit the attendant. We all deny it, but by then it's like a mud-throwing contest so the bouncers drag us all into a side office and call the police.

Nell
Mel didn't hit anyone. One of the girls starts screaming that Mel did it and because everyone knows Melanie, she gets the blame.

Jonnie Welbourn-Jones, owner of Jonnie Jones Microbrewery
Yeah, I was there that night. It was good catching up with Mel. We hadn't seen each other for a few months. She looked good that night.

I remember she was wearing these black leather hot-pants and a slinky silver top. It would have looked like overkill on anyone else, but on Mel it just looked hot.

Jessie
So we're standing in this tiny office and the coke girls are crying their eyes out, telling the bouncers over and over that they weren't even involved and—

Lola
And then they just let them go. Honestly, the smile on their faces as they leave. I could've punched them.

Jessie
You? Ha! You can't even swat a fly.
So they leave before the police even get there. We said over and over that it wasn't Mel who hit the bathroom attendant but the bouncers have already made their minds up.

Lola
Poor Melanie. She's hysterical when the police show up. She keeps talking about how it's going to be this big story in the papers like the last time and she's freaking out about what her dad will do.

Jessie
Melanie gives me her phone and asks me to call her dad. Nell doesn't want me to. She goes on and on about how he doesn't need to be involved and it won't do Melanie any good in the long run if he finds out.

Lola
Which was stupid, because of course he was going to find out. I mean, the police actually arrested Melanie. Handcuffs and everything. They

frogmarched her through the club with everyone watching. Of course the media were going to hear about it.

Jessie
Sir Peter was really nice on the phone. He was obviously worried about Mel but grateful we'd called him too.

Twitter
15 February 2007

Amy B @GirlAboutTownBlog
OMG!!! Melanie Lange has been arrested! Punched an innocent woman.
Looks like someone is finally showing their true colours! #MelanieLange

Nelson H @BigN983
I'd show Melanie Lange what a real punch feels like. Stupid rich
bitch! #MelanieLange

SazzP @Sarah1994_01
OMG! About time she got what's coming to her! She's so stuck
up and isn't even that pretty any more. #MelanieLange

Rianne Jacobs @RianneJacobs-Greene
Whatever happened to innocent until proven guilty?
#MelanieLange

Amy B @GirlAboutTownBlog
No smoke without fire! #MelanieLange

Barbara T @Barbara366
Melanie Lange is an ugly tramp! How does she live with
herself???

SIR PETER LANGE —
MY SIDE OF THE STORY (UNPUBLISHED)

*Interviews between ghost writer Ryan Morris
and Peter Lange, 7 October 2022*

Ryan: Good morning, Sir Peter. How are you? Ready to start?

Peter: I'm ready to get back to running my businesses, but since that's impossible right now, yes, let's start. Fire away.

Ryan: All right then. Can we go back to the night of Melanie's second arrest? Her nineteenth birthday?

Peter: [Sighs] The minute Mellie left in that limo I knew it was a bad idea. I couldn't sleep and I was awake when one of Mellie's friends called. I was making a bolognese, Mellie's favourite, and worrying about Mellie in her new place and how I wouldn't know if she got home safe. I was already regretting giving her the apartment and feeling bad for not trusting her more.

I can't remember which friend called me, only that it wasn't Nell. Anyway, Mellie's friend tells me Mellie has been arrested for punching a bathroom attendant in a nightclub. It was like history repeating itself. Straight away I called my lawyer Frank. Again we met at the station, where there was a crowd of photographers this time.

Ryan: What was your reaction when you heard about the assault?

Peter: My first thought was that it couldn't have happened. Mellie doesn't have an aggressive bone in her body. There was no way she punched anyone. Nell, maybe, but not Mellie. My second thought, I'm ashamed to say, was OK, maybe she did punch this woman, because how well did I really know my own daughter at that point in time? Of course my initial instinct was correct.

Ryan: The charges were dropped the following day, is that right?

Peter: Not before all the front pages ran a photo of a sixty-year-old woman with a puffy eye next to a photo of Mellie in handcuffs.

Mellie was questioned that night and released pending further investigation. She should never have been arrested in the first place. The problem was, a bouncer at the club claimed to the first officers on the scene that he'd witnessed the assault. It wasn't until the following morning that the police actually thought to show the bathroom attendant a photo of Mellie, and the attendant confirmed that Mellie had nothing to do with it. It was a massive balls-up from start to finish.

Ryan: Did the papers run a retraction?

Peter: A retraction for what? They said she'd been arrested. She had been. Did they run a follow-up story with the truth? No. The second story heavily implied that the charges had been dropped because the bathroom attendant had been bought off.

Ryan: How was Melanie when you collected her from the police station?

Peter: Distraught. It was horribly unfair what happened to her, and she took it very hard. Partly, I'm sure, because she'd been drinking so heavily. Mellie isn't a happy drunk. She sobbed uncontrollably for the entire journey home. It was four or five in the morning by that point and I took her back to the house. Zara was awake and made us bacon sandwiches before sending us both to bed.

I fell asleep, and when I woke up there was a note in the kitchen from Mellie telling me she was sorry for causing so much trouble and she'd gone to her apartment to sleep.

I left it until lunchtime and then I called Mellie. She didn't answer. I assumed she was sleeping off her hangover, and then I thought she was probably licking her wounds, but I kept calling. By the evening I was worried and decided to check on her. I'd suggested to Mellie that she leave a spare set of keys at the house in case she ever lost hers. I took them with me and Zara came too. When Mellie didn't answer the buzzer, we let ourselves into the building and knocked on the door. There was no answer. I remember half hoping and half dreading that she was out again.

I open the door and . . . straight away I know something is wrong. There are empty wine bottles all over the kitchen and Zara points out the newspapers on the floor. All those headlines about Mellie.

We run into the bedroom and find Mellie on the bed surrounded . . . surrounded by empty pill packets. Seeing her like that felt like my heart was being ripped out of my chest. It was Janet all over again.

[Coughs]

I really thought she was dead. Her skin was so pale, almost translucent. I'll never forget that.

I think I went into shock seeing her so lifeless. I just stand in the doorway while Zara calls an ambulance and finds a pulse, before sticking her fingers down Mellie's throat and forcing her to throw up. A stream of liquid and tablets pours out of Mellie and she comes round. She sees our faces and starts crying. She tells us she can't cope with the whole world thinking she's a person who can punch someone. I put my arm around Mellie and I tell her it's going to be OK, that I'll look after her no matter what. We were both crying by that point. I promised myself there and then that I'd never let that happen to Mellie again. That I would always protect her, no matter what.

The ambulance arrives and I go with Mellie to the hospital. Zara stayed and cleared up the apartment before joining me with the car.

Ryan: Can we be very clear here, because this has never been reported before – are you saying that on the fifteenth of February 2007, the day after her nineteenth birthday, Melanie tried to kill herself?

Peter: Yes. The doctor at the time wasn't sure she'd taken enough to cause serious harm, but there were unopened packets. If we hadn't been there, she could have woken up and carried on.

Ryan: That must have brought up some terrible memories for you about your sister?

Peter: Yes. It was my worst nightmare. Everything I worried about had come true. Mellie spent the night in hospital having her stomach pumped and the next day I drove her straight to a private clinic.

Ryan: And that was Beaumont Court, a mental health and rehabilitation clinic in Tunbridge Wells, Kent?

Peter: Yes.

Ryan: There's been a lot made of your choice of treatment facility for Mellie.

Peter: I know. Another mistake on my part. The guilt over that decision hasn't been easy to live with. You have to remember that I was operating on zero sleep. I was emotionally wrung out and exhausted. My sole focus was getting Mellie into a treatment facility that would offer her privacy while she dealt with her suicide attempt.

Zara and I made a number of calls and Beaumont Court seemed like the best choice. I wanted a place that dealt with addictions as well as mental health problems. In today's world, if someone in the public eye stands up and says they've got depression or some other mental health problem, they're given a lot of support and it's accepted for the most part. Back then, when Mellie was nineteen, it was still a taboo subject. I thought it would be hard for her to come back from that and so we made sure everyone thought she was in the clinic for an addiction to prescription painkillers.

Beaumont Court was very private, very secluded. Visits were limited. I didn't want a journalist wandering in there and learning the truth. I also knew from my own experience with Mellie that routine and structure were key for her stability. Beaumont Court offered that, and it focused on the teenage bracket, allowing Mellie to be with her peers.

It broke my heart when Mellie told me what was happening there. I offered to send her to therapy, but she wouldn't take it. She blamed me for sending her to that place. I blamed myself too.

Ryan: How long was her stay at Beaumont Court?

Peter: Originally, we decided on four weeks. After three weeks she was doing so much better, so we decided to extend her stay to twelve weeks.

Ryan: When you say 'we', who do you mean? Melanie's doctors?

Peter: Yes, and Mellie too. She was an adult, don't forget. When I went to visit, she was quiet, but she agreed to stay. She told me she liked the fact that she was nobody special. She liked that her face wasn't being plastered across every newspaper. She said she was happy and I believed her. It was only later when she told me everything that I realized I'd never been left alone with her on that visit.

Ryan: It was a year before the abuse at Beaumont Court came to light. What kinds of things did they do to Melanie?

[Pause]

Peter: I'm sorry, I can't go into details. That's really Mellie's story to share. What I can say is that I reported the clinic and I made damn sure it was investigated.

Ryan: How long did she actually stay at Beaumont Court for?

Peter: It was around six weeks in the end. Thanks to Nell, her stay was cut short. It's probably the only time I've been grateful for their friendship. In hindsight, I should have told Nell the truth about Mellie and why she was at Beaumont Court, but it didn't feel like my place to explain, and quite frankly I didn't trust Nell. Presumably Mellie didn't either.

[Knock at door]

Female voice: Sorry to interrupt, Sir Peter. I have Zara out here and she says it's urgent.

Peter: Fine. Sorry, Ryan. I'll just be a moment.

RECORDING STOPPED

Netflix Original Documentary:
Melanie Lange – The Ugly Truth

INTERVIEWS RECORDED 19–22 SEPTEMBER 2022
(220 DAYS SINCE MELANIE'S DISAPPEARANCE)

Narrator
On the sixteenth of February 2007, Melanie was admitted to Beaumont Court, a private medical facility and rehabilitation clinic in Kent. While no official statement was made by Sir Peter Lange, sources close to the family reported that Melanie was being treated for an addiction to prescription painkillers. Not everyone believed these rumours to be true. Just one year later, in 2008, Beaumont Court was closed by the local authority after numerous reports from former patients of abuse and mistreatment.

Nell
I was Melanie's best friend then. I'm her best friend now. And I can say with 100 per cent confidence that Melanie did not have, nor has she ever had, an alcohol or drug addiction.

Melanie did not need to be in rehab, and let me tell you something else – Beaumont Court was no rehab clinic. The way Mel spoke about it, it was more like a group home for naughty teenagers.

I still feel sick thinking about Melanie in that place. It took her a long time to get over her treatment there. She was never quite the same though. It was like it broke part of her spirit.

Vic Watson, tabloid editor
Melanie went into hiding after her second arrest, not that I blamed her. Whatever was left of her public image at that point was in tatters. A privileged rich girl assaulting a low-paid nightclub worker didn't look good. There was a mini PR campaign underway from

everyone but Melanie. Nell Stevens and Melanie's other friends were all in the weekly magazines with their side of the story. The bathroom attendant had a double-page spread in the *Mirror* claiming Melanie was trying to stop the fight.

The public lapped it up, but there were plenty of rumours flying around about pay-offs from Sir Peter.

Jonnie Welbourn-Jones, owner of Jonnie Jones Microbrewery
Personally, I thought Mel went to rehab to get a break from the tabloids and to show the world she was turning over a new leaf. Everyone loves a sob story like that.

These rehab places for the rich and famous are all spas and luxury anyway.

Nell
I believe Sir Peter forced Melanie to stay at Beaumont Court to keep her out of trouble for a few months. It was practically a prison. They didn't allow visits or access to the internet. Sound familiar?

There was one pay phone but they could only use it for ten minutes every other night, and Mel told me afterwards that they listened in on the calls to make sure no one was badmouthing the place.

When she called the first time, I cried hearing her voice. It sounded . . . it sounded like she was only half there.

I asked her when she'd be coming home, and do you know what her reply was? It was, 'Whenever my dad decides I'm allowed to leave.'

At first I was all like, 'Come on, you're nineteen, you can walk out of there. They can't stop you.'

Do you know what she said to me? She said, 'Yes, they can.'

After that I knew I had to get her out.

I kept asking and asking what was going on, but she wouldn't say. She just asked me to write to her. She later told me they were monitoring calls but didn't open letters sent to residents.

Former treatment assistant at Beaumont Court

[Face obscured for anonymity]

If your troubled kid was thirteen to twenty-one and you had the money, you sent them to Beaumont Court. Therapy was centred around a strict routine. Everyone had to be awake and dressed at 5 a.m. Then it was a group exercise class for an hour. All food was bland and additive-free.

It specialized in behavioural issues, trauma, depression, anxiety, addiction, the works. We had kids who were there for killing their cats and we had kids who were there for no other reason than their parents wanted a break. Everyone was treated the same, and yeah, it was tough love most of the time. A lot of those kids had been given a long leash and we had to bring them back in.

Nell

At the time, I had a job working for a commercial marketing company. It was admin stuff, filing and answering phones, organizing events, but I liked it. I booked a day off work for the following week and then I wrote to Mel. I told her I'd be parked outside Beaumont Court all day and all evening on that particular day and if she wanted to leave and could get away, I'd take her wherever she wanted to go.

And that's what I did. I drove down there really early when it was still dark. I sat in my car and I waited. I didn't know if she got my letter – I didn't really know if she wanted to leave, or even if she could.

It was getting later and later and I kept telling myself, 'Five minutes. Just give it five more minutes.'

Then at five to midnight, the passenger door flies open and Mel throws herself in the car and screams at me to drive. I do as I'm told and we get out of there. Twenty minutes later, I pull over to the side of the road and give her a hug. She bursts into tears and keeps saying, 'Thank you, thank you.'

I was crying my eyes out too.

Former treatment assistant at Beaumont Court

[Face obscured for anonymity]

We had a few patients who had additional needs on top of the therapy, but for the most part, like I said, it was routine and rules.

I worked at Beaumont Court for around four years. I was there in 2008 when they came and closed us down. Some kid complained that they were subjected to regular beatings by members of staff. It was a big scandal in Kent. One of the local newspapers even called it The House of Horrors. Suddenly it was abuse that kids were having to exercise before breakfast every day.

Times change, practices change, and the style of care offered at Beaumont Court went out of fashion. People can say what they want about it now, but I've worked with troubled teens all my life and the only time I ever consistently saw real change, positive change, was through the strict routines and rule-based care given to them at Beaumont Court.

Nell

Mel stayed with me for a few days after our jailbreak. She was so quiet. I'd wake up in the morning and she'd just be lying there, staring into space. She didn't want to talk about what happened but I saw the bruises on her wrists from restraints. There was something deeply wrong with that place. She never wore a watch or a bracelet again after that. I tried to talk to her about it once, check she was OK. She told me wearing a watch made her feel like she was back there. I suggested she should talk to a professional but she closed me down. She said, 'It's all in the past now.' But I never felt like it was.

After those first few days, Sir Peter showed up on my doorstep. I asked Mel if she wanted me to stay but she said she was OK, and so I went out for a coffee. When I came back, Mel's eyes were red but she was happier. She said, 'I don't have to go back there, as long as I move home for a while.'

I tried to convince her to stay at mine anyway. I didn't like the control Sir Peter had over Mel, but she said he'd explained things to her about his past and she understood. She didn't say what things and I dropped it in the end. Mel didn't need me telling her what to do on top of her dad. She needed a friend, someone who would be there for her no matter what. I was that person and I still am.

Melanie Lange video 6/9
Published on Melanie Lange YouTube channel on 5 August 2022

I'm Melanie Lange. I'm being held captive by my father – Peter Lange. I want to tell you about how he tricked me. Twice. The first time was when he brought me here and convinced me to post my apology on YouTube, and the second time in June when he told me that he wanted me to do a photo shoot on the beach for the launch of my new perfume. He said it would be a test. If I could get through the day without 'incident', as he called it, then I could start making steps towards returning to my life. He promised me I would see my boys. So I agreed, because he had all the cards and I had none.

The photo shoot was surreal. I'd spent over three months alone and then to be suddenly surrounded by people, it made me anxious. I just kept telling myself, 'Get through it, Mel, and then see your boys.'

It was a small crew. The bare minimum really. A photographer, a make-up artist, a lighting tech and one assistant. I've worked in the industry for decades in one form or another but I didn't know any of them, which I believe was my father's doing.

About half an hour before the crew were due to leave, I panicked. I could see everything being packed away, and I knew they would leave and I would be all alone again. And so I scribbled a note and gave it to the photographer. It said, 'Get me help. I'm being held prisoner here. I'm not free to leave.'

[Sighs]

What I didn't know, but I should have guessed, is that my father told the crew I was experiencing problems with my mental health and they shouldn't accept any notes or believe anything I said to them. So when I handed the photographer that note, the first thing he did was give it to my father. And at the same time that was happening, this girl, this amazing assistant who'd not even spoken to me, came over to say goodbye and pushed this phone into my hands.

I freaked out. I thought it was a trick set up by my father and I tried to give it back. Then she said, 'Nell wants to know you're OK,' and I just knew it was real and that somewhere out there people were worried about me.

My father handed me the note I'd written and left without a word, and I knew he was never going to let me go.

I know that if these videos ever get released, then he'll pull out those photos of me and say, 'Look, she's fine. She's smiling and happy.' But I'm not fine. I promise you. There is nothing fine about this place.

SIR PETER LANGE —
MY SIDE OF THE STORY (UNPUBLISHED)

Interviews between ghost writer Ryan Morris
and Peter Lange, 7 October 2022

Peter: Right, where were we?

Ryan: Melanie's stay at Beaumont Court was cut short.

Peter: Yes. Thanks to Nell.

Ryan: You mentioned in one of our previous interviews that it was around this time that you told Melanie about your sister's suicide.

Peter: That's right. She came out of Beaumont Court and stayed with Nell for a few days. I went to visit her there. This poky little one-room apartment in Soho. It didn't even have a sofa. Just the bed. Anyway, Mellie was quite shaken and angry about the conditions she'd endured. I was too when I found out. She obviously blamed me, and rightly so as it was me who found Beaumont Court. I apologized, and then I told her about Janet and the effect her suicide had had on me. I think it helped Mellie understand where I was coming from. And she moved home after that. We kept the apartment for when she was ready. She still saw Nell and her friends, but only at her apartment or at the house. She didn't go out shopping or for lunches. She didn't attend any bar openings, and as far as I know she didn't touch a drop of alcohol for at least six months. And then one night towards the end of that summer she asked to join the business.

Ryan: Why didn't Melanie go to university?

Peter: For the same reason Mellie didn't do anything – first and foremost because she didn't want to, but also because I wanted her to. And Mellie liked to do the opposite of what I wanted most of the time. I wanted her to get out of London and experience different people, different friendships – a world away from me, from Lange Hotels, from Nell as well, obviously. I even suggested travelling – backpacking around the world, experiencing different cultures – but Mellie said she didn't want to do any of that and wanted to come and work at the business like Zara had done.

Ryan: How was your relationship with Melanie after her spell in Beaumont Court?

Peter: It was hard. There was a lot of blame and a lot of guilt. It made making decisions hard for me. I felt a constant pressure not to take a wrong step or say or do the wrong thing with Mellie. She was . . . delicate, I would say. She took everything to heart. Everything I said was taken as an insult, but worse were the stories about her. I could see her confidence was shattered and reasoned that working in the business, the normality of it, might help build Mellie's self-worth.

That's not to say there weren't times when we all got on. There were some family dinners together that didn't end in throwing accusations at each other, but whenever there was peace, it felt tentative. So I agreed to Mellie joining Lange Hotels, with two conditions. Firstly, she had to grow up and realize I wasn't the enemy. Secondly, she had to do the job she was given. No skipping off for long lunches.

Ryan: And she accepted?

Peter: 100 per cent, and things did get better. It was a good decision. It helped her find herself again.

[Knock at door]

Female voice: Sir Peter, you wanted me to tell you when it was time to leave for your meeting.

Peter: Thank you, Denise. Tell my driver he can go home. I'm driving myself tonight. Ryan, we're going to have to stop early today.

Ryan: Not a problem. If you're driving somewhere though, I'm happy to come with you and we can continue in the car.

Peter: No. Let's pick up tomorrow morning. It's Saturday though, is that OK?

Ryan: Of course.

RECORDING STOPPED

Twitter
30 September 2007

Amy B @GirlAboutTownBlog
Melanie Lange has got her first job! Working for Daddy! Bet that was a gruelling interview (NOT!) #MelanieLange #CelebrityGossip

> **Tammy S @TammySunflowers**
> Typical! Does she have any idea how many people are struggling to find work that she's just trampled over?

> **Trisha Aitken @TrishaVAitken**
> I can just imagine her cleaning hotel rooms too!! Hope that's the last we hear of her!

> **Rachel Bond @NotJamesBond77**
> I was a year below Melanie in school. And you're wrong if you think she's going to be cleaning! She's going to shake things up.

> **Nelson H @BigN983**
> Was she spreading her legs for every man in London back then too?

> **Natty H @NataliaLH**
> Why does Melanie Lange wear her hair tied back all the time now? It makes her look tired! #MelanieLange

> **Tammy S @TammySunflowers**
> Still dresses like a tramp though!

Netflix Original Documentary:
Melanie Lange – The Ugly Truth

INTERVIEWS RECORDED 19–22 SEPTEMBER 2022
(220 DAYS SINCE MELANIE'S DISAPPEARANCE)

Narrator

In September 2007, Melanie joined her father, Sir Peter Lange, and her sister, Zara, and began work at Lange Hotels. After a rocky few years, life for Melanie appeared to be settling down, but after three years at Lange Hotels everything changed again for Melanie with the launch of her own business – Lange Cosmetics.

Terri Byford, retired teacher

Melanie always had a spark for business in a way Zara never had. Zara was very mathematical, very logical. Melanie was creative. When she was in Year Seven, so eleven years old, the whole year group took part in an annual business project we do. Every child is given five pounds to start up their own business. We try to give them plenty of freedom and as long as it's not gambling or illegal, we let them get on with it. There's a fair in the hall each week that's open to the whole school, and the children are able to sell whatever they've used their money for. At the end of the month, the person with the most money wins.

Melanie took that money, bought beads and string, and in the first week she sold bracelets. Now, all the other kids carried on selling the same thing each week, but Melanie took the money from the bracelets and bought something else and something else. In the final week she hired a photo booth with lots of fun props – wigs and floppy hats, that kind of thing. There were flyers all around school about it and kids lined up to have a photo with a friend. She made five thousand pounds in that one month. The second best amount was two hundred pounds. She saw what the kids wanted and she supplied it. No, in fact, she told them what they wanted and then she gave it to them. A lot of parents complained that Melanie had help from her father, but she didn't.

Nell

Was I surprised that Mel joined the family business? Not at all. It was a stepping stone. She told me her plans and I was excited for her.

Bruno Kowalski, former Chief Operating Officer for Lange Hotels Limited

I'm sure there was resentment towards Zara when she joined Lange full time, but Zara had been helping out a lot over the years and had proved her worth by hard work and solid decision-making. Maybe she skipped a few steps on the ladder after completing the graduate scheme, but she always worked as hard as anyone did and I certainly don't think she faced half as much animosity as Melanie when she joined Lange Hotels.

It didn't help that Melanie had hardly spent any time in the business before joining. People knew who she was, of course. Everyone knew Melanie's face. And then instead of starting her at the bottom in admin and on reception, Sir Peter put her in marketing. My niece was working on reception at the time. She'd been helping out the marketing team a lot. It was no secret that she wanted to move on to the team, but then Melanie comes along and takes the job. So straight away, most of the women in the office hate her.

SIR PETER LANGE —
MY SIDE OF THE STORY (UNPUBLISHED)

*Interviews between ghost writer Ryan Morris
and Peter Lange, 8 October 2022*

Ryan: Good morning, Sir Peter. Thank you for taking time out of your weekend for this. Are you all right? You look—

Peter: I'm fine. Coffee? Denise – bring some coffee, please.

Ryan: We were talking yesterday about Melanie joining the business. Where did she start?

Peter: I didn't put Mellie on the graduate scheme like I did with Zara, who by that point was working almost like a gatekeeper to me. If someone wanted a decision on something, they'd invite Zara to the relevant meetings. She'd gather all the information and either make a decision or summarize it for me to make the final decision. It was a format that worked.

But Mellie was never going to follow the same path as Zara. So I spoke to the relevant heads of departments and designed something else for her. Mellie wanted to be more creative and I knew she had some business ideas of her own, so I started her in marketing where, quite frankly, she shone.

It wasn't easy for her, going into the business. I wasn't blind to what people thought – the boss's spoilt daughter coming to get a salary without doing any work, but that wasn't Mellie. There were others too, those who read the magazines and wanted to get close to Mellie for the wrong reasons. Her first year at Lange was very lonely. It was hard for her to find her place, but she kept her head down and worked hard. I was proud of her. I was proud that she wanted to work with me and be part of something that meant so much to our family.

Ryan: How soon after Melanie started working at Lange was the idea of Lange Cosmetics first introduced?

Peter: Mellie had obviously been thinking about it for a while, but the first time she mentioned anything to me was about a year after she'd started in the business.

We had a small team that was looking into ways the business could diversify. There was a start-up in the US who were making waves with a new model for holidays. I could see very early on that it would have a huge impact on hotel stays if it took off. That company was Airbnb and I was right.

Mellie was spending two days a week in the business diversity team and I was aware she was researching her own ideas.

One day, Mellie comes over for dinner and says she has something to talk to me about. You worry as a father when your daughter has something to tell you that it's going to be an unplanned pregnancy or an engagement to one of the worthless boyfriends she continued to date, but then she tells me about her plans to launch her own cosmetics brand – face creams and serum, body washes, soaps. She's got it all mapped out and takes me through this entire business plan. It was a good pitch. A very good pitch.

Then she tells me she's leaving Lange to set up the business on her own, which is when the alarm bells start ringing for me. Mellie had been doing so well. The press was still out to destroy her but she was paying less attention to it. She'd really grown in confidence since joining Lange Hotels. The thought of her working on her own, finding investors, it felt like a lot of things could get out of control and I wanted to stop that from happening. I wanted to protect her.

So I suggested to Mellie that she could set up her business under the Lange Hotels umbrella. She'd have all the resources, all the investment.

But Mellie is no fool. Lange Cosmetics was her baby and she

wasn't going to hand over control to anyone. In the end we reached a compromise we were both happy with. There was a lot of back and forth, a lot of meetings with the board of Lange Hotels, and it was eventually agreed that they would be a shareholder in Lange Cosmetics. They would make the initial investment and own 49 per cent of the business. Mellie kept the 51 per cent for herself. She had the final say in all decisions.

It took a bit of arm-twisting to get everyone on the board of directors to agree, but I did and very quickly it became clear that Mellie was on to something. It was and still is a genius business model. By reimagining the Avon lady sales rep, Melanie circumvented any competition with the big brands. She didn't have to fight or pay for any shelf space in high-street stores, she didn't have to change her branding or compromise in any way. She knew people would fall in love with the products and she knew her fans would want to sell them to everyone they knew.

It was a good investment for Lange Hotels. It still is.

Ryan: How did you feel when Lange Cosmetics began to outshine and outperform Lange Hotels?

Peter: When Lange Cosmetics started to do well, it was good for all of us. I wasn't jealous, if that's what you're asking. Imagine it like two children. I was proud of both businesses.

Ryan: Even though Lange Cosmetics was actually Melanie's business?

Peter: It's in her name. It was her creation, but without me and Lange Hotels, without the Lange name, it wouldn't have got off the ground.

Nell

It was around a year into working for her dad that Mel takes me to lunch and tells me about her plans to launch a cosmetics brand. She'd talked about it in the past but now it was really happening. She was so passionate about it. That lunch was the most excited I'd ever seen her, and that includes her wedding day.

Then she says, 'You have to come and work for me. I need you, Nell.'

And I say, 'I'm your best friend and I'll always be your best friend, but I need to earn money and there's no way your dad is going to employ me.'

That's when she says – and this is really important for what's happening to Mel right now. This is the reason I believe Sir Peter has Mel imprisoned – she says, 'Lange Cosmetics is my business. I'm the majority shareholder. I can hire whoever I want.'

And so I handed in my notice and went to work for Mel. Lange Cosmetics launched the following year, in 2010. Officially, I had the job title of personal assistant, but I did everything from research and marketing to hiring and firing. I was right beside Mel, helping to create the first product line.

Later, I was Mel's eyes and ears in the business while she was on maternity leave. It was a job Zara was after and one she thought should rightfully be hers. Zara and Mel were civil to each other at that point when their paths crossed in the office and at social events. Outwardly, I'm sure people mistook them for being close, but beneath the surface it was all rotten. Mel never trusted Zara after that photo from the party hit the papers, and Zara . . .

[Laughs]

She resented the hell out of the fact that her little sister had been the one to swoop in and save Lange Hotels, when Zara had been slogging her guts out there for years.

Danielle Lamont, editor of *Beauty* magazine
Lange Cosmetics launched in the spring of 2010. No one in the industry took it seriously. Behind closed doors there were a lot of jokes about what looked essentially like a vanity project instigated by Sir Peter Lange to keep Melanie out of trouble and make it appear as though she had an actual job. I wasn't interested in Lange Cosmetics. I ignored all the invites to testing sessions in the run-up to the launch. I didn't believe the products would be any good, and I also didn't like that Melanie Lange, who was all of twenty-two at the time, was elbowing her way into an industry using Daddy's money and Daddy's contacts. I didn't want to give her any more of a leg-up than she was clearly already getting.

And then one day, three months before Lange Cosmetics was due to launch, Melanie Lange herself walks into my office in a tailored white business suit and four-inch heels, looking every bit the model she once was, and just says, 'You have every right to think that I'm a spoilt brat who has no business launching a cosmetics brand, but I'd really appreciate five minutes of your time so I can convince you otherwise.'

It took balls to do that, so I waved her into a seat and made a point of checking my watch.

She pulls out one product. Just one. It's the Lange Eye Expert. She hands it over and tells me to dab a tiny amount under just one eye. So I'm dabbing away and Melanie is chatting at a hundred miles an hour about the Lange Cosmetics ethos. Natural, responsibly sourced ingredients. Recycled, reusable packaging, cruelty free, vegan.

This was 2010, don't forget. Cruelty-free products were a big thing, but not natural or responsibly sourced. It was barmy. I was convinced it would never take off. People didn't care about that stuff enough. They just wanted to look good. And I was about to tell her that when she pulled out a compact mirror and held it up. I couldn't believe the difference. That cream took five years off me.

I gave her five minutes to convince me that Lange Cosmetics was a serious business. She sold it to me in two. The Eye Expert serum is still my go-to product every morning.

Based on that one product, I offered Melanie a double-page spread. Then I ask her what other products she's got and what retailers she's signed to, and get this, she says, 'None.' Then she gets this big smile on her face and tells me about this plan to reinvent the Avon calling lady. She says, 'I want the people who believe in my products to be the ones to make money from it.' I still get goosebumps thinking about it.

Melanie Lange could have sold her products in any of the big department stores and she could have sold that eye cream for eighty pounds a tub. Do you know what its original retail price was? Seventeen pounds. When she told me that, I swear my jaw hit the desk. I've been in the beauty business in one way or another for most of my life, and nothing shocked me as much as Melanie Lange did that day.

We ended up offering free samples to every customer, along with a call to action for sales reps, who she signed up by the truckload. Melanie and I became good friends after that meeting. She has been underestimated her entire life, she's had more mud thrown at her by the tabloid media than anyone else in the world, but make no mistake, Melanie is a phenomenal businesswoman. Even then, in her early twenties, she knew exactly what she was doing. When she left my office, I thought to myself, 'Woe betide anyone who gets in that girl's way.'

I truly hope Melanie is all right. I don't know what to believe, to be honest. Save Melanie and Help Peter are all I see on Twitter at the moment. Whatever is going on, I hope she's OK.

Twitter
6 October 2022

Matty Venus @Filmjunkie2000
I've been watching the #MelanieLange videos all night and the more I
watch them the more I wonder if the whole #SaveMelanie thing is wrong.
#HelpPeter

    Kaitlyn M Davids @Mummyrulestheroost
    No way! If her dad had said which health facility she was in, none
    of this would have happened! It's all too weird!! #SaveMelanie

    Cristen Watts @CristenPWatts
    You're the one who is mentally ill @Filmjunkie2000! This woman
    has been imprisoned by her dad for months. There is no other
    way to see it! #SaveMelanie

Netflix Original Documentary:
Melanie Lange – The Ugly Truth

INTERVIEWS RECORDED 19–22 SEPTEMBER 2022
(220 DAYS SINCE MELANIE'S DISAPPEARANCE)

Narrator

In late 2010, six months after its launch, Lange Cosmetics became one of the leading cosmetics brand in the UK, winning numerous awards for both its products and its ethos. Twenty-two-year-old Melanie became a regular guest on *This Morning*, *Loose Women* and *BBC Breakfast* discussing beauty products and trends, as well as women in business.

Between 2010 and 2012, as Melanie was making a name for herself in the cosmetics industry with Lange Cosmetics, media outlets ran over six thousand stories, comments and photographs about Melanie. These stories focused on two topics – Melanie's appearance and Melanie's relationships.

Nell

About a year after Lange Cosmetics launched, Mel was approached by ITV about becoming a TV beauty expert on the daytime shows. She said no at first. Mel has always seen herself as a businesswoman not a celebrity, but the marketing team put together a pretty convincing pitch for why Mel should do it. In the end, she did it to raise the profile of Lange Cosmetics. But she made it clear right from the start that she would appear as a business leader and beauty expert and would not answer questions about her personal life. Those *Loose Women* hosts really tried to get something out of her, especially when it came to who she was dating, but Melanie always stuck to the brand.

When it comes to dating, Mel had been photographed so much by then that the entire country knew her type. I mean, even I forgot the names of these men sometimes. They all looked the same. Skinny jeans, unwashed hair, black clothes, and all of them misunderstood or wronged in some way. I think because she lost her own mum so young, Mel had this desire to mother or fix these boys she found. They were washed-up strays. They'd move in with Mel for a few weeks, a month, and then when they didn't change, they'd move out again.

Then Finn Parker comes along, and he is the exact opposite of every single man Mel has ever dated.

Vic Watson, tabloid editor
Just when you think things are going to get boring, Melanie throws us a huge bone. I think it was in May 2011 Melanie attends a cocktail bar opening. She walks into the bar with one of her usual boyfriends on her arm. An hour later she walks out with Finn Parker. Now, this man is wearing a suit, he owns his own business and he is incredibly handsome. So we run both photos – Melanie walking into a bar with this bloke in baggy jeans who looked like he'd pass for a homeless person, and then Melanie walking out with a Bruce Wayne type. He's like a knight in shining armour. It all seemed too good to be true, and it turns out it was. Sir Peter paying a man to date his daughter! Not even we'd make up a story like that.

Twitter

13 May 2011

Amy B @GirlAboutTownBlog
HOT GOSSIP!! Melanie Lange has a new man and he is hooooot!
#MelanieLange #WhoIsMelanieDatingNow

> **Patsy Hanson @LeicesterWeddingPhotography**
> OMG imagine how beautiful their children would be!

> **Jennifer S @JenJen88**
> He's cute!

> **Natalie-Claire Olson @NattyClaire_Olson**
> I thought she was dating that TV quiz host.

> **Amy B @GirlAboutTownBlog**
> That was last week! Hard to keep up with Melanie's love life.

Leslie Riley-Moor @FashionistaFan_Blogger
I wish #MelanieLange would change her wardrobe up a bit. Those black
dresses she always wears are so boring.

> **Laura V @LauraLostHerPhone**
> Black hides the weight gain. Look at her face and the chubby
> cheeks. Wouldn't kill her to smile though!

> **Shannon Grant @CoffeeLova1000**
> Melanie Lange is not fat!!! What is wrong with you? I'm a healthy size
> 12. According to you that would make me clinically obese, would it?

Danny Boy @DannnyBoyBeats
This dude looks too clean-cut for Melanie. She's a right filthy bitch! I can
always tell, LOLs.

SIR PETER LANGE –
MY SIDE OF THE STORY (UNPUBLISHED)

Interviews between ghost writer Ryan Morris
and Peter Lange, 8 October 2022

Ryan: Lange Cosmetics launched in 2010 to rave reviews, but the personal side of Melanie's life was still being played out weekly in the media. How did she cope with building her cosmetics range alongside being a public figure?

Peter: Like most people, Mellie had good days and bad days. She tried to accept the media attention. It wasn't always easy, but she was now the face of Lange Cosmetics. Mellie might not have enjoyed the tabloid attention, but she recognized the benefits of her fame. She made the decision to model her own range and it was a good decision because she was a very recognized face. An entire generation of women had grown up right alongside Mellie and seen her on the front pages of the magazines they bought, and despite every effort made by the British media to drag her down, she was popular. Those girls who wanted to be Melanie Lange when they were sixteen were now women in their twenties with a disposable income.

Mellie became a guest on some of the daytime TV shows chatting about women's health, beauty, business, all sorts of things. She was very clear with every interview that she would not discuss her private life.

It didn't stop the tabloids from hounding her on a daily basis. They just couldn't leave her alone. They'd spent years portraying Mellie as a party girl, but as soon as Mellie stopped going to clubs, they had to change their focus, and they were ruthless. They'd take a photo of Mellie leaving work or going into a restaurant and they'd Photoshop it to include whatever idiot boy they wanted to tell the world she was dating.

Ryan: So none of the stories were true?

Peter: Mellie was a beautiful young woman in her early twenties looking for love. It wasn't easy. A lot of men wanted to date Mellie because of who she was.

Ryan: Last year your ex-son-in-law, Finn Parker, made a rather scathing accusation in a magazine interview regarding your role in the start of their relationship.

Peter: He did.

Ryan: He claimed that in 2011 you invited him and several other men to interviews at Lange Hotels under the guise of partnering with their businesses, when in actual fact you were looking to hire them to date Melanie. You've never refuted the accusation, so I have to ask if there's any truth to it?

Peter: There is.

Ryan: It might seem to some – or even to many – to be quite an odd thing to do. Tell me what was going through your mind at this point in your own relationship with Melanie?

Peter: Let me start by telling you what I wasn't trying to do. I wasn't trying to find Mellie a husband. It wasn't an arranged marriage. I wasn't even trying to find her a relationship. My first priority with Mellie, with both girls, is happiness and health. I had no intention of interfering with Mellie's love life.

Lange Cosmetics was doing well. Everyone was excited about it. The board of Lange Hotels were happy, but they were nervous too. I felt like I was spending half of my working life trying to placate their worries about whatever story was running about Mellie that week. I understood their concerns. Lange Cosmetics had gone from a pet project investment as a favour to me to being a huge earner for us, at a time when there was a downward trend in hotel stays. The investment in Lange Cosmetics was becoming more important and they wanted to protect it.

The UK Business Awards was a few months away. We had two tables booked – one for Lange Hotels and one for Lange Cosmetics. Lange Cosmetics was up for a lot of awards that night. All the directors were going to be in attendance. It felt important at the time that Mellie didn't have one of her usual sorts on her arm that night.

I keep saying it because it's true, but Mellie was and is the face of Lange Cosmetics. It works because of her. She models for it, she's the spokesperson, she's the queen bee of all these workers who sell her products for a percentage of the profits and a discount off their own purchases.

The demographic of these women is twenty-eight to forty-nine: mothers, housewives looking to make a little extra money. These people were her army. They believed in her as much as her products, and she made each and every one of them feel like a valued member of the team.

There is no Lange Cosmetics without Mellie. And Mellie, for all her business sense and innovation, couldn't see that when she turned up places with some shaggy-haired lowlife on her arm it risked damaging the brand.

I wanted Mellie to have a date for the awards that wouldn't draw any unwanted attention. Zara had the idea that we could hire a male model, someone in a suit who looked the part. It was a good idea, but there was no way Mellie would agree to it.

But Zara's idea planted a seed that perhaps there was a way to step in and help Mellie. I knew I would have to be discreet. If Mellie got even a whiff that I'd had a hand in finding her a date, she'd turn around and find the most inappropriate man she could to be by her side just to spite me, and she'd probably marry him.

Ryan: So Melanie had no idea about this plan?

Peter: None at all. And before anyone goes and accuses me of being a heartless businessman, it wasn't just the image of these men I had a problem with. They were leeches who sucked Mellie dry of her energy and her money. She was forever trying to save them from themselves, which, believe me when I say, is an impossible and thankless task.

Ryan: Can you talk me through what exactly you hired Finn Parker to do? Presumably he had to deceive Melanie and convince her to take him to the awards?

Peter: In the spring of 2011, three months before the awards ceremony and the launch of Melanie's second line of products, Zara arranged for us to interview four men under the guise of a vague business partnership opportunity. They were entrepreneur types, self-starters. Real go-getters like Mellie. They were men who on paper looked like they were going places and didn't need Mellie to take them there.

Ryan: What were the requirements exactly?

Peter: Smart, normal-looking men.

Peter: By normal-looking, do you mean attractive?

Peter: They had to look right standing beside Mellie, so yes, a certain level of attractiveness was important. One of the men lied about his height on the application and was sent home straight away. The other three were invited to an all-day workshop.

It was . . . an unusual day. We gave them a lot of different tasks. I wanted to see how they'd react to a powerful woman. I wanted to see how they'd react when they were angry or challenged, and I wanted to see how they'd handle a person in crisis. By the end of the day, we'd narrowed it down to two men. When I called the first man in and explained what I was looking for, he walked out straight away.

Ryan: The second man was Finn Parker?

Peter: Yes.

Ryan: In his interview, Finn said he was offered money to date Melanie and likened the proposal to being pimped out.

Peter: [Sighs] I read his interview. There was some truth to what he said and some outright lies, which is why I've never spoken publicly about his accusations. No money ever changed hands between me personally or Lange Hotels and Finn. What I offered him was better than a cash handout. I offered him access to my business contacts in exchange for getting to know Mellie, and if they were both amenable to it, taking her out on a date.

Ryan: Was the UK Business Awards mentioned?

Peter: I believe it was, yes.

Ryan: So it was more than just one date. It was several dates and a focus on an invite to the business awards together?

Peter: Yes, but I was very clear that things should only progress if both parties wanted to. I suppose I had a second motive alongside the date for the business awards. I struggled to understand why Mellie only dated a particular type of boy – and they were boys, not men. I wanted her to see what dating a strong man could be like for her. I wanted her to be treated right in a relationship by someone who respected her and put her needs before their own. I was sure that if she could see what that kind of relationship looked like, then she would stop searching out the idiots to date.

I never expected Mellie to fall in love with Finn and for their relationship to become what it did.

Ryan: And at no point did you or Zara tell Melanie that you'd been the one to set her up with Finn?

Peter: No. By the time I realized Finn and Mellie were serious, it felt too late to say anything. She found out with the rest of the world in Finn's ill-timed, ill-mannered *Hello!* interview last year.

Ryan: How did Melanie take the news?

Peter: Not well, which I can understand. In hindsight, I can see that I shouldn't have interfered in Mellie's love life. If I could go back and do it all over again, believe me, I'd do a lot of things differently.

Netflix Original Documentary:
Melanie Lange – The Ugly Truth

INTERVIEWS RECORDED 19–22 SEPTEMBER 2022
(220 DAYS SINCE MELANIE'S DISAPPEARANCE)

Narrator

On Thursday the twelfth of May 2011, Melanie met clean energy entrepreneur Finn Parker at a cocktail bar opening in London. At the time this seemed to be a chance meeting that would lead to marriage, the birth of two children and a decade of media attention. But in a tell-all magazine interview in September 2021, Finn Parker made damning accusations surrounding the start of his relationship with Melanie and the role Sir Peter played as matchmaker.

Finn

I'm just going to say it and get it out of the way – yes, Sir Peter offered me a lot to date Melanie.

Nell

I'm still completely lost for words about the whole thing. There is no line that monster won't cross to keep control of Mel's life, but this is exactly what I mean about Sir Peter. He has to have control over every part of her. I just wish Melanie had seen the truth sooner, but by the time she really opened her eyes to what her dad was capable of, it was too late. She started making steps to pull her business and her life away from him, but he had her locked in that place before she had the chance.

Finn

I first met Melanie at the invite-only opening of VOC, a new cocktail bar near King's Cross that Sir Peter had got me tickets for. The place was tiny – one of those narrow, exposed-brick places where the bar runs down the entire length of the building. It was rammed to the hilt with people getting pissed on free booze. There were waitresses in skimpy sailor outfits with trays of weird seventeenth-century cocktails that no one had heard of, and there was Melanie perched on a barstool drinking a glass of red wine.

The attraction was instant. I knew right then that regardless of how our paths had crossed, Melanie was someone I wanted to get to know a lot better. Melanie was and still is stunningly attractive. Intimidatingly so. I remember wondering at the time if that's why she seemed to date weird guys. Maybe all the decent men were too afraid to approach her.

Anyway, Mel's wearing a black backless number with her hair piled on top of her head. Everyone in the room is looking at her, but she's cool as a cucumber drinking her wine.

She's with a guy – the only bloke in the place not wearing a suit – and he keeps disappearing outside to smoke and leaving Melanie at the bar. I remember thinking, if I was with Melanie, there's no way I'd leave her alone like that.

It's maybe like the third time she's on her own, and I turn to the friend I'm with and I say, 'Sorry, mate, I need to go over there.' He just laughs and wishes me good luck in that way mates do when you both know there's no way you've got a chance.

I walk over to Melanie, and my heart is racing and my palms are clammy. I'm a confident guy, an easy-going guy, but walking up to Melanie that night, I was nervous. I sit down beside her and she turns to me and tells me the stool I've just sat on is taken.

I say, 'I know, but if I was on a date with you, I wouldn't keep leaving you alone. Someone might try to steal you away.'

She laughs and asks me if that's my best line. But she's smiling too and so I say, 'I know a great Chinese just around the corner,' which was a total bluff. I didn't really expect her to say yes, but she grins and stands up and we just walk out together. I wave down a black cab and ask him to take us to Chinatown.

She says, 'I thought you knew a place around the corner?' It became an inside joke after that about my definition of what 'around the corner' meant. Even when she was giving birth to Sebastian, she asked, 'How much longer?' and I rubbed her back and said, 'Not much longer,' and she laughed. Even in that much pain, she laughed and said, 'If "not much longer" is the same as "around the corner", then I'm in trouble.'

Nell

Finn was like a Ken doll compared to Mel's other boyfriends. You know the type? The real strong jaw, clean-shaven, big smile and whiter-than-white teeth. His hair always looked like it had just been cut. I used to wonder if he went to the hairdresser's weekly. And he always wore a suit. And I mean, always. I think the first time I saw him wearing jeans and a polo shirt was when Sebastian was born and I went to visit Mel in the hospital.

It's hard for me to think about the Finn I met back then and what I thought of him. There's a lot of unresolved shit, a lot of anger we've had to put aside to focus on Melanie and what's happening to her right now.

Finn

When we're in the taxi, Melanie keeps looking behind her and I notice three or four men on motorbikes following us. As soon as we're on the street, cameras are flashing in our faces. They're shouting at us too. Asking for my name and if I'm Melanie's new boyfriend.

Melanie grabs my arm and pulls me into the first restaurant we find. It's plain inside. Brown tables, no tablecloths, but the food smells amazing and the manager finds us a table upstairs, away from the flashing cameras.

Mel is apologizing to the manager and to me as though it's her fault. I try to tell her it's OK, but she's shaken. I was shaken. The manager disappears and comes back with two beers and a bowl of prawn crackers on the house.

I say it must be because he feels sorry for us, and Melanie gives me this wry smile and says, 'It's because he knows that tomorrow the name of his restaurant will be in the papers and that means more business for him.'

I say something about having a lot to learn, and she nods and says, 'Welcome to the circus.'

Vic Watson, tabloid editor

The paper went to town on the night Melanie and Finn met. News was slow and we had pages to fill. The front page showed Melanie entering a bar with one man and leaving with another. The Mystery Hunk, we called him. Inside we did a two-page feature on twenty-four hours in Melanie's shoes. A little timestamp over every item or photo.

Finn

I'll be honest, even though I knew of Melanie Lange – I don't think there was a man in his twenties who didn't – and obviously over the years I'd seen the stories about her and knew she was famous, I didn't appreciate what that fame really meant. What it felt like. I thought it was all standing outside bars and smiling.

Nell

Straight away, Mel was different about Finn. We're chatting at her desk the day after they meet and she says to me, 'Nell, I've met this guy. I really like him, but I don't think I should see him again.'

I was so happy that she'd finally met someone she really liked. I said, 'Mel, if you like him, then see him,' but she was worried about dragging him into her crazy world. She had one of the papers open in front of her and there's all these photos of Mel. The last one showed Mel walking down the street, supposedly leaving Finn's house in the early hours of the morning. The implication being that she'd stayed the night.

They were always making up stuff about Mel.

Finn

We had an amazing meal. The food was delicious and we had the entire upstairs to ourselves. We went back there to eat every anniversary after that, and every time the manager gave us the same table, the same free drinks and prawn crackers.

Mel spent a lot of the evening talking about Lange Cosmetics, and it was clear how passionate she was about sustainable resources and chemical-free products. I told her about my business and my drive to make companies more energy efficient. We weren't exactly Greenpeace, but it felt like we were both trying, you know? It connected us.

At the end of the meal she told me it would be better if she left alone, and that's exactly what she did.

She gave me her number, thanked me for dinner and left.

She didn't come back to my house. We didn't even kiss that first night.

The following week, Melanie invited me over for dinner. I was pretty surprised by her apartment. It was really nice. These big white walls and huge windows, but it was small as well, and I remember wondering why she didn't have a bigger place when it was clear she could afford it.

I ask her if she's seen the article about the two of us and she does this cringe-look that she does anytime she feels uncomfortable. It's like a grimace and a shrug all at once. I ask her if she's contacted the paper and demanded a retraction for claiming we slept together. Oh, how she laughs at that. She laughs until she can't breathe. Until tears are rolling down her face and she's waving her hands in front of her eyes trying to stop her mascara running.

When she stops laughing, she says, 'I don't want to mess you around. If we're going to date, then you need to know that the British press are vultures. They are poison to everyone who tries to get close to me. It means your name in the paper, your ex-girlfriends selling their story, your skeletons out for the world to see. It means your business could suffer, and I don't want that for you. So if you want to walk away right now, then I don't blame you. If I could walk away from my life, believe me, I would, and if I was in your shoes right now, I'd already be walking away.'

I think about those words a lot. 'If I could walk away from my life, believe me, I would.' There was a point when I wondered if that's what she'd done, you know? Just walked away. But Mel would never leave Sebastian and William. That's how I know she's in trouble.

Anyway, Mel makes the speech and then excuses herself and disappears into the bathroom, like she's actually giving me time to think about it, and I knew it wasn't just something she said to people. She really wanted me to think and so I did. I thought about how my life was pretty sweet. My business was growing and I felt like I was on the cusp of something, and staying could mean the end of that. Then I wondered how many times Melanie had given that speech and how many times she'd walked back into the room and found it empty. I thought about this amazing woman I was trying to get to know and how much she seemed like she needed someone in her corner.

Sometimes I wonder what would have happened to both of us if I'd walked away that night. But we had a happy marriage for a long time and two beautiful boys who are my world, so of course I'm glad I didn't, but I'd be lying if I said it's been easy being Mr Melanie Lange.

Lola
Oh, Finn. Lovely Finn.

Jessie
No, no, no. We hate him now, remember?

Lola

Oh, right. Yes, we do. He was nice at first though, wasn't he? He was good for Mel.

Jessie

He was perfect. Do you remember that garden party at Mum and Dad's house? We invited Mel and Nell, and Mel brought Finn too.

Lola

The way they were looking at each other. God, it was like true love. They were both so passionate about their businesses. I think that's one of the reasons they worked so well at the beginning.

Jessie

They really respected each other, really listened when the other one was talking.

Lola

Exactly.

Nell

Even though I was happy for Mel, there was a part of me that felt a bit wary of anyone new coming into Mel's life. Things were going so well for her and she had some of her old confidence back. I didn't want anything to rock the boat. But I'll admit Finn was good for Melanie. He didn't need fixing or mothering. I hoped it would allow her to be more of herself in the relationship, but it seemed to me at times as though she wasn't trying to be herself, she was trying to be someone else, or maybe she was just growing up. We both were.

I was living with a guy from the accounts team. I felt really grown-up and settled and I wanted that for Mel. I wanted her to find that happiness. I'm not going to pretend I thought Finn was Mel's perfect match, or that I saw eye to eye with him all of the time, because I didn't.

Finn

Did I stay that time at Mel's apartment because Sir Peter had made certain promises to me about sharing his business contacts? No.

The only thing I ever did for Sir Peter was to go along to that bar opening with an idea that I'd date Melanie and Sir Peter would help with my business, and then we'd all go our separate ways, but I was expecting some airhead of a beauty. Nothing could have been further from the truth.

Within seconds of meeting Melanie, I knew she was special. Her father and Zara may have been the ones to set us up, but if they were looking for an ally, they didn't find one in me.

It took about three months before the tabloids really honed their attention on me and started ripping away at my business. Accusing me of unethical practices and a load of bullshit. I was radioactive. I had to become a silent partner in my own business. That was tough. But I was madly in love with Melanie by then so I knew it was worth it. Lange Cosmetics was really taking off. I joined Lange myself in a business consulting capacity for a while, looking at how they could reduce the carbon footprint of their hotels. It was a pretty exciting job. You wouldn't believe how much energy hotels burn. Just by changing to sensor-controlled lights in their communal areas it saved the business thousands in electricity bills.

It was a sacrifice. I made it for Mel because I wanted to be with her, I wanted a life together. We both made sacrifices to make that happen.

Nell

There are things Finn did to Mel at the end of their marriage that I will never forgive him for, but he wants Mel back for the boys as much as I do.

Finn

I never thought I'd trust Nell further than I could see her, but she'd do anything for Mel and on this one thing, right now – Save Melanie – we are united.

From: Zara.Lange@LangeHotels.com
To: Peter.Lange@LangeHotels.com
Date: 8 October 2022
Subject: Call me!

Dad,

I know you said you were all right this morning, but you didn't sleep at all last night! How many batches of bolognese did you make?

I don't think talking to this ghost writer is a good idea right now. What if you say something you regret? Can you trust him?

Z x

SIR PETER LANGE —
MY SIDE OF THE STORY (UNPUBLISHED)

Interviews between ghost writer Ryan Morris
and Peter Lange, 8 October 2022

Ryan: Can we talk about the wedding in July 2013? You chose Finn as a match for Melanie, so you must have been pleased when they made plans to marry?

Peter: I had my reservations about Finn. No matter who you are or how close you are to someone, you can never know what goes on inside their relationship with another person. Mellie said she was happy and she certainly looked it. So I tried to make peace with her decision.

Ryan: Tell me about the wedding. We've talked a lot now about how private Melanie is as a person, but then she agreed to have a very public wedding featured in *Hello!* magazine. Why was that?

Peter: That was all Finn. He got greedy and Mellie wanted to make him happy. I can say quite confidently that she hated every moment of that day, which I've always thought was a shame, but she wanted the marriage and the relationship and was willing to give up her idea of one perfect day for Finn.

The entire thing was a giant spectacle.

I pulled Finn aside a few weeks before the wedding. We were at the tailor's having final adjustments to the suits Mellie had chosen for us. I wanted to make sure he was marrying Mellie for the right reasons.

Ryan: What were they?

Peter: Love, obviously. And happiness. That's all I've ever wanted for both girls. I suppose I was concerned that because I'd had a hand in the creation of their relationship, perhaps Finn was trying to cash in on Mel's fame and her money. Finn took my concerns seriously and told me very clearly that he loved Mellie and wanted a life with her. I still had my doubts about the two of them, but perhaps all fathers do.

Melanie Lange video 7/9
Published on Melanie Lange YouTube channel on 6 August 2022

I'm Melanie Lange. I'm being held prisoner by my father. The house is modern. There's a private beach which I used to be allowed to visit. A guard would accompany me down the cliff path and I could sit and watch the waves. That was until I saw two kayaks coming around the headland. The next day, I was told the beach was out of bounds.

So I started walking the grounds of the property. Sometimes it was just to be outside in the fresh air and sometimes to search for signs of life outside this property. Then yesterday after breakfast, I went to go outside, but . . . [crying] the door was locked.

I'm trapped in this house.

More and more things are being taken away from me. Last night I was given a bowl of wholegrain rice. Nothing else.

It's like I'm being punished.

[Crying]

I . . . I feel so trapped and alone.

[Gasp]

The guard is at the door. He's knocking. I have to go. I can't let them find this phone.

Twitter

25 July 2013

Amy B @GirlAboutTownBlog
HELLO! wedding pics are out!!!!! Melanie Lange looks beautiful
#MelanieLange #Melanie&FinnWedding

> **Laura V @LauraLostHerPhone**
> That dress swamps her. She's lost so much weight! She looks like
> Skeletor from that kids' cartoon!

> **Amy B @GirlAboutTownBlog**
> LOL

> **Leslie Riley-Moor @FashionistaFan_Blogger**
> Wish she'd worn her hair up. It looks messy.

> **Tammy S @TammySunflowers**
> This is such a fake wedding!!! They only did it for the money. You
> can tell from the way they're posing that they're miserable.

> **Natalie-Claire Olson @NattyClaire_Olson**
> Her lips look weird. Has she had something done to them?

> **Amy B @GirlAboutTownBlog**
> Absolutely!

Netflix Original Documentary:
Melanie Lange – The Ugly Truth

INTERVIEWS RECORDED 19–22 SEPTEMBER 2022
(220 DAYS SINCE MELANIE'S DISAPPEARANCE)

Narrator

On the twentieth of July 2013, 250 guests gathered to watch Melanie and Finn marry in a lavish ceremony estimated to have cost over £300,000. Photographs from the day were sold exclusively to *Hello!* magazine for £1.5 million.

Finn

Melanie wanted to get married in the same church her parents married in. Then she wanted a small reception in the garden at her dad's house. Just family and close friends. Twenty people tops.

It was me who wanted more. It sounds naive now that I say this, but I was only planning to get married the one time and I wanted it to be a big celebration of our love. Mel was always trying to make herself smaller. She didn't like drawing attention to herself. That's not how I wanted her to feel about her wedding day. I wanted her to feel like she could be the shining light. I didn't want either of us to look back and have any regrets.

As soon as the engagement hit the news, *Hello!* approached us with an offer. They wanted exclusive rights to the wedding photographs. We both said no. And then they came back with a bigger offer – enough to buy our dream house. Which is when I thought about how many people wanted to see our wedding.

If we handed the rights to the photographs over to *Hello!*, then we were in effect stopping the tabloids from using them, which is what Mel wanted.

Looking back, it was pretty over the top, but it was still a brilliant day for both of us.

Lola

Mel looked stunning in her wedding dress, didn't she?

Jessie

Flawless.

Lola

The dress was designed by Vera Wang exclusively for Mel and it really showed. The way it just hung from her body.

Jessie

It was really quite simple. A silk shift dress in ivory white. She wore her hair half pinned up with all these tiny little pearls. I remember thinking she looked like a Greek goddess.

Lola

Oh my god, you're right, she did. Finn looked rather handsome too, didn't he? A grey suit. No top hat or tails.

Jessie

Thank God. So old-fashioned.

Lola

The bridesmaids wore black which looked so classy. It was us and Nell, of course, and Zara.

Jessie

Not that Zara did anything except pose for photos. She wasn't even in the suite with us when Mel was getting ready. It was Mel's wedding day when we fell out with Nell.

Lola

Because she was in a mood all morning. I even heard her ask Mel if she was sure she wanted to go through with it. We pulled her to one side and super nicely told her to get her shit together because this was Mel's day not hers.

Jessie

She didn't take it well. She accused us of not caring about anything beyond ourselves.

Lola

Which was way harsh. We kept up all the smiles for Mel that day but we didn't see Nell for ages after that.

Nell

I don't remember Lola and Jessie talking to me. I thought we'd just drifted apart. The thing I remember most about Melanie's wedding day was this moment just before the ceremony when everything was ready and it was just the two of us standing in this waiting area. We could hear all the people shuffling about in their seats waiting for a glimpse of Mel.

She looks at me and she smiles, and I know without her telling me that she's nervous, and I feel this weight of responsibility, like I need her to know I've got her back. So I say, 'Are you sure he's your guy? My car is outside – we can be on a plane to Barbados in no time.'

She takes my hand and smiles again and says, 'Finn sees the best version of me and he makes me want to be that person all the time. I love him, Nell.' She goes all misty-eyed before she says, much more Mel-like, 'And if it all goes tits up, then we'll cash in on this bloody magazine deal and all the rest and then we'll get divorced. I'm the face, I'm the brand – Finn is along for the ride for as long as I say.'

I thought, 'Right, well you've got your head screwed on.' Although it turns out she was wrong, because what that man did with her boys is nothing short of criminal.

Vic Watson, tabloid editor

From the moment the engagement was announced, the nation became obsessed with wedding fever. They wanted to know every tiny detail about the wedding plans. They wanted to know the fights and the fallouts, who was going, who wasn't going and why. I feel like I lived and breathed that wedding for nine months.

And the very moment Melanie was married, things really changed for her in the stories we published. Overnight she became Martha bloody Stewart in the nation's eyes. The photos that sold papers were not of Melanie out on the town – although she was still a part of that scene; she was only twenty-five after all – but shopping in Waitrose. People wanted to know what she was cooking Finn for dinner. They wanted to know every single detail about Melanie's married life. She seemed to give a lot of women hope. A single girl who is clearly attracted to no-good musicians. And then along comes a handsome businessman to sweep her off her feet. That was the story they wanted to read, and that's what we gave them for quite a while.

Miranda Dickson, lead seller for Lange Cosmetics 2012

Every quarter, Melanie invites all the sales reps to a roadshow event at one of the Lange hotels. We get to sample any new products, we get sales training and we get support. Proper support and not just about sales stuff. There are mortgage advisers, financial advisers and therapists at these things. Melanie really looks after us. And she comes to every roadshow and chats to us all individually. At least, she did up until this year.

Even so, I couldn't believe it when the invite to the wedding came through the door. There was a handwritten note from Melanie. It said, 'Thank you for all your hard work. I would be honoured if you and your family could celebrate my big day with me.'

And that is one of the many reasons why I love Melanie Lange. She invited all of her top sellers and their partners and kids to her wedding. We weren't stuffed in the corner either. We were treated like any other guest. Melanie came over at one point, looking absolutely beautiful, and spent some time with all of us. She even did some colouring with my daughter.

Vic Watson, tabloid editor
It goes without saying that the entire nation was holding its breath for baby news.

Finn
We both wanted children and started trying pretty much straight away, but it didn't happen as quickly as we expected. There was a lot going on behind the scenes. I think people would be surprised to know how fragile Melanie was at times during our marriage. I don't know the full details of what happened to Mel at that place her dad sent her to when she was nineteen. She hated talking about it, but it left its mark on her emotionally. She couldn't sleep unless there was a hall light on outside the bedroom, and when she got nervous she'd rub her wrists, like people do in films when they have handcuffs taken off.

I remember once, she had to present to the shareholders – the board of Lange Hotels – on how Lange Cosmetics were going to be sold moving forward. There was growing pressure to move away from the sales rep model they'd been using and stock the products in retail outlets, but Melanie was adamant that the products and sales should remain in the hands of her reps. She always said, 'These people believed in me when I was starting out, and now it's my turn to believe in them.'

The problem was that Zara, who had nothing to do with Lange

Cosmetics, went rogue and lined up huge deals with the high street shops and supermarkets to sell Lange Cosmetics. They were offering advertising and prime shelf space. It was potentially a big money-maker and Melanie knew she had a fight on her hands. She went into the office in these skyscraper red heels and her favourite black power suit, as she called it. It was an all-day meeting. She brought in her own experts and some of her sales reps, and whatever Mel said, it did the job. Lange Cosmetics remained off the high street.

Mel should've been on cloud nine. It was a big win for her, but she came home practically shaking with exhaustion. It was like the day had sucked the life out of her. She just sat on the sofa and cried. I didn't know what to do. I thought we'd be popping champagne and going out for dinner. It made me feel really helpless.

When Melanie fell pregnant and launched Baby Lange, it added a lot of pressure. There were times when I really worried about her.

Twitter

7 October 2022

Matty Venus @Filmjunkie2000

WOW. Just watched #TheUglyTruth. Can't believe the shit that went on #SaveMelanie

> **Meg Hillis @MegHillis88**
>
> I can't believe Finn showed his face after what he put her through. It's clearly all his fault. #SaveMelanie
>
> **Amy B @GirlAboutTownBlog**
>
> So humbled by #TheUglyTruth! I've never stopped to think how I might be part of the problem. I'm truly sorry for some of the comments I made about Melanie over the years. I won't make excuses, but I was going through some bad stuff back then. #SaveMelanie
>
> **Jessie W @Jessiebakescakes4U**
>
> Someone else who wants to make a woman imprisoned for 8 months about them! #SaveMelanie
>
> **Kimberly F @Kimberly_T_Filch**
>
> Exactly this! If @GirlAboutTownBlog was truly sorry, why is she still on here spouting all her crap?

SIR PETER LANGE —
MY SIDE OF THE STORY (UNPUBLISHED)

*Interviews between ghost writer Ryan Morris
and Peter Lange, 8 October 2022*

Ryan: What was life like after the wedding?

Peter: It was a golden time. I think it was the first time since Mellie stepped on to the red carpet at the launch party for Lange London that the tabloids seemed on her side. Lange Cosmetics continued to grow from strength to strength. A make-up line was added, so was perfume. Mellie was happily married; life was very calm for her during that period. I think it helped that she spent more time at home with Finn than out with Nell, and like I said, even the tabloids stopped trashing her, although it was a brief reprieve. This went on for maybe a year, and then Mellie has this idea for a new range of products she wanted to call Baby Lange. A whole new line of skincare products with exactly the same ethos as Lange Cosmetics but for pregnant mothers, babies and children.

No one doubted Mellie like they did at the start of Lange Cosmetics. Whole new teams of people were hired. Samples were tested, designs were done. Then about five months before the launch, Mellie announced she was four months pregnant and so she modelled for the pregnancy products herself.

Ryan: The following year, in 2016, your hotels reported their first ever annual losses. How did that feel?

Peter: I won't pretend it didn't sting because it did. But as I said, we'd been expecting a downturn for several years. We'd seen the profits gradually decline over the course of five years. We had fierce competition from every side. More people were choosing to stay in Airbnb apartments rather than hotels, and those who wanted hotels were choosing the low-cost options. Our model of affordable luxury wasn't working any more. Which is why I'd been so keen to diversify and why we'd invested so heavily in Lange Cosmetics. In 2017 we made the difficult decision to sell a number of our hotels and invest the money in spas, gyms and conference centres for more of our establishments. Lange Cosmetics provided their products and Mellie led the team that developed the treatments the spas would offer. It was an exciting new direction for Lange Hotels. We were adapting to a changing market, which we'll continue to do.

Ryan: Would it be fair to say that Melanie's business saved Lange Hotels?

[Pause]

Peter: That's a very simplistic way of looking at it. I prefer to think that we invested wisely for this eventuality.

Ryan: What do you say to people who suggest that without Lange Cosmetics, Lange Hotels wouldn't be a viable business?

Peter: If you cut off the arm of a world-class tennis player, are they still a world-class tennis player? No, of course they're not. These people think of Lange Hotels and Lange Cosmetics as being separate businesses, and obviously they are registered that way for tax purposes and the like, but to me they are one body, one organism. They need each other to survive.

Ryan: I think your critics would argue that Lange Cosmetics doesn't need Lange Hotels for anything.

Peter: For God's sake, are you even listening to what I'm saying?

[Pause]

Sorry. Let's take a break. I need some lunch.

RECORDING STOPPED

Netflix Original Documentary:
Melanie Lange – The Ugly Truth

INTERVIEWS RECORDED 19–22 SEPTEMBER 2022
(220 DAYS SINCE MELANIE'S DISAPPEARANCE)

Narrator

Melanie's second business venture, Baby Lange, launched to rave reviews in August 2015. On the fifteenth of that same month, Melanie gave birth to her first son, Sebastian Parker. Support for Melanie poured in on every social media platform as her fans waited for the first glimpse of her newborn son.

Nell

Mel is an amazing mother. She's so intuitive and so fun. She would hold these mini discos in the living room, and she and the boys would dance and play silly games.

When Sebastian was born and I went to see her in hospital and hold him for the first time, Mel was pretty teary which is totally normal. Finn goes to find a midwife because Sebastian is having trouble latching on to her nipple and Mel is getting upset. When it's just the two of us in the room, she tells me she's scared.

I say, 'What are you scared of?'

She says, 'I'm scared how much I love Sebastian. I'm scared how much he needs me. I'm scared I won't be as good a mother to him as my mum was to me.'

I tell her that everything she is feeling is normal. I'm sure all first-time mums are scared, but I don't think that fear ever went away for Mel.

Vic Watson, tabloid editor

The timing was perfect, wouldn't you say? Baby Lange launching the same week Mel gives birth. Everyone was clamouring for that first baby photo.

Finn

People always tell you that the second baby is easier, but that wasn't the case with us. Sebastian was born at 2.55 p.m, weighing seven pounds six ounces. He was perfect. Completely and utterly perfect.

I'm not saying we didn't have sleepless nights with him because of course we did. It was exhausting and it was hard, but he very quickly fell into a good routine. He was sleeping through the night from about six weeks and he slotted into our lives like he'd always been there.

Mel's intention was always to take a year's maternity leave and I'd carry on working, but Baby Lange was launching and it meant so much to Mel. She was getting calls every ten minutes about this product or that. There were interview requests pretty much daily.

I come home one day when Sebastian is three months old and I find Mel in her office. She's on the phone doing a radio interview while feeding Sebastian. She laughs her way through the interview, makes a joke about juggling her two babies, and when it's over, she hangs up and bursts into tears.

She tells me about the baby group she'd wanted to go to at the local church and how she was running late because Sebastian needed a feed, and then a change, and then he was sick and she had to change too. When she finally made it out the door, she was surrounded by photographers. A new mum on her own with a baby in a pushchair, and these sharks shove a camera in her face and give her no choice but to go back inside the house.

It seemed obvious to me that the answer was for me to stay at home and Mel to go to work. It took quite a bit of convincing, and it was hard for Mel. Really hard. She would call me crying in the toilets at the office because she missed Sebastian so much, but my business didn't need me the way Mel's did her. And I didn't get anywhere near the same attention leaving the house with Sebastian as Mel did. It just seemed like the right thing to do for Mel and Sebastian and me.

One of the hardest things for Mel was how much it divided opinion. For every person who supported a businesswoman returning to work so soon after the birth of her child, there was another person telling Mel she was an unfit mother. She couldn't win. And it didn't help that in both types of stories I was portrayed as the hero stay-at-home dad saving the day.

Mel's confidence took a knock. She began to doubt her decisions, at home with Sebastian and at work.

Narrator

Twelve months after its launch, Baby Lange became the leading brand of baby skincare products in the UK. Between 2015 and 2016, turnover for Lange Cosmetics increased by over £18 million. This jump in profits is largely attributed to the Baby Lange product line. After the birth of her first son, Melanie remained at the helm of Lange Cosmetics and continued to promote the products herself with modelling and TV appearances.

Nell

Yeah, that was a crazy time for us. But in a good way, I think. We were all working flat out in the business, and on top of that Mel was being badgered to do *Strictly Come Dancing*, *I'm a Celebrity*, *Dancing on Ice*, *Celebrity Big Brother*. She turned them all down. There was no way she was leaving Sebastian any more than she had to, but she carried on her regular slots on the morning shows.

The only celebrity show she did was a charity special of *Who Wants to be a Millionaire?* She raised money for MIND. People couldn't believe she got as far as she did. One question away from the million. £500,000 for charity in less than an hour, with Lange Cosmetics promising to match whatever money she raised. No matter what she did or how hard Mel worked, the British press still wanted her to be the washed-up model, which couldn't have been further from the truth.

It wasn't until Sebastian's first birthday party that I started to worry Mel was taking on too much.

Lola

Sebastian was the cutest baby ever.

Jessie

No surprise there. Just look at his parents.

Lola

Mel invited us to Sebastian's first birthday party.

Jessie

We hadn't seen her for ages, had we?

Lola

Nope. I saw her more on the TV that year than I did in person.

Jessie

The party was at their house in South Kensington. They had the barbecue going and Finn in an apron. It felt so normal, you know? After the extravagance of the wedding, we weren't sure what we were going to walk into at that party.

Lola

We were so overdressed. There's us in Gucci dresses like we're going to Ascot, and Mel opens the door in a pair of denim shorts and a white T-shirt. Barely any make-up, hair tied back.

Jessie

She looked tired, didn't she?

Lola

Absolutely wiped out. And there was a funny atmosphere. Like there'd been an argument ten minutes before we arrived and Mel was putting on this false joviality.

Jessie

It wasn't a big party. I remember wondering why Mel had invited us. Sir Peter was there and Zara, plus Finn's parents and brother, Nell obviously, and us. We made a bit of small talk with Nell, which was also weird. We hadn't seen her since the wedding.

Jessie

She was in a right mood at the party, wasn't she?

Lola

Everyone was. Nell just wasn't hiding it. Anyway, the sun was shining, and little Sebastian was crawling around the lawn and being passed between the guests for kisses. Then Mel brings out this Thomas the Tank Engine cake and we all sing 'Happy Birthday'. Mel and Finn help him blow out the candle and then Finn says, 'While we've got you all together, we've got one extra present to give to Sebastian.' And he pulls out this little blue T-shirt, and on it is written 'I'm the big brother'.

Jessie

That was a bit cringe actually. If they'd just said, 'Mel's expecting,' then we'd all have jumped up and congratulated them, but the T-shirt thing fell pretty flat.

Nell

It was Finn that made the announcement about Mel's pregnancy. All eyes were on him as he slipped this little blue T-shirt over

Sebastian's head. I was the only one looking at Melanie and what I saw on her face was pure fear.

Finn

We both wanted more children. I think Mel would've waited another year or two before trying, but there's only eighteen months between me and my brother and we've always been close. Whereas there's four years between Mel and Zara and they'd never gelled. Zara was always there at the family stuff and in the office, but she and Mel just didn't connect. When I explained it like that, Mel agreed.

Mel and I talked about how we would manage the childcare and Mel was very clear that she wanted to take more time off this time, which I was happy to support.

Nell

Of course I was happy for Mel and Finn. I guess I was worried about how much Mel was adding to her load with a second baby so soon, because I knew she already felt so stretched.

Narrator

In the early hours of the first of February 2017, two weeks before Melanie's twenty-ninth birthday, she gave birth to her and Finn's second child – William Parker.

Finn

The labour with William was a lot longer. Mel's waters broke at six in the morning and shortly after that she got her first contraction. We called our nanny, who came straight away to take care of Sebastian, and I drove Mel to hospital. I remember in the car we were talking about what we'd do for dinner that night. I think we both assumed we'd be home by lunchtime, but the labour went on and on.

Then there were some concerns about William's heartbeat and Mel was rushed in for an emergency caesarean.

It wasn't a great start and Mel needed a lot of support to recover from the surgery. She found this tough. She'd always been a hands-on mum and it was hard for her not being able to pick up Sebastian, and play and dance with him the way she usually did.

Even after a few weeks, Mel was crying a lot and just wasn't herself. I suggested we up our nanny's hours, but Mel was adamant that she wanted to use her maternity leave to look after her own children.

It was hard work. William did not like to sleep at night. He struggled to feed, and I mean struggled. It felt like he was permanently fixed to Mel's boob. Then he had reflux and would throw it all back up. What I'm saying is, I should have picked up on how much Melanie was struggling a lot earlier than I did, but we were both sleep-deprived and exhausted, trying to care for a toddler and a newborn.

Nell

Like I said, Mel is a brilliant mum, but it ripped her in two being a mother. On one side, she wanted to be the same mother as her mum had been to her. A homemaker, someone who was always there for the boys. And at the same time she wanted to be ploughing ahead with her brands. She hated that she wasn't in the office to keep an eye on things. She spent a lot of time worrying that if she wasn't in the office, then Sir Peter or Zara would muscle their way in and change the fundamentals of her business. She called three or four times a day, and I would normally pop round on my way home to give her a full debrief of the day's meetings.

Mel wanted me at the business all of the time, but I wish I'd been there for her more. I wish I'd seen how sad she was. I'm surprised Finn didn't.

Twitter
5 May 2017

Natty H @NataliaLH

Er what is with Melanie Lange? She used to be a MILF and now she looks like a tramp. #MelanieLange

> **Amy B @GirlAboutTownBlog**
>
> Agree! She could make an effort.

> **Shannon Grant @CoffeeLova1000**
>
> What's up with Melanie Lange? She's just had her second baby!!! And is probably exhausted.

> **Patsy Hanson @LeicesterWeddingPhotography**
>
> The pressure on women to bounce back after childbirth is insane! Leave the poor woman alone.

> **Laura V @LauraLostHerPhone**
>
> Totally! Good for her for not bothering! She'll be back at work next week anyway. Not sure why she bothered having kids.

> **Tammy S @TammySunflowers**
>
> As if she's doing any of the childcare herself!! Bet she's got an army of nannies. Probably only sees the kids for photo ops. #MelanieLange

Netflix Original Documentary:
Melanie Lange – The Ugly Truth

INTERVIEWS RECORDED 19–22 SEPTEMBER 2022
(220 DAYS SINCE MELANIE'S DISAPPEARANCE)

Lola

William was about four months old and we hadn't had a chance to visit. We had a home visit with a client around the corner from Mel's and we thought we'd just ring the doorbell and see if Mel was in. Take her some flowers and say hi.

Jessie

I'm so glad we did that.

Lola

She opened the door and just burst into tears. William was crying in her arms and Sebastian was colouring on the walls and the place was a tip. Mel looked about ten seconds away from a nervous breakdown. I took William, and we sent her upstairs and told her to take a break. Sleep or shower, whatever.

Jessie

We cleaned up a bit and I played with Sebastian. Mel came downstairs an hour later looking a bit better. We made her eat a sandwich and have a hot cup of tea. Then she told us how hard everything was and how low she was feeling.

Lola

And how lonely she was. It can't have been easy making friends.

Jessie

It was me who suggested it might be postnatal depression. I'd gone through it after the birth of my daughter, Kitty, the year before.

Lola

You thought all new mothers had postnatal depression.

Jessie

Not all mothers, but a lot, and so many mothers struggle through it without realizing that it isn't normal to feel that way. Besides, I was right, wasn't I?

Lola

We'd recently launched a fashion YouTube channel – Lola & Jessie – and I told Mel about it that day. She told me that Lange Cosmetics were thinking about launching something similar and I told her that it didn't need to be a business thing per se, and that perhaps she'd get something out of connecting with other mothers.

Vic Watson, tabloid editor

So here is a woman who never does interviews about her personal life, who claims all she wants is privacy, but then she'll happily go on all the morning shows when it suits her. She times her first child to coincide with the launch of her baby range, and then she sets up a YouTube channel after the birth of her second child. And what does she talk about? Herself. Forgive me if I'm just a little cynical.

VIDEO FOOTAGE. SOURCE:
YOUTUBE, MELANIE LANGE CHANNEL

Date posted: 6 June 2017

Hi. Hey. I'm Melanie Lange. I've set up this YouTube channel because I want to talk about how hard I'm finding motherhood right now. I really thought, 'Well, I've done it once,' so I thought I knew what I was letting myself in for. I thought the second time would be easier.
   [Laughs]

I can't believe that now. It's not easier. It's a million times harder. It's taken me a few months to realize my exhaustion and emotions are more than just 'baby blues' – God, I hate that term.

I had some friends pop over this morning. They were brilliant. They sent me upstairs for a shower and I got a little bit of time to myself. When they left, I felt so much better and I thought, 'Right, I can do this. I can go to the supermarket to get a few things.' I'm down to like three nappies, and I'm sure you guys know that getting that low puts you at risk of an exploding bum. It's like they know, right?

So I think to myself, 'I've got the whole afternoon, I can do this.' But then William needs a feed and by the time we actually make it to the supermarket, it's getting close to Sebastian's dinner time and he's getting whiny.

I get one of those monster trollies with the seat for Sebastian and the little baby chair for William. It was stressful, but William fell asleep so I could at least get what we needed without him screaming the place down. Then I got back to the car and Sebastian tried to climb out of the seat before I was ready, so I grabbed him under one arm as I unlocked the car. There was another mum waiting for my space and she looked as stressed as I felt, so I hurried. I hopped in the car and left. I was almost out of the car park before I realized – before I remembered – William. I'd left him and the shopping in the trolley.

Can you believe that? I left my newborn baby – one of the most precious things in the world to me, and I left him behind. I drove back and he was there with my shopping, exactly where I left him.

I see all these stories about what a terrible mother I am because I went back to work when Sebastian was so little, or because I stopped breastfeeding or because I use the wrong kind of nappies. All mothers feel that judgement, but to have it written down in the magazines and online, it hurts. It makes it that much harder to believe in myself as a mother.

The mum who I gave the parking space to was with William, and she gave me a big hug and told me not to worry, that she'd done the same thing once, and that I was doing OK. I wish I'd got her name. I wish I could tell her now how much those words helped me, and how her compliment feels like the biggest compliment anyone has ever given me.

Her support made such a difference to me.

There are days right now when I don't even think I can get dressed, let alone care for my beautiful boys. I sat in my car for a few minutes after that, and then I drove straight to my doctor's, where I was diagnosed with postnatal depression.

And even though I've got some medication that I'm going to take, that I know will help, just having that diagnosis, the recognition that I'm not supposed to feel this way, has helped already.

Now, I know this video is going to make lots of headlines, I know I'm going to be judged and ripped apart, but I'm doing it anyway because I want all the mums out there who are having a shit time of it like me to know that they're not alone, and because I'm one of those mums having a shit time of it, and I want to know that I'm not alone. This is me reaching out. Hello and help!

Finn

I was cautious about the YouTube channel. I didn't want it to backfire on Melanie when she was in such a delicate state. But it actually did her the world of good. She would post videos at 3 a.m., and in the mornings, no make-up, hair a mess, and tell it like it was. She did it for herself, but it really helped a lot of mothers.

Vic Watson, tabloid editor

I'm not saying that Melanie's YouTube channel was a stunt. Even I could see that the emotion in those videos was real. I'm just saying that from a PR standpoint, it was a genius move. We ran a story. I think the headline was something like: 'Melanie leaves baby in supermarket'. We got thousands and thousands of complaints about that story. We were slammed on Twitter for it too. It was like a national movement of Melanie fans came flooding out of the woodwork. The paper got boycotted and we lost a lot of readers. The nation spoke and they told us to stop trashing Melanie, and so we did. We became her number one fan instead, right up until the story broke about her marriage in 2018. Her fans didn't care what we printed then. They were as desperate as we were to find out what was going on.

Melanie Lange video 8/9
Published on Melanie Lange YouTube channel on 6 August 2022

Nothing has changed. I'm so tired today. I don't do anything but I'm so tired. I just wanted to say that I'm still here.

I'm Melanie Lange. Don't forget about me.

SIR PETER LANGE —
MY SIDE OF THE STORY (UNPUBLISHED)

*Interviews between ghost writer Ryan Morris
and Peter Lange, 8 October 2022*

Ryan: So Lange Cosmetics is grossing millions every quarter. Baby Lange is one of the top-selling baby brands on the market. Melanie is married and has two children of her own. Everything was going well. When did it all change for Melanie?

Peter: It's hard to pinpoint an exact date. Melanie was back at work after her maternity leave with William. She was exhausted and quite emotional. She'd lost some of her edge, which was understandable. But it wasn't until the nanny story broke over Christmas 2018 that things really turned for Mellie.

Ryan: Did you believe the nanny's claims?

Peter: The public certainly did. I thought perhaps there might be some truth, but also a lot of exaggeration.

Ryan: And Melanie? Did she believe it?

Peter: I didn't ask and she never said. The priority for Mellie has always been taking care of her boys and her business.

Netflix Original Documentary:
Melanie Lange – The Ugly Truth

INTERVIEWS RECORDED 19–22 SEPTEMBER 2022
(220 DAYS SINCE MELANIE'S DISAPPEARANCE)

Narrator

For several years Melanie rode a wave of popularity. Her YouTube channel grew to over a million subscribers and for two years running, in 2017 and 2018, she was voted Celebrity Mum of the Year. But six days before Christmas 2018, everything changed for Melanie when the *Sun* made damning accusations about Melanie's marriage and her mental state.

Vic Watson, tabloid editor

As an editor there are going to be stories which you break, and there are going to be stories that other papers break, and some of them hit me right in the gut. The Aoife Duffy story was the latter. I still get this feeling right here in my chest, this frustration that we weren't the paper that broke that story.

Was it true? I don't know and I don't care. True or not, the cracks in Melanie's marriage started to show.

Finn

Aoife Duffy was an eighteen-year-old girl who Mel hired in the summer of 2018 for four months while our regular nanny, Laura, went travelling across Asia. Aoife was a good kid, she was good with the boys, and she was happy to work whatever hours we needed her.

When Laura returned from travelling, Aoife asked if we'd keep her on and even though we liked her, for whatever reason, Laura felt like a better fit with us, and so sadly we let Aoife go, but we offered to write her a good reference. I think Mel even put her in touch with a couple of mums she knew.

We hear nothing from her for months, and then out of nowhere this story breaks that I had an affair with Aoife during the time she worked with us.

It was absolute nonsense. Not a word of truth to any of it, and Mel knew that. I'm not saying our marriage was perfect, because no marriage is, but she knew it was lies.

Nell

Of course Finn denied it. All men deny shagging the nanny. God, it's such a cliché and so humiliating for Mel. There were just so many details in the story. Like Finn's birthmark on his arse, for God's sake. How else would she have known that if it wasn't true?

Finn

I was in the shower once and William came toddling in buck naked. Aoife rushed in to grab him because he didn't have a nappy on and wasn't potty trained at that point. We were very British about it and both started spluttering our apologies, despite the fact that neither of us had done anything wrong. It was just one of those stupid things that happens when you have another person coming in and out of your home all the time. You forget they're there. I cupped my privates and turned my back to her to maintain some modesty, so she would've had a clear view of my bottom and the birthmark. I told Mel at the time and we both laughed about it.

Nell

So this girl rushes into the bathroom to grab William and rushes out again, and in those brief few seconds she was able to see through a steamy shower cubicle and notice Finn's birthmark? That's super-human powers of observation.

I wouldn't go as far as to say that Mel believed every word of the story. She knew what the tabloids were like in exaggerating, but one of the reasons Mel didn't ask Aoife to stay in the first place was because she didn't like how Finn acted around her. Whether it was true or not, William wasn't even two and Sebastian was three. They were both so young and Mel didn't want to rip their lives apart because of a stupid girl. She loved Finn and she chose to put it behind them and work on the marriage for the sake of her kids. She really did try to keep her family together.

Lola

It was total rubbish. Anyone with half a brain could see that. Mel didn't believe it for a second. You only have to look at Aoife's desperate attempts to become famous to see what her motives were.

Jessie

She got a bloody boob job straight after selling her story and took her kit off for one of the men's mags. Any credibility she had was gone after that.

Lola

I think the worst thing about that whole story was the stuff the nanny said about Mel.

Jessie

Worse than saying she was shagging Finn?

Lola

I know, I know, it was all awful, but I always felt like everyone knew Aoife was lying about that, while the stuff she said about Mel being hysterical really stuck. The media really latched on to that. Every week they were poking at it, questioning Mel's choices and mental state.

Jessie

God, yes. If she stayed in her house, they'd say she was agoraphobic. If she was out at a restaurant, then she was drowning her sorrows.

Nell

The whole thing knocked Melanie at a time when she was getting her life back after the postnatal depression. I took her out as much as she'd let me and tried to give her a safe space to vent and have a laugh, which she did, but it was still hard. She told me once that she felt like she was holding her marriage together with sticky tape.

The boys were her absolute priority though. I don't think the tabloids ever got wind of this, but she used to take them sightseeing at the weekends a lot of the time. She'd wear a big hat and glasses and she'd sneak out the back of the house and spend all day with them, going on the London Eye or just riding the top of the bus around the city.

Finn

When I look back at the last few years of our marriage, it seems clear to me that Mel never properly recovered from her postnatal depression. She became very insecure and worried constantly. There were days when she would stand in front of her wardrobe and cry because she didn't know what she should wear. I'd take her by the hand and we'd talk about her day and then I'd help her choose something.

There was other stuff too. Mood swings. Clingy one minute and snapping at me the next. There was one winter – 2017, I think – when she wanted a light on in every room all night. She hated the dark. I know it was related to that place Sir Peter sent her to, but I guess my patience was wearing thin.

Look, Mel was a fantastic mother. Even with all the stuff going on, she never let things slip with the boys. I was forever walking into the house and finding she'd converted the living room into a makeshift fort with them.

[Laughs]

But for me, it was exhausting being this constant rock of support. I think . . . well, it was a relief to chat to Aoife sometimes. I guess we did get close. We shared the same sense of humour. We didn't have an affair, but there was a night when Aoife kissed me. It was a stupid mistake on both our parts and it never happened again. She apologized the next day and we got over it. I didn't tell Mel at the time because she was already struggling with so much.

On top of everything else, when Melanie went back to work a year after William was born, she became obsessed with what people were saying about her. She'd come home from work, she'd read to the boys and put them to bed, then she'd pour herself a glass of wine and scroll through every comment written about her online. And I don't just mean the tabloids. I mean everything. She'd spend hours on Twitter crying because some nobody from Newcastle said her hair looked crap or she was looking old. Mel took everything to heart. The scrutiny destroyed her, and in the end it destroyed us.

Twitter
5 May 2019

Amy B @GirlAboutTownBlog
Who spotted the photo of Melanie Lange stuffing her face with a Pret baguette? No wonder Finn strayed #JustSaying #MelanieLange

> **Leslie Riley-Moor @FashionistaFan_Blogger**
> She dresses like she's still 21! Those clothes do nothing for her.

> **Laura V @LauraLostHerPhone**
> Their marriage is a sham anyway! They'll be cashing in on a divorce story next!

> **Tammy S @TammySunflowers**
> Finn is such a hot dad. You can tell he really cares about those boys. Melanie always looks so miserable when she's photographed with them.

> **Laura V @LauraLostHerPhone**
> I bet the kids aren't even hers. They probably faked the whole thing for publicity and got a surrogate.

> **Natty H @NataliaLH**
> I bet she doesn't even remember their names, LOLs.

SIR PETER LANGE –
MY SIDE OF THE STORY (UNPUBLISHED)

Interviews between ghost writer Ryan Morris
and Peter Lange, 8 October 2022

Ryan: Melanie and Finn's marriage officially ended in early January 2021. Were you surprised at the announcement?

Peter: Not particularly. I don't think there was a single person in the country surprised when Mellie broke the news. The only surprise was that they carried on for so long after the affair story broke.

Ryan: How was Melanie at the time?

Peter: She put a brave face on it, but Mellie's divorce was hard. It was hard on her. It was hard on the business.

Ryan: Sales were affected?

Peter: Yes, unfortunately. Lange Cosmetics saw a profit drop the year Mellie and Finn divorced. It was a reminder of how important Mellie was to the business. There were meetings, of course. Zara and several of the directors felt strongly that Mellie should take a step back as the face of Lange Cosmetics. They thought a small rebrand and new models would help. There were a few questions over Mellie's ability to run the business, but that's not unusual. When you're at the top, there's always someone looking to push you off. Even more so when it's a woman at the top.

Ryan: What was your view on what the business should do?

Peter: I was torn. As a father, I could tell Mellie was in a dark place. I was worried about her. There was a morning not long after her divorce announcement when I found her sitting in my office. I asked her how long she'd been waiting for me and she made a comment about how she hadn't realized it was morning already. Then she walked off. I've no idea what she was doing in my office or how long she'd been there for, but it was worrying behaviour. I could see Mellie's fragility creeping back in. I didn't know how to help her. I think it was around that time that I purchased a house on the coast with a thought that it could be a place for Mellie if she ever needed space. It was a back-up plan, I suppose, a way to feel like I was helping. But that feeling, that helplessness as a father, is terrifying.

It was that part of me that wanted Mellie to take a step, not back, but to the side. For her own health, I thought she needed a break. Mellie was adamant she was absolutely fine, and it was her decision. She, more than anyone, knew she was the face of Lange Cosmetics and Baby Lange, and she stood by her products. She said, 'People might try something because of me, but they'll stick with it because it's a good product.'

With my business hat on, I was keen to cushion how any fallout would impact Lange Hotels. We did a successful advertising campaign around romantic spa breaks using slightly older models and wording that suggested it wasn't their first love. We also focused on girls-only weekends, which were very popular. We live in a country where divorce is very common, and that's before the added pressures that were on Mellie and to a lesser extent, Finn. So I thought the sales dip was most likely a blip, and that things would pick up with the right advertising and when everything calmed down.

Ryan: Except things didn't calm down.

Peter: No, they didn't.

Netflix Original Documentary:
Melanie Lange – The Ugly Truth

INTERVIEWS RECORDED 19–22 SEPTEMBER 2022
(220 DAYS SINCE MELANIE'S DISAPPEARANCE)

Narrator

The rumours of Melanie's marriage troubles continued into 2019 and 2020, but it wasn't until January 2021, after months of media speculation, that Melanie Lange and Finn Parker officially separated, with Melanie announcing the news via her YouTube channel.

VIDEO FOOTAGE. SOURCE:
YOUTUBE, MELANIE LANGE CHANNEL

Date posted: 7 January 2021

VIDEO TITLE: SAD NEWS FROM ME!

Hi everyone. God, this is a hard video to do. A part of me didn't want to come on here and record this, but you guys have been on my motherhood journey with me now for so many years, and I've found so much support here. I know you'll help me through this next thing.

OK. Deep breath. Here goes. I'm very sad to say that Finn and I are separating. It's been a long time coming. There have been stories in the press about the state of my marriage from day one, so I know I don't need to tell you not to believe a word they say. I don't!

I'm not here to badmouth Finn or rake over the details of our separation. I'm trying very hard now to look forward and find a harmony and happiness that the boys will thrive in.

As you can see from the change in the background, I'm in my new place. It's really close to the house, which Finn is keeping, and the park the boys love, and Sebastian's school. I've got this cute little room here and all the toys they like.

Finn and I might not love each other in the same way any more, but we both want to do what's best for Sebastian and William. I really hope this is it.

Parenting is so much harder than I ever thought it would be, and we've just gone and made it a hundred times harder. I . . . I haven't adapted yet to the fact that there will be nights, whole days and weekends when I don't see my precious boys, when I don't kiss them goodnight and read them their favourite story five times before sleep. I can't get used to how cold it feels waking up without a little person snuggled beside me.

Does it get easier? A part of me hopes so, but another part of me doesn't.

Finn

All married couples argue. We were never the type to let things fester. We'd get it all out and then we'd get over it. That was our way. It was when we stopped arguing that we were in trouble. We stopped trying. We limped on in our marriage for the sake of the boys, but there came a point when the atmosphere at home was just too much. There was no laughter. No joy. I felt very sad about that. So did Mel.

Nell

What broke Mel and their marriage was Finn and his gaslighting. He completely denied and took no responsibility for an affair which obviously happened, and then made out Mel was paranoid for not believing him. He poked and poked at every little thing about her, making her second-guess what she should wear every day, and worst of all whether she was a good mother or not.

He was such a waste of space. He didn't even have a job as far as I could tell.

In their final months, Finn decided to really cut down the hours of Laura, their nanny, and look after the boys himself. Then out of nowhere he tells Mel he wants a divorce, and as the main caregiver he should stay in the house with the boys.

Mel didn't want to move out, but she was trying to do what was best for the boys, and so she moved into an apartment down the road while she looked for a house for her and the kids.

Finn

We sat down at the kitchen table one night in November 2020 and we both agreed it was the end. It was sad, but I think we were also relieved in a way.

We wanted the boys to have one more family Christmas, but we began making plans to separate. Mel found a really nice apartment about fifteen minutes away. She got bunk beds for the boys, which they loved, and kitted the place out with all their favourite stuff. One Sunday morning in January 2021, we went out for a walk and Mel showed the boys the apartment. Sebastian was five at that point and William was three. Sebastian asked if this was going to be our new home. Hands down, talking to the boys that day, it was the hardest thing I've ever had to do in my life. I got a lump in my throat so Mel did most of the talking. I knew it was just as hard for her, but she wanted to show the boys we were fine. She says, 'You boys are going to have two homes now. This one is your home with me, and the house is your home with Daddy.' She reassured them that we loved them, that it wasn't their fault. They both took it in their stride. There were nights later on when the reality sank in for them, when Sebastian cried. William started wetting the bed too. I hated it. I hated how much it affected them.

Nell

At first, it looked like Finn and Mel were going to have a really good relationship. They shared custody. Mel had the boys for four days one week and three the next. Mel increased Laura's hours again. Laura would look after the boys in whatever house they were in.

Jessie

The divorce was horrible. Melanie was in pieces.

Lola

And it didn't help that Nell was constantly telling Mel that she was better off without Finn. I mean, maybe she was, but Nell didn't need to keep reminding her.

Jessie

We don't know that she did.

Lola

That's what Mel said though, wasn't it?

Jessie

I guess, but I think Nell was just trying to boost Melanie's confidence in her usual bullish way. She doesn't always stop to think. Melanie found the days she didn't have the boys really hard. She asked us out for dinner one Friday night and it was like old times.

Lola

I feel sick even thinking about the hangover from that night.

Jessie

We went to Skylon for dinner and cocktails, and I thought that would be it. Then Mel suggests heading to one of the old bars to go dancing. We were so drunk. We thought it would be a laugh.

Lola

But everyone was so much younger than us.

Jessie

You still got chatted up though, didn't you?

Lola

We all did. These young boys were throwing themselves at Mel.

Jessie

It was a brilliant night. It reminded me that I was still fun.

Lola

What are you talking about? Of course you're fun.

Jessie

When I'm in bed most nights by nine thirty with a herbal tea, it's easy to forget. After our night out, we had the usual texts the next day. All those 'Oh God, did we do such and such' messages flying back and forth. Sharing all the photos we took. But then Melanie suggested doing it again the following week, and I just thought, 'I'm too old.' A one-off every now and again is great, you know? But not every week.

Lola

Mel was just so lost without the boys. She was ugly-crying by the end of the night. We suggested lunch and shopping instead but she didn't reply for ages.

Nell

Of course Mel found it tough not seeing the boys every day. But she also relished the freedom it gave her being out of Finn's shadow. We'd go dancing once a week, or get a takeaway at her apartment and crank the music up and dance, just the two of us. She said to me once, 'Towards the end, when I was with Finn, I stopped dancing. I don't know why that is.'

I did. Because he sucked all the joy out of her life.

The tabloids lapped up Mel's single status. It was all, MEL'S WILD NIGHTS, and WHO'S MEL DATING NOW? Finn hated it.

But when she had the boys, she was just focused on them. She took a lot of time off to take them to school and be there to pick them up. I remember she did this treasure hunt for them on the way home once. They had all these clues to follow and spent hours charging around the park until the final clue – pizza night.

[Crying]

Sorry. I can hold it together pretty well, but talking about what a great mum Mel is, it's so hard. I keep thinking about what Sebastian and William have missed out on this year and how much it's killing Mel not to be with them.

Finn

I really didn't care what Mel did in her free time. It was only when it affected the boys that I had a problem.

SIR PETER LANGE –
MY SIDE OF THE STORY (UNPUBLISHED)

*Interviews between ghost writer Ryan Morris
and Peter Lange, 8 October 2022*

Peter: They say things get worse before they get better. In Mellie's case, things got worse and then worse again. The media ripped Mellie apart on a daily basis. Sales continued to dip. I became very concerned about Mellie and the businesses. She was very erratic. Some days she'd be in the office at 5 a.m., other days she would forget to show up to meetings. I began to spend more time on the Lange Cosmetics floor, taking on some of Mellie's workload. There was a feeling among the staff that Mellie was a ticking time bomb.

Ryan: This was last year, in the summer of 2021?

Peter: Yes.

Ryan: And then it came out in a magazine interview that you'd hired Finn to date Melanie. Did Melanie approach you after the interview?

Peter: Of course. Finn didn't give Mellie any warning, so she found out with the rest of the world that I'd had a hand in her relationship with Finn. Mellie is someone who has a lot of empathy for others and their situations and because of that she rarely gets angry, but when she burst into the house on that Tuesday morning, she was furious.

The first thing she asks is: 'Did you pay Finn to date me?'
Which I deny.

So then she asks, 'Did you interview Finn to be my potential boyfriend?'

I tell her that part is true, and then I make us coffee and I explain everything the same way I did to you. She was still mad when she left, but I think it was more at Finn's story and being blindsided by it than the actual events.

Netflix Original Documentary:
Melanie Lange – The Ugly Truth

INTERVIEWS RECORDED 19–22 SEPTEMBER 2022
(220 DAYS SINCE MELANIE'S DISAPPEARANCE)

Nell

Just as Melanie is getting her life back on track and finding some peace in being on her own, Finn decides to do a tell-all interview in *Hello!*

No warning. No 'Just so you know, Mel, I'm going to air all our secrets to the world.'

Not only does he announce to the world that Sir Peter was the matchmaker for their relationship, he also says he never even loved her. Saying all this crap about how he fell in love with the idea of Mel.

That interview nearly destroyed Mel. To spend so much of your life worrying that your family are trying to work against you, and then to find out that they actually are, and they're doing it with the man you thought loved you, was crushing.

After all their years of marriage, after seeing day after day how much the media stories affected Mel, to do that to her was just cruel. The only silver lining to the whole thing was that Finn received a lot of rightful criticism about his own conduct.

Lola

Oh my god, that interview was totally shocking. I swear my jaw hit the floor reading it.

Jessie

But Finn didn't actually say that he took any money from Sir Peter, did he? I know Sir Peter offered it, but he didn't take it.

Lola

No, but he should've told Mel years ago, and he definitely should've told her himself.

Finn

I was in a bad place last year and early this year. I was seeing photos of Mel having all this fun and it hurt. My business had ceased trading, and I let the loneliness and the bitterness get to me. I felt that I'd given up a lot to be married to Mel and she didn't even see that.

Then this freelance journalist approaches me. She says she's got a source that's willing to go on record that mine and Melanie's marriage was all a sham. The journalist knew everything about Sir Peter's fake recruitment day.

I could see how crushing it was going to be for Mel and so I offered her my own story, just to get the truth out there. She agreed and we sold the story to *Hello!* magazine. It was supposed to run in the November issue. I thought I had time to tell Mel myself what happened, but they released the story early and screwed everything up.

I was angry over the end of our marriage. I said things I didn't mean. Of course I loved Mel. I would never have married someone I didn't love. We were good together but I lost sight of all that. I directed that anger in the wrong place. I thought it was Mel I was angry at, but now I think it was the situation. Our relationship never stood a chance, not with the scrutiny we faced on a daily basis.

Nell

Without Mel, Finn had no income. They shared custody so there was no child maintenance coming his way. Finn needed money and he wanted to hurt Mel. That's why he did the interview. And when he wanted more money and to cause more hurt, he filed for full custody of Sebastian and William.

SIR PETER LANGE –
MY SIDE OF THE STORY (UNPUBLISHED)

*Interviews between ghost writer Ryan Morris
and Peter Lange, 8 October 2022*

Ryan: How did Finn's revelation affect your relationship with Melanie?

Peter: Mellie became very closed off after that. It was difficult to get a read on how much of her behaviour was due to a lack of trust she felt between us, and how much was to do with her struggles with her mental health, which went downhill very quickly towards the end of 2021 and the start of 2022.

Ryan: Which is when the property you mentioned previously became more than just a back-up plan?
   [Silence]
   Sir Peter? Are you OK?

Peter: Yes. Sorry. What was the question?

Ryan: I asked about the property you mentioned and when it became more than just a back-up plan?

Peter: It was around that time.

Netflix Original Documentary:
Melanie Lange – The Ugly Truth

INTERVIEWS RECORDED 19–22 SEPTEMBER 2022
(220 DAYS SINCE MELANIE'S DISAPPEARANCE)

Narrator

In February 2022, a year after the breakdown of her marriage and just twenty-four hours before Melanie Lange disappeared, Finn Parker won an emergency order granting him full custody of their two children: Sebastian, who was six at the time, and William, who was five. A supervised visitation order was also granted. Under this court ruling, Melanie was only allowed to see her children during supervised hours in the presence of a social worker.

Finn

It was an awful time. It all got so toxic. Mel had her lawyers whispering in her ear, I had mine doing the same. We lost track of what was important, and that was the boys. I might not love Mel any more, and there have been times when I haven't liked her, but she's always been a really good mother and I forgot that for a while.

For a year after our separation we shared joint custody, and that system worked for both of us. I had them three days one week and four the next. But then Mel started dropping them back later than the agreed times. She was clearly upset about not being with them, but it messed up their bedtimes and it wasn't fair on them. I got frustrated and it was at a time when we weren't communicating at all. Mel was still angry with me about the *Hello!* interview, which, looking back, I can understand.

There was one particular time when I dropped the boys to her apartment and she was clearly hungover and reeking of wine. I'm not saying I was perfect all of the time, but I saw signs of trouble ahead. We started bickering about stupid things. She had a real go at me once when Sebastian turned up wearing a T-shirt with a hole in it. She accused me of neglecting them, which really made me mad. It was his favourite T-shirt. He didn't care it had a hole in it.

Nell

Finn and Mel had this system where Finn would drop the boys to Mel and she'd drop them back. And then he started dropping them off late. There was always some excuse, like a kid's party that Finn had to take them to. I mean, Mel's their mum. She could've taken them. He was messing her around and would get really narky with her if she was five minutes late dropping them back.

Mel was tearing her hair out over it, and so I suggested she talk to her lawyer and get their custody arrangements set in stone so that Mel had the backing of the court if Finn was consistently late.

Vic Watson, tabloid editor

One of our journalists started hanging out in the coffee shop near Melanie's lawyers' office a few times a week. He hears these two secretaries chatting about Melanie's custody battle and whether she's got any chance of winning full custody. Of course we run the story.

Finn

I saw that headline – 'Melanie files for full custody' – and I saw red. I called my lawyers and we filed for full custody that day. That was in January, a month before Mel's birthday weekend and the emergency custody hearing.

Look, I shouldn't have believed the story. I should've talked to Mel, but we were both so angry with each other. I wasn't thinking straight.

Nell

Mel didn't want full custody and she never applied for it. She knew the boys needed their dad just as much as they needed her. Shock horror, the papers got it wrong.

Finn

After that, things got really bad between us. We were only speaking through our lawyers and used Laura to shuttle the kids between us.

I think we had a lot of pent-up anger towards each other from the failure of our marriage. We'd put it aside for a long time and focused on the children, and only when they were settled into the new routine did it surface. That's the only way I can really give some meaning to the anger I felt towards Melanie last year. It doesn't seem logical now. Nothing we did was logical.

Then Melanie's birthday weekend happened. She was due to have the boys. Laura was off sick and so I dropped them to Mel. We managed to be civil and I even asked her if she had any birthday plans. She laughs and says, 'Does watching the Disney *Cars* trilogy count as plans?'

I tell her that if she changes her mind and wants to go out, then I can swap days and have the boys back for a night, but she's adamant she's got no plans.

I go home and cook myself some dinner and watch a couple of films. I'm just going to bed when this news alert pops up on my phone saying Mel's been rushed to A&E because she fell over while drunk at her birthday celebrations. I couldn't believe it. I couldn't understand why she hadn't told me she was going out. I would've helped with the boys.

It's about midnight when I call Mel, and she's clearly drunk and starts trying to tell me that Nell is the one who's hurt and that she, Mel, has just gone in the ambulance to be with Nell. It sounded like total bollocks. I ask about Sebastian and William and she says it's fine, the babysitter is with them. I ask which babysitter and Mel says it's someone from an agency.

A total stranger.

I didn't want Sebastian and William to wake up and wonder where their mum was. I was so angry with Mel for lying to me and for leaving the boys like that. So I drove over to her flat and brought them home with me. I called my lawyer early on the Sunday morning and he filed an emergency injunction for full custody. There was a short hearing. My lawyer really laid it on thick. All the news accounts worked in our favour. He even talked about the time in the supermarket when William was just a baby. I was granted a temporary custody order.

It all happened so fast. I didn't stop to think what it would do to Mel or if it was the right thing.

Nell

Just because it was one of Mel's nights with the boys, it didn't mean she wasn't allowed out of the house. It was her birthday weekend. Laura was going to babysit, but then she was ill, so Mel called the babysitting agency she'd used a few times before and booked a babysitter. She put the kids to bed and made sure they were asleep before she went out.

After a really bad few years, she wanted to go dancing on her birthday.

We're out and we're having a great night. Tequila shots and champagne and dancing. It was the first time in ages that Mel let her hair down, and for the first time in a long time, I saw flashes of the old Mel.

It was nice, you know? Mel had been up and down. The divorce, the childcare, the business, it was enough to push anyone to the brink, but add in the constant pressure from the British media – I mean, she was OK, she wasn't off the rails and she certainly wasn't having a breakdown, but she wasn't quite herself either.

It's about eleven when Mel starts to worry about the boys, so we head off. But of course the photographers are outside the club and they surround us the second we're out the door. This bouncer steps in to help and starts shoving the guys away. One of them falls right into us and we go down like dominoes. Mel was fine but I smashed my head on the pavement and it knocked me clean out.

The next thing I know, I'm waking up in the back of an ambulance with Mel holding my hand.

About 2 a.m. I get admitted for monitoring and I tell Mel to go home to the boys. She looks at me a bit funny and says she doesn't need to because Finn picked them up from the babysitter. I can tell she's upset but she doesn't want to worry me.

She stays by my side until the next morning when I'm discharged. We're in a taxi on the way back to my house when she turns her phone on and straight away it starts ringing. She answers it and it's her lawyer telling her about an emergency custody hearing taking place about custody for the boys. We get the taxi to turn around, but by the time we get to the court it's all over.

Neither of us could believe it. Finn's lawyer made out Mel had left the boys with a total stranger. It was a babysitting agency, for God's sake. Who the hell did Finn leave the kids with while he was in court?

Mel's lawyer starts talking about an appeal and how the judge was clearly influenced by the tabloid stories about Mel. She's really reassuring and thinks it will be reversed within weeks, but it crushed Mel all the same.

I offered to go home with her, but she told me to get some rest.

[Pause]

I should never have left her.

[Crying]

Narrator

The emergency custody order was granted at 11.21 a.m. on the thirteenth of February. At 3 p.m. the same day, a distressed Melanie attempted to visit her children, causing an altercation with the police.

Rebecca Gainsborough, Finn Parker's neighbour

It was me that called the police, but it wasn't on Mrs Parker – I mean Melanie Lange – like those papers said. It was on the reporters. They were on my driveway, leaning over the fence to get a shot of Melanie at the front door of Mr Parker's house. They trampled all over my daffodils and ignored me when I told them they were trespassing on private property. It was awful when the police showed up.

I had no idea at the time what was going on. Melanie was banging on the front door. I couldn't understand why Mr Parker didn't let her in.

Melanie was very upset. She kept shouting, 'You can't do this to me!' And then she was begging him. Saying, 'Please, Finn. I can't live without them.'

The police arrive and get the photographers off my property and make them stand across the road from the house. Then they go over and talk to Melanie. They take her over to the police car and she sits down in the back seat with the door open, and one of them gives her some tissues and a bottle of water. She calms down quickly and she leaves.

She wasn't arrested. I called every single one of the newspapers that reported it wrong, but no one listened to me.

Narrator

A statement from the Metropolitan Police read: 'On Sunday the thirteenth of February, officers were called to Mr Parker's address following reports of a disturbance. No arrests were made.'

Vic Watson, tabloid editor

The first headline we ran with was 'MELANIE ARREST?' The question mark is there for a reason. We had the story of Finn Parker winning an emergency custody order and then we had the photos of Melanie banging on Finn's door and crying in the back of a police car. So in the end we ran with 'MELANIE LANGE: MOTHER OR MONSTER?'

When the video of Melanie announcing her mental health breakdown appeared on her YouTube channel on Monday afternoon, we were already well into the story.

Nobody was surprised when Melanie Lange did a runner. Celebrities do it all the time. They go off to find themselves and pop up a month later with a new haircut and a seven-figure book deal.

SIR PETER LANGE –
MY SIDE OF THE STORY (UNPUBLISHED)

*Interviews between ghost writer Ryan Morris
and Peter Lange, 8 October 2022*

Ryan: You've mentioned Melanie's declining mental health a few times in relation to the time period after her divorce. Were you concerned she might try to harm herself again?

Peter: Every day. Every night. Every second. That was what I worried about.

Ryan: Did you try to talk to her about your concerns?

Peter: Yes. But Mellie didn't trust me. She closed up when I tried to talk to her. Even so, a week before her birthday, Mellie and I had a meeting together that ended at lunchtime and I suggested we get a bite to eat. There's a little Italian around the corner from the office that I used to take both girls to when they'd come with me to the office during school holidays and the take your daughter to work days. It felt quite nostalgic going back together. Mellie even ordered her old favourite, spaghetti carbonara. We shared a bottle of wine and I asked her outright how she was doing. She visibly slumped in her chair and told me every day was a struggle.

She must have seen the worry in my face because then she added, 'I'm OK, Dad.'

I said, 'And if you ever feel not OK?'

She replied, 'You'll be the first person I call.' And I was. When Mellie got herself in trouble on her birthday weekend, it was me she called.

Ryan: This was the fourteenth of February, Melanie's birthday? What happened?

Peter: She called me in the early hours of the morning. My phone rang and I knew straight away it was Mellie. It might have been fifteen years since those nights I used to wait for my phone to ring, but it all came rushing back.

It feels like a repeat of her nineteenth birthday. I'm throwing clothes on and rushing out of the door before she's even said anything. At first all I can hear is her crying. Then she tells me she's sorry. She's messed up and she's had enough of the world. She says without her boys she's nothing and she might as well be the screw-up the whole world thinks she is. And then she hangs up.

Ryan: So what did you do?

Peter: I did what any father would do. I protected her, and what Mellie needed protecting from most was the world. I drove over to her apartment, and on the way I made a phone call to the staff I'd hired for the house. I told them I was on my way.

Ryan: This was the house you purchased in 2021 when you were worried about Mellie's mental health?

Peter: Yes. It's a beautiful property. Very private. I'd had it refurbished and staffed. I made sure it had everything Mellie needed.

Ryan: Are you OK, Sir Peter? Would you like to take a break? Are you feeling all right?

Peter: I'm fine.

Ryan: So, this house you'd bought and staffed, had refurbished just in case Mellie needed it. That's quite an expense. Did Mellie know about it prior to her birthday weekend?

Peter: No. No one knew. I . . . I know it sounds odd, but I wanted somewhere ready for her.

Ryan: I'm sorry to keep going over it, but I want to make sure I completely understand. You bought a secluded beachfront property and converted it into what? A mental health facility for Mellie? Staffed and ready twenty-four-seven on the off-chance she'd need it?

Peter: Yes. It wasn't an off-chance. I saw how she was spiralling. I knew she'd need it at some point. I wanted to be ready.

Ryan: Why not just check her in to an established facility?

Peter: I couldn't. You must see that. After the last time – Beaumont Court. Nell collecting her so easily just when Mellie was making progress.

Ryan: But the place was abusing patients. You told me that yourself. You said you were heartbroken by how they had treated Mellie.

Peter: I was. I am. They took it too far, but their fundamental principles were spot on. The structure, the routine. It worked for Mellie back then. She was getting better before Nell took her away.

Ryan: So this house you bought is like Beaumont Court?

Peter: No, not at all. It's different. It's . . . it's just for Mellie. For Mellie's own safety and wellbeing, there are things I can't talk about, but I want to do everything I can to explain. I want people to understand the situation I've been forced into. The choices I've had to make. It hasn't . . . It's not been easy. I know I'm seen as the villain by those Save Melanie campaigners, but they don't know. They don't have the first clue what I've been through to protect Mellie. I couldn't let what happened to my sister happen to Mellie. That's all that matters in all of this – keeping Mellie safe.

Netflix Original Documentary:
Melanie Lange – The Ugly Truth

INTERVIEWS RECORDED 19–22 SEPTEMBER 2022
(220 DAYS SINCE MELANIE'S DISAPPEARANCE)

Nell

What Finn did that weekend is unforgivable. She wanted to see her boys. She's their mother. It was her weekend with them, and he took them away and got a ridiculous court order. Mel just wanted to give them a hug and tell them she'd see them soon.

Finn

I should have let Melanie into the house that day. It's easy to look back and say that now, but I messed up big time. I was still so angry with Mel for leaving the kids, and my lawyer at the time was telling me not to give her an inch because her lawyers would use it to prove I thought she was a fit mother. So when she came to the front door and started banging and screaming, I packed the boys up and took them to my brother's for the night. We went out the back door. We weren't even there when the police came, but I'm glad about that. I wouldn't have wanted the boys to see it. My mum called me that night and gave me a stern talking-to. She said, 'Finn, you're my son and I love you, but Melanie is a good woman and a good mother, and I'm disappointed in you for losing sight of that and what's best for your boys.' I don't think there are many mums out there who would give it to their sons so straight, but I was glad she did. I lay awake all night thinking. I knew my mum was right. Melanie is an amazing mum. The boys . . .

[Pause]

Sorry. The boys need her.

The next day – Melanie's birthday – I fired my lawyer and I texted Mel to tell her I was sorry and I'd undo it, and she could see the boys anytime.

That message was never read.

SIR PETER LANGE –
MY SIDE OF THE STORY (UNPUBLISHED)

Interviews between ghost writer Ryan Morris
and Peter Lange, 8 October 2022

Ryan: What happened when you arrived at Melanie's apartment?

Peter: The door was unlocked, thank God. I rushed in and found Mellie unconscious on the bed. She was still breathing, just out of it. I gave her a shake but she wouldn't wake up. I scooped her into my arms and carried her to my car, just like when she was a little girl and would fall asleep in our bed. I carried her to my car and I drove her to the house.

Ryan: What do you want to say to Save Melanie campaigners?

Peter: I want to tell them that I love my daughter. I wish I could love her back to health, but I can't. She has to do that for herself.

Ryan: Did you watch the new Netflix documentary, *Melanie Lange – The Ugly Truth*?

Peter: No. I didn't want to watch that . . . that fiction.

Ryan: Is the house where Melanie is staying a registered mental health clinic? What safety protocols are in place to make sure she is being treated properly?

Peter: Mellie is safe. She is physically well. You can see that quite clearly in those ridiculous videos of hers.

Ryan: Are you holding Melanie against her will?

Peter: [Shouting] Haven't you been listening to anything I've said? I'm trying to protect my business.

Ryan: Your business?

Peter: [Heavy breathing] My daughter. I meant to say my daughter. I'm trying to protect Mellie.

Ryan: You said—

Peter: These interviews are over. Stop recording.

RECORDING STOPPED

From: Zara.Lange@LangeHotels.com
To: Peter.Lange@LangeHotels.com
Date: 9 October 2022
Subject: Call me!

Dad,

I'm getting really worried!! You're not answering your phone. When are you home? Why won't you tell me what's going on?

Have you been to see Melanie today? How is she? Is she getting better?

Please call me!!!!

Z x

Twitter
9 October 2022

Matty Venus @Filmjunkie2000
Can anyone part of the #SaveMelanie campaign give us an update please?

> **Jessie W @Jessiebakescakes4U**
> Why? What have I missed?

> **Matty Venus @Filmjunkie2000**
> I heard on a FB group the police have reopened the investigation!

> **Meg Hillis @MegHillis88**
> Hopefully they'll arrest Finn Parker! I didn't trust him for a second watching #TheUglyTruth.

> **Amy B @GirlAboutTownBlog**
> Guys!!! Things ARE happening right now! I'll do my best to post news as soon as I can!!

Connie Rose @Wannabeawritergirl
Just seen the news!!!!!! OMG! #SaveMelanie

> **Jessie W @Jessiebakescakes4U**
> What's happened???????????

Melanie Lange video 9/9
Published on Melanie Lange YouTube channel on 6 August 2022

I'm Melanie Lange. I'm a prisoner. I haven't left this property for five months. Today Dr Sam asked me how I would live my life differently if I were allowed to leave. If. That's the word she used. Not 'when' but 'if'. What kind of psychiatrist or counsellor or whatever she's supposed to be says 'if' to a patient? Surely the goal is to see me leave this place.

I've spent a lot of time thinking about why my father is doing this, and I think . . . I think in some warped part of his mind, he's telling himself that by doing this, by keeping me locked up, he's protecting me. I'm sure that's what he's telling everyone. But this is about my businesses and how much he stands to lose if I take them away from him. Zara – you know this makes sense. You have to speak to him! Please!

I know I was a mess in February. I was having a difficult time after my divorce. Losing custody of Sebastian and William in the way that I did, it hit me really hard. I'm still coming to terms with that. The media were splashing my problems across their front pages like it was entertainment.

[Crying]

Those stories were impacting me, obviously, but I was not suicidal. I was not a danger to myself or to anyone else. I was just a woman having a hard time, and now I'm locked away and I . . . I don't think I'll ever be free.

[Door opening]

Shit.

Oh God.

Go away. GET OUT. NO. You can't take it. You—

PART III

Seaview Clinic staff report

Date: 15 February 2022
Staff member initials: SS

Patient distressed.
Temporary sedative administered.
To be reassessed weekly.

Journal
Page 1

March (I think)
I'm trapped here!!
    No one will tell me anything. I don't how long I've been here.
Everything feels foggy.
    WTF!!

Dr Sam gave me a stack of notebooks today. 'Write down your
thoughts and your progress. Bring the notebook to our daily chats.'
    They are not chats. They are not voluntary.
    I don't trust her. I'm scared.
    What will they do to me?
    Why am I here?

Seaview Clinic staff report

Date: 7 March 2022
Staff member initials: SS

Patient showing compliance to treatment.
Sedative dose reduced.
Writing therapy commenced.

Journal

Pages 2–3

Locked doors. Guards watching me all the time. What is this place?

How long have I been here? Weeks???? Can't keep track of days.

I'm going to write in one of the notebooks for Dr Sam (BITCH!). I'll fill it with the kind of bullshit psychobabble crap she goes in for.

But this notebook is for me. I need to keep track. Keep sane.

I'm going to keep it hidden under my mattress when I'm not writing in it. I'll have to be careful when I swap them round so the guards don't see. Especially the woman with the frizzy grey hair. She watches me so closely. Why?

Dr Sam asked me how I was feeling today. I filled a page of her notebook with some crap about feeling clear-headed and tranquil. I wanted to scream at her, 'How do you think I'm feeling?'

I want to leave.
I want to leave.
I want to leave.

I miss my boys.
I miss my boys.
I miss my boys.
I miss my boys.

I miss my boys.
I miss my boys!!!!!!!

Netflix Original Documentary:
Melanie Lange – The Ugly Truth

INTERVIEWS RECORDED 19–22 SEPTEMBER 2022
(220 DAYS SINCE MELANIE'S DISAPPEARANCE)

Narrator

On Sunday the thirteenth of February 2022, on the eve of her thirty-fourth birthday, Melanie left the doorstep of her ex-husband Finn Parker's house and walked home. These are the last known movements of Melanie Lange.

Nell

I spoke to Mel about 6 p.m. on that Sunday night. She was very upset. Very tearful and also angry with herself. She hadn't been able to see the boys and she knew that by going to the house she'd potentially made the situation worse. Certainly she knew the photos taken that day would look pretty damning.

We chat for about an hour, and I tell her things will look better in the morning and, whatever she does, she shouldn't read the stories. She says she's going to have a glass of wine and a bath and go to bed. And then she says, 'Tomorrow I'm going to wake up and I'm going to start a war. There is no way Finn is taking my boys away from me. No way!'

That is the Melanie I know and love. That is the Melanie I expected to see sitting in her office when I walked into work on that Monday morning.

Finn

I was pretty surprised that Mel didn't read my text message or call me on that Monday. I thought maybe she'd broken her phone in a moment of anger or was keeping a low profile after the 'mother or monster' breakdown stories.

I take the boys to school and head back to the house before phoning Mel's office. It's Nell that answers. She says, 'Mel isn't in yet,' which we both think is odd, but Nell makes a point of adding that Mel is probably having a meeting with her lawyer, which I thought was a pretty fair thing to say.

Seaview Clinic staff report

Date: 15 March 2022
Staff member initials: SS

Patient exhibiting mild agitation during therapy.
Meeting with patient's father. Treatment to continue.

Journal

Pages 4–5

March (I think)

Things Dr Sam refuses to talk about with me:

1. Who is paying her
2. Anything related to the conditions I am living in
3. When I'll be able to leave
4. WHY SHE IS THE ONLY ONE WHO TALKS TO ME
5. Where I am
6. The date
7. The fact that I have been here weeks and I'm not allowed to leave or make a FUCKING phone call!!

What kind of name is Dr Sam? It sounds like a chat show host. How is this not breaching a million ethical rules?

Is she even a doctor?

She comes to see me every day, Monday to Saturday. The door from the kitchen unlocks and she appears. Always at 9.30 a.m. sharp. Always wearing a hideous pastel suit. Always lipstick smudged on her teeth.

I've started listening out for a car or the bang of a door in the morning. Nothing! This part of the house is so quiet. I think it's been soundproofed. I never hear a car pulling up or delivery vans. WHERE AM I?

Does she live here? Are there other patients? The house is big enough. When I'm in the garden I can see a second floor, lots of rooms. But if Dr Sam lives here, then what does she do for the twenty-three hours in the day she's not talking to me?

Journal

Page 6

Dr Sam mentioned sedatives this morning. 'Do you think you'd benefit from a short course to calm you down?'

It was a threat.

I don't want to feel foggy and lose days again. I have to be careful, but I'm so angry today. Furious. Red rage kind of angry. Angry at myself for being duped into this. Angry at everyone here. Why will no one but Dr Sam talk to me? Why are there round-the-clock guards?

I'm angry at Finn too for taking my boys and starting all this. Maybe I'm being unfair blaming Finn, but I can't help it. What he did that weekend, I can't forgive him.

But mostly I'm angry at Dad. He's why I'm here. Why I'm trapped. He alone has done this to me.

It's all about money. Lange Cosmetics.

He saw what was happening in my personal life and he used it as an excuse to get me here! I'm so angry.

Scared too.

Petrified!!!!!! How long will he keep me here?

Netflix Original Documentary:
Melanie Lange – The Ugly Truth

INTERVIEWS RECORDED 19–22 SEPTEMBER 2022
(220 DAYS SINCE MELANIE'S DISAPPEARANCE)

Narrator

Melanie Lange has not been seen publicly since Sunday the thirteenth of February 2022. Despite numerous attempts to contact Melanie, her mobile phone has remained off, her apartment empty.

Nell

I spend most of that Monday calling Melanie. Every time it clicks on to voicemail I get more worried. I call her lawyer, Lucy Winn, but she hasn't heard from her either. It's 3 p.m. and I'm about to head over to Mel's apartment when Zara appears on the Lange Cosmetics floor. She's dressed in a new grey Prada suit and her hair's been done differently. The fact she's even on the Lange Cosmetics floor is almost as weird as the fact she's wearing Prada, because Mel hasn't let Zara anywhere near her business since Zara went behind her back and tried to get Lange Cosmetics in the high-street stores.

Zara walks up to me and hands me an empty box. She tells me I'm on leave until further notice. Just like that. In front of everyone. She tells me to clear out my desk and to expect a call from HR later.

I refuse, of course. Zara has no authority in Lange Cosmetics. I say, 'The only person who can fire me is Mel.' Zara makes this big show of how I'm not being fired and that Mel knows all about it. Then two security guards appear at Zara's side and I just about manage to grab my bag before I'm frogmarched out.

Later that day I get a pretty shit redundancy package from HR, and all I can think about is where the hell is Mel? The minute I'm outside the building, Sir Peter calls me. Another first. He doesn't say anything about me being fired. He says, 'Nell, I'm sorry to tell you this, but Melanie isn't very well. She's in hospital having treatment for a breakdown.'

I ask which hospital, but he says he can't tell me because they don't want the press to find out where she is. Then he says, 'Look at Mel's YouTube channel,' and hangs up. That was the last time I spoke to Sir Peter.

Finn
Zara calls me on the evening of Mel's birthday and tells me that Mel is in hospital following a breakdown. I ask her if I should bring the boys to see her and she says not yet. She'll call me again soon. I felt terrible when I heard that. Really, the worst I've ever felt in my life.

Lola
I saw the video Mel posted saying she's taking some time away to work on her mental health. My friend sent me the link and I sent it to Jessie.

Jessie
We weren't surprised.

Lola
Not at all. Just sad.

Jessie
I called Finn to see if he knew where Melanie was so I could send her a care package, but he didn't know. He was really cut up about it and blaming himself.

Lola
Good.

Jessie

I'm not saying he isn't in part to blame for her breakdown, but I think it's more the straw that broke the camel's back.

Lola

Yeah, I think you're right.

Jessie

I told him about the voice message Mel left me the week before and he asked to hear it. After that, he wasn't as upset.

Seaview Clinic staff report

Date: 29 March 2022
Staff member initials: SS

Update call with patient's father. Visit discussed.
Patient responding well to writing therapy.
No further changes to medication at this time.

Journal
Pages 7–8

March/April???
I WANT TO LEAVE.

The silence is a form of torture! What did I do to deserve this?

I miss my boys. I miss Nell. I miss people. I miss being hugged and being seen and talking and laughing.

Dr Sam wasn't happy with me today. She asked me how I was finding my journal and what I was writing about. I said, 'Mostly you.' She gave me her displeased smile, her you-can-do-better smile.

Dr Sam has a lot of smiles. She'd be a terrible poker player. A terrible businesswoman! There's her what-do-you-think smile where her thin left eyebrow hooks up like the top of a question mark. Her isn't-it-a-wonderful-day-to-be-alive smile. That one is fucking annoying. I like to reply with my I'm-still-a-prisoner look and the smile dies a slow death on her lips. The worst smile is her I'm-not-going-to-answer-that smile where her lips purse like a Jack Russell's arsehole, and she narrows her eyes and waits a beat before beginning again like my question never existed.

Every day the same.

Dr Sam likes to start every session with the same question. 'Why do you think you're here, Melanie?'

I'm here because I'm a prisoner. I'm here because this is where my father has locked me away from the world.

Wrong answer.

I hate her, but on Sundays when she doesn't come to visit me, the silence half kills me. If only the guards would talk to me and tell me what's going on.

It's Groundhog Day!

Same visit from Dr Sam.

Same bland food.
Same FUCKING silence.
What are they going to do to me?
How long will they keep me here?
HELP!

Netflix Original Documentary:
Melanie Lange – The Ugly Truth

INTERVIEWS RECORDED 19–22 SEPTEMBER 2022
(220 DAYS SINCE MELANIE'S DISAPPEARANCE)

Narrator

Melanie's disappearance has fuelled intense speculation among her fans and the media. While some believe Melanie is being held against her will by her father, there are many who see Melanie's videos as an elaborate hoax or the act of a mentally ill woman.

Nell

What do I say to people who think this is all a hoax? I say, why? Why would anyone do that? Mel doesn't need the money. She has never been an attention-seeker and she certainly isn't doing this for fame. Lange Cosmetics and Baby Lange are crushing the market. She has two sons who she loves more than life itself. What motive does Mel have for keeping herself hidden and pretending to be a prisoner? To deny herself seeing her children for all these months? None. There is no reason in the world Mel would do that.

But let's look at the other side of this and think about Sir Peter for a minute. Does he have the means to do this? Absolutely. He's one of the richest and most powerful businessmen in the country. He can do whatever he likes. I don't think it's an oversight that the police haven't bothered to investigate Melanie's disappearance properly, even with video evidence of her telling the world she's being imprisoned by her father.

Sir Peter has the means and he also has form for doing this exact thing. It isn't the first time he's locked Melanie away. He was the one who sent her to Beaumont Court. That's a fact.

As for a motive – it's business to him. It's public knowledge that Lange Hotels is haemorrhaging money. Just look at the accounts. If it wasn't for Melanie's business, Lange Hotels would have ceased trading years ago. Melanie has 51 per cent control of Lange Cosmetics. She makes the decisions. Sir Peter doesn't like that.

I have to be careful what I say here because I've signed a confidentiality agreement with Lange Cosmetics, but saving Mel is my number one priority and I can't see what difference it makes now.

About a year ago, Mel hired a consultancy firm to do a business check on Lange Cosmetics. Like an MOT kind of thing. Business was going great, but Mel is super savvy and she always gets outside opinions and advice. She always wants to be at the top of her game and she wanted to make sure the creative teams weren't just agreeing with her because she was the boss.

I think we were both expecting the consultancy firm to suggest freshening up the design team, that kind of thing, but they did a thorough check and looked at everything, which is when they found that Lange Hotels had been charging Lange Cosmetics way over the odds on rental space in the building and other stuff. Like quadruple what it should have been. Lange Hotels was effectively stealing from Lange Cosmetics. There were other things too, when Mel started to look. It scared her, I think, to see how deeply Sir Peter had his claws into her business. She wanted to make some drastic changes and started having secret meetings she wouldn't even tell me about. If Sir Peter heard about those meetings, and I strongly suspect he did, it would've given him cause for concern with regards to Lange Hotels' role in the future of Lange Cosmetics. It's also no secret that he and the other directors hated the negative attention Mel got in the press, as if it was her fault. So not only does keeping her locked up mean he has control of her business, but it also ensures that sales aren't affected by the negative stories, because there aren't any stories. Mel has dropped off the face of the earth. He obviously didn't foresee the Save Melanie campaign. I don't have the first clue what's going through Sir Peter's mind right now, but I'd bet anything he's not happy.

That's why Mel is locked away. So she can't take her business from him. He has complete control over Lange Cosmetics and he has complete control over her.

Finn

I know what Nell thinks. She thinks Sir Peter has Mel locked up because of the business. For me that feels a bit far-fetched and playing into the hands of Melanie's conspiracy theory fans on Twitter. Personally, I have no qualms that Sir Peter has Melanie imprisoned somewhere in this country, but I don't think it's because of business or money. I think he's got Mel locked up because in the weird world of his mind, he thinks he's helping her. He's always been an overprotective father. This is a whole new level of crazy overprotective, but it's still what I think.

Seaview Clinic staff report

Date: 3 April 2022
Staff member initials: LV

Patient distressed. Reported to SS.

Journal
Pages 9–10

March/April???

How many Sundays have I been here? Six? Seven? Nearly two months. That feels impossible.

I asked one of the guards what date it is earlier. The nice one I call Augustus. I don't know why I think he's nice. He's the same as the others. He doesn't speak, but there's pity in his eyes when he looks at me. When he didn't answer, I begged him to say something. Tears sprang from nowhere. SILENCE.

In the garden I can see the daffodils being squashed out by an army of tulips. It's not so cold.

I cling to these clues. I constantly search for them, for any sign of time and change, but every time I find something, it feels like I'm being stabbed in the chest over and over. Time is marching on. I am not. Then I think about Sebastian and William. I think about whether Sebastian's favourite book is still *The Hundred-Mile-an-Hour Dog* or if Finn is reading him *Harry Potter*. I wonder if William has managed to get all the way across the monkey bars at the park by himself or if he's still falling two rungs short. I think of all the things I don't know about my children. MY CHILDREN!!! And it eats me up inside.

Netflix Original Documentary:
Melanie Lange – The Ugly Truth

INTERVIEWS RECORDED 19–22 SEPTEMBER 2022
(220 DAYS SINCE MELANIE'S DISAPPEARANCE)

Narrator

On the sixth of August 2022, amid growing pressure from the general public and the media, the Metropolitan Police released the following statement: 'We are aware of the videos online of Melanie Lange and we have opened an investigation into her whereabouts. While the investigation remains open, we are satisfied with our initial findings that Melanie Lange is safe and well.'

Nell

That so-called police investigation was completely bogus. People don't understand the power Sir Peter has. I mean, he even had the Prime Minister mention Melanie's wellbeing during Question Time last week, saying some utter crap about how he personally knows that Melanie is safe and well. Then dodging any other question on how he knows this. The police aren't a bit interested. And they've used the same language as the PM. Safe and well.

Mel is a prisoner and those in power are doing nothing about it. This is not someone who has been placed in the care of a psychiatric hospital or under the care of medical professionals. This is not even about Melanie's mental state. Melanie is not in a hospital. This is not a conspiracy. This is real and it's terrifying.

Lola

I mean, the police say they're satisfied. So maybe there isn't anything going on.

Jessie
Yeah, but it is a bit worrying, isn't it?

Lola
It's the police. They don't really take pay-offs like Nell would have everyone believe. This is real life, not some ITV crime drama.

Seaview Clinic staff report

Date: 7 April 2022
Staff member initials: SS

Patient requested call with father.
Request noted.

Journal

Pages 11–15

Same question from Dr Sam today. 'Why do you think you're here, Melanie?'

I'm here because my father kidnapped me in the middle of the night and this is where I woke up.

Wrong answer again.

What did happen that night?

Dad said I called him, threatening to kill myself. I don't remember but I'm sure he's lying.

I remember being at the hospital with Nell after her fall on our night out. It was my fault. Me those photographers wanted. Nell was collateral damage again.

I didn't sleep, fuelling myself on coffee and chocolate from the vending machine and thinking about Finn's call and his rage. My own fury that he'd gone to collect the boys, but the relief as well that they were with him, that I could stay and take care of Nell.

Then the journey home. It was hot in the back of the taxi. Nell was dozing, her head resting on my shoulder. My phone rang. My lawyer's number.

Lucy didn't even say hello. She said, 'Mel, where are you? I've been calling. You need to get to Southwark Crown Court now. Finn's lawyer has arranged an emergency custody hearing for Sebastian and William.'

My blood ran cold as ice, and Nell woke up and we screamed at the driver, and he turned around and we were on our way. Twenty minutes too late.

Lucy apologized. She'd tried to delay, but the judge was on Finn's side from the start. She told me how he'd cited the tabloid headlines. My drunken night out that ended in chaos. My every little mistake or choice or nothing at all amplified beyond recognition.

Finn knew it was bullshit. It's always bullshit. But he used it anyway.

I sent Nell home with the taxi and went back to the apartment. I hate that place. It reminds me of the one Dad bought me. I was desperate for a house with a garden but nothing felt right. Was I still hoping Finn might change his mind about us? Maybe.

Despite the sickening realization of how our relationship started – that bloody magazine interview he did. Despite my suspicions of his infidelity and how awful the final months of our marriage were – when I couldn't breathe without annoying him – I think I was still clinging to the smallest of hopes that we might find our way back to how it used to be. For the boys and for us too. I'm an idiot.

I should never have gone to the house. But the boys had fallen asleep to the sound of my voice reading to them, and they'd have woken at the house with Finn. They must have been confused and I wanted to give them both a big hug.

The paparazzi were there. I should have turned around but I pushed past them and knocked on the door. It was impossible to ignore the heckles of the photographers. 'Is it true you've lost custody of the boys? Are you having a breakdown, Melanie?' I wanted to scream at them that I didn't know.

I could hear William shouting, 'It's Mummy!' from somewhere in the house. Finn came to the door and without opening it, he told me to leave, like I was one of the photographers – an annoying journalist and not the mother of his children, the woman who'd provided for him for years and never once asked what he did with his time or all the money he spent.

I kept knocking and the paparazzi closed in, and I couldn't walk away even if I'd wanted to. I was an animal in a cage being watched and taunted. The desperation to escape was like a bomb about to go off inside me. I needed to get inside the house, not just for the boys any more. I banged and banged and pleaded, but Finn didn't let me in.

Then the police came and pushed the photographers back. They were so kind. A man and a woman whose names I didn't get. I sat down in the police car for a while and pulled myself together. They knocked at the house to speak to Finn but he didn't answer, and I realized he'd gone out the back gate. We'd done it so many times before.

I pictured him sitting on his brother's sofa with a beer, the boys playing with the wooden train track they keep there. Warm. Safe. And me on the street sitting in a police car. I should've been angry but I didn't have room beyond the tearing sadness at what was happening around me.

How could he take my boys from me? Did he really think I was an unfit mother?

I went home and had a bath and a glass of wine. I chatted to Nell. She gave me one of her pep talks on picking myself up and fighting the good fight, and she was right and that was my plan, but first I wanted to drink and wallow. I took a Xanax. Not a great idea with the wine and the exhaustion. It must have knocked me out because that's all I remember.

The next day I woke up in this prison, my head fuzzy. Dad waiting for me at the table with a laptop. He was so full of concern that when he told me I'd tried to kill myself, when he begged me to take a break, to rest in this house, I looked out of the window and I took in the rustic garden and the grey sea beyond, and it felt easy to agree.

I saw myself alone with a full fridge of my favourite foods. I pictured myself running along the coastline in the early morning before working at the table, managing things remotely, talking to Lucy and arranging a new court date. Just a few days to get my head straight, away from London and the press.

Why didn't I notice that there was no door to my bedroom? Or that I couldn't see the kitchen or an upstairs? Why didn't I try the door to the garden and realize it was locked? Or check the wardrobe and find it already full of clothes for me? Why didn't I run for my life?

Dad suggested the video for my YouTube channel. 'Just so your fans don't worry about you,' he said.

I trusted him to think clearly at a time when I wasn't.

After the video, he gave me two tablets. Paracetamol, he said. It wasn't. When I woke up, I was in bed again and there was a woman outside my room, sitting on a fold-out chair with a book on her lap. Her eyes moving back and forth across the page and then up to me.

My mouth was dry, my head light. I wanted to freak out. A total stranger watching me. But everything was foggy. I think I asked her who she was. What she was doing?

She didn't reply, and before I could scream and yell and rage or try to run, sleep took me again.

Netflix Original Documentary:
Melanie Lange – The Ugly Truth

INTERVIEWS RECORDED 19–22 SEPTEMBER 2022
(220 DAYS SINCE MELANIE'S DISAPPEARANCE)

Lola

I'm not saying we're not worried about Melanie. Of course we're worried. I'm just saying, Nell has blinkers on when it comes to anything to do with Mel. She refuses to even consider things that are right in front of her.

Jessie

Exactly. She's like a mama bear protecting her cub.

Lola

Of course we want to know Melanie is OK and we want to visit her. But we also know that she really wasn't well. The entire world has witnessed Melanie's ups and downs, you know? She's been relentlessly pursued by the paparazzi for two decades. The more interest they show her, the hungrier her fans—

Jessie

And critics.

Lola

You're right. The hungrier her fans and critics are for more. It's a vicious circle and it put huge pressure on Melanie. That level of pressure for that length of time is always going to have an impact.

Jessie

It seemed obvious to us when we saw Melanie for lunch in January that she was not herself.

Lola

Totally. We ordered a bottle of white wine and Melanie drank most of it herself before ordering another one. I didn't have more than a glass because I was driving.

Jessie

I had maybe two glasses at the most.

Lola

It wasn't just the drinking though. She was saying a lot of stuff that wasn't making sense. She seemed paranoid, if I'm honest. She was talking about making some business changes and kept looking over her shoulder like someone was listening in.

Jessie

And a few weeks later, about a week before she disappears, I get this voicemail on my phone.

VOICE MESSAGE AUDIO FROM
MELANIE LANGE TO JESSIE YANG

Date recorded: 5 February 2022

Hey Jessie, I'm sorry I'm calling so late. [Sniffs] I just wanted to talk about . . . about clothes. There was this thing on Twitter. All these people saying I dress like I'm still seventeen. I know I shouldn't listen but . . . look, can you help me? [Crying] I need help. I need to look like . . . Fuck it. I don't know what I need. I need not to be here, that's what I need. I need to be out of my head for a while. This fucking world. I hate it.

   [Crying]

   Sorry. I shouldn't have called.

Lola

I feel so sad every time I hear it. She sounds so low. What the hell was she doing, reading all those Twitter posts and letting it get to her? That's what really worried me. I knew the tabloid stories used to upset her sometimes, but she'd never let some nobody on Twitter upset her before. These people didn't treat her like she was human, like she had feelings. Mel knew that. She knew to ignore it, and the fact that she wasn't sent alarm bells ringing for me.

Jessie

I called and called the next day, but she never picked up. That was the last time we heard from her. So you can see how Melanie posting a video saying she needs a break makes total sense to us.

Nell

I've heard the voicemail, but I don't interpret things the same way as Lola and Jessie. It sounds like Mel's had too many glasses of wine and is thinking of getting a wardrobe revamp. Sometimes the negativity got to her. It was like a scab she kept picking at to make it bleed, but she'd always laugh it off the next day.

Seaview Clinic staff report

Date: 9 April 2022
Staff member initials: SS

Patient requested call with father again.
Patient agitated. Monitoring dosage of sedatives.

Journal

Pages 16–17

April (I think)????

It was warm today. The sun a milky yellow in the sky. I walked down the wooden steps to the cove and sat on the sand.

There's a bookshelf in my room. It's stocked with happy novels. Romantic fiction and a few bonkbusters. Not my usual style. I imagine Zara choosing them with a great amount of satisfaction, thinking how annoyed I'll be with them.

Zara! My sister!

Where is she in all this?

How much does she know about this place?

We've had our issues. That's probably an understatement. She wanted a bigger role in Lange Cosmetics. Maybe I should've given it to her. I've always told myself she doesn't understand our ethos. Too corporate. Or was it pettiness on my part? Payback for something a million years ago.

Would she stand by and let Dad do this to me?

I don't know.

If it was her who chose these books, then she was wrong. I enjoy them. They're the only company I have.

I took a Marian Keyes book down to the beach with a plan to read, but instead I stared at the sea tumbling on to the shore, wondering how far I'd get before the guard caught me or I drowned.

If I stare at the sea for long enough, maybe the nose of a boat will poke around the side of the cliff and I can scream the word that circles my mind in my sleep.

HELP!

Seaview Clinic staff report

Date: 13 April 2022
Staff member initials: SS

Patient uncommunicative in therapy.
Increasing antidepressant dose.

Journal

Pages 18–19

April (still not sure)

I can't stop thinking about everything that went on in the last few years.

Why did I let myself get dragged into the meaninglessness of people's opinions? Those stories, the comments, Twitter – it was a riptide. Every day I chose to stand on the beach and wade right into the middle to get sucked away by it.

I didn't think I had a choice.

Once upon a time I did a better job of ignoring it. I remember there were times when I was seventeen or eighteen and I'd see a story about me or a blog post, and I'd be horrified by the lies and comments, by how exposed those stories made me feel. Sometimes I wondered if they were all true and it was me who was lying to myself.

But there were also days, weeks, months when I wouldn't even look at the papers, the magazines. And there were days when I'd see the comments from the trolls, from everyone who thought they had a right to talk about me like I wasn't a human being, and I would laugh. I would pity them and their pathetic lives where all they had was me to pick on.

When did I start taking it all to heart? Why did I let myself do that? When the boys were born, I guess. Motherhood dented me, I think.

Finn tried to stop my obsession. There were countless evenings when he'd pull my phone from my hand and put it face down on the side before dragging me into the living room to watch some nonsense TV. But I'd slip out of bed when he was asleep and go back.

Finn told me once I was obsessed with knowing every single thing that was said about me. He called me selfish and vain. He called it self-harm and said that if I didn't stop, then he wasn't sure our marriage could survive.

I told him he was overreacting, but he wasn't. He was right. I was obsessed. I was self-harming. It doesn't excuse what he did to me!

When I leave here (IF!!!), I will buy a little house somewhere. High fences and a big garden. Just me and the boys. The irony is that this house is all of those things. If Sebastian and William were here with me now, would this still be a prison?

Will I ever see them again?

Netflix Original Documentary:
Melanie Lange – The Ugly Truth

INTERVIEWS RECORDED 19–22 SEPTEMBER 2022
(220 DAYS SINCE MELANIE'S DISAPPEARANCE)

Nell

So on one hand we're supposed to believe that Mel had a breakdown and is in hospital. She's too ill for visitors. Too ill to see her best friend or even her children. On the other hand she's posted a video on her YouTube channel telling her fans, me, the world, that she's taking some time out. Look at that video of her. Look at her face. She is not a woman too ill to see her children.

Finn

For a while I was pretty angry at Mel for leaving that video. I know I wasn't her favourite person that day, but surely one phone call to tell me that she's going away wouldn't have been hard. Sorry. I know I sound selfish. I'd just stopped Mel from seeing the boys. Who was I to talk about communication? But as I said, I was in a bad place earlier this year. There was a lot of crap I hadn't dealt with properly. I think taking a sidestep away from my own business to take care of the children emasculated me. Such a cliché, right? It made me insecure and mean. So yeah, for a while, like a month after she disappeared, I was just pissed off with her.

It's been hard for me with the boys, day in and day out. I told them Mummy was poorly and needed to stay away until she was better. Sebastian took it in his stride but William kept forgetting, and then he'd ask me when he was going back to the bunk bed flat to see Mummy.

I think it was the end of March when I called Lange and left a message with Sir Peter. He didn't get back to me, but a week later Zara turned up one evening totally out of the blue. That was a weird night.

Seaview Clinic staff report

Date: 14 April 2022
Staff member initials: SS

Meeting with patient's father. Visit agreed. Treatment to continue.

Journal

Pages 20–21

April (I think)

Dad is coming tomorrow. Dr Sam just told me.

He's coming to take me home.

I'm still so angry with him. The rage so red hot I think lasers will shoot out of my eyes and kill him dead. The relief is greater though. This pulsing relief that makes my breath catch in my lungs. Dad is coming. I can go home.

Just knowing I'll be seeing Sebastian and William tomorrow night floods my body with joy. Hugging them. Breathing them in. There will be time for anger and shouting and retribution another day. Right now the boys are all that matter.

Going home day

It's 8 a.m. and I'm bouncing off the walls. Dr Sam said he's coming for lunch, but Dad has this thing he does where he likes to disarm people. It's one of his business tricks. He always tells me and Zara, 'Turn up when you're not expected and you'll see what's really going on.'

So I'm sitting at the table ready and waiting. I've braided my hair and put on a little make-up I found in the bathroom. I look good. I look healthy. I am so mad at him for doing this to me, but even I can see that there has been a benefit to this extreme detoxing. He's forced me to cut out everything, go cold turkey. Alcohol, crappy food, social media, life. I've gained so much perspective. The only thing that matters to me is my children.

I can't stay here another day.

Netflix Original Documentary:
Melanie Lange – The Ugly Truth

Finn

Things between Mel and Zara have always been frosty. It wasn't outright nastiness, but you could feel the temperature drop if they were in the same room together, which was usually at family events or the odd board meeting.

I'd never really thought about why. Plenty of my mates have brothers and sisters they don't speak to. But one night, when Mel and I were two bottles of wine in, I asked her what the problem between them was.

It turns out Mel blamed Zara for ending her modelling career and hated that Zara kept trying to muscle in on Lange Cosmetics.

I never told Mel this, but I always thought she was exaggerating things. I used to think there were two sides to every story, and I was pretty sure Zara hadn't always had it easy living in the shadow of Mel's fame and the drama that came with that. And you'd have to be blind not to see that Sir Peter treated Melanie like a precious doll and Zara like his personal assistant.

Then, at the start of April, six weeks after Melanie vanished, Zara appears on my doorstep one evening, proffering an expensive bottle of red wine like she's done it a hundred times before, which she hadn't. I can count on two hands the number of times Zara had been inside the house.

She says she's come to see Sebastian and William and bring them a present, which is weird because she's never paid them much attention before. It's already gone eight so I tell her they're fast asleep. But she asks if she can come in anyway for a chat.

I open the wine and pour us both a glass, and when I walk into the living room, Zara has taken her jacket off and kicked her heels to the floor.

I ask Zara if she knows how Mel is doing but she just shrugs. So I ask if she knows when she's coming back. Zara says, 'Mel will come back when she's better and when we've cleaned up her mess.'

Then she says, 'Mel did this once before. Went off the rails and stayed in a hospital for a few months when she was nineteen after getting into a fight in a nightclub.'

I say, 'Melanie told me all about that a long time ago, but Mel isn't a teenager any more.'

Zara says, 'Yeah well, you were good for her. When you guys split, I knew it was only a matter of time before she went off the rails again. She's not well, Finn. Dad is looking after her.'

I say, 'But Mel wouldn't leave the boys for this long.'

She says, 'I thought you said she's an unfit mother. That's why you went for full custody, wasn't it?'

Her comment hurt to be honest, but I didn't know how to reply. I couldn't get a read on Zara. She was so jittery. She seemed less sure of herself. Like she was trying to convince herself, not me.

Then she says, 'Mel will come back when she's better and then it will all start again.'

I didn't really know what she meant, but she seemed a bit tipsy by that point. I'm doing lots of yawns and hoping Zara takes the hint, when she slides her hand up my leg and says, 'Ever wonder if you chose the wrong sister?'

Thank God William woke up right at that moment and saved me from answering. I made my excuses about getting William back to sleep and showed Zara out.

I went to bed that night and thought about everything Zara said about Mel going off the rails, and how it just didn't tally with the person I'd been married to.

Zara's visit woke me up; I stopped being angry at Mel. I put aside everything I'd read about her and the things Zara and Sir Peter had told me, and I focused on the Melanie who would sing a thousand verses of 'Cows in the Kitchen' to William when he had colic, because it was the only thing that would soothe him. I thought about the woman who started an entire ethical cosmetics business out of nothing and took the world by storm. And then I called Nell.

Seaview Clinic staff report

Date: 15 April 2022
Staff member initials: SS

Patient agitated.
Increased dosage of sedative given.
To be reviewed weekly.

Journal
Pages 22–23

April

I'm still here.

Dad's visit didn't go well.

I WANT TO LEAVE!!!!!!!

He arrived in the late afternoon. No clocks in the house, but the sun had dipped over the side of the house. By the time he appeared from the door into the kitchen, carrying two plates of club sandwiches and French fries, I was near tears, convinced he wasn't coming.

The food smelled heavenly. Bread and chips! God, it tasted like heaven. Dad looked good. His hair had turned from grey to white but he'd cut it short. It suited him. He had a tan too, and I wondered where he'd been while I was stuck here.

He motioned for me to sit and we ate our lunch like it was any other normal day. He went on and on about how well my brands were doing. I should've asked who was looking after my business. I hoped it was Nell, but I knew the answer was Zara and I didn't want to hear it. I don't care. I don't care. I don't care!!!

When lunch was over, I asked if he'd seen Sebastian and William. He took his time answering and my heart was in my mouth the whole time. He said, 'They're doing really great, Mellie. They're happy.'

I was so relieved to hear it that I didn't think to ask what that even meant. Had he actually seen them? Spoken to them? Was his comment a dig at me? Did I not make them happy? I wish I could undo that last weekend with them. Everything went so wrong.

Then Dad asks how I'm doing.

I say, 'I'm doing really well. Thank you for arranging this. It's taken me some time to appreciate how much it's helped me to be here, but I'm ready to leave now.'

But he says, 'It's doing you so much good, Mellie. I don't think it's time yet.'

I could tell by the steely look in his eye that he meant it. No point arguing with that look.

The tears, all that pent-up anticipation and anger, come pouring out and I can barely get the words out to ask how long he's planning to keep me here.

He says, 'Until you're stronger.'

So then I shout something like, 'You can't keep me here like a prisoner for the rest of my life.'

He says, 'You know it's not like that.'

But the look on his face is telling me that he can do whatever he likes. And that's when I try to grab him. Just like Sebastian used to cling to me when I would take him to nursery. I couldn't let Dad leave without me. But the more I fought, the more upset I got. It was like I was playing right into his plan, like he knew I'd prove his point. One of the guards prised me away and he left without a backwards glance.

I don't think I'm ever going to see him again. I don't think I'll ever be free.

Journal
Page 24

Too tired to write. I'm all alone. I'm trapped here.
Alone

    Alone

        ALONE

            ALONE

                ALONE

                    ALONE

Nell

After being forced to leave Lange Cosmetics by Zara, I gave it two weeks for Mel to get in touch. I thought, 'If I don't hear from her in that time, then I know something is wrong.' It was the hardest two weeks of my life. I had spare keys to her flat so I went round there to take a look. Everything was spotless and smelled like lemon cleaning products. I found her bag. Her purse was still in it. The only things missing were Mel and her phone. Look, I'm not someone who believes in spirits or ghosts or anything and I'm not sure what I'm even trying to say here, but there was a weird feeling in that flat. It gave me the creeps and I left really quick. After that I started calling all the clinics, all the health spas, all the hospital psychiatric units. It was a waste of time. None of them would confirm if she was there, but I thought I might be able to hear it in their voices.

Seaview Clinic staff report

Date: 22 April 2022
Staff member initials: SS

Sedative dose reduced.
Meeting with patient's father. Treatment to continue.

Journal
Pages 25–27

April

Lost track of days again. Can't think straight. Everything feels blurred. Are they drugging me? Antidepressants? Sedatives? Both?

I need to remember to write in Dr Sam's notebooks as well as this one. I can't let them get suspicious. I can't let them find this. It's all I have.

Can't stop thinking about Dad's visit, dissecting every second, thinking of all the things I should have said and didn't. It's really dawning on me – I'm in trouble.

For the two months I've been here, I've been holding on to the hope that in his own very extreme way he's been trying to help me, but I was right before. This is about Lange Cosmetics. It's the only thing that makes sense.

I had a dream last night that I was back in Beaumont Court. That place! I thought it was hell on earth, but looking back I feel almost wistful about the freedoms I was given. A phone call to the outside world. TV time. Talking to the other patients. God knows what we found so funny about that place, but we laughed a lot in our dorm rooms. I guess we had to. It was laugh or cry. I'd give anything to be back there now over this place. Just to be around other people. Trapping me like this, keeping me isolated. If I'm not careful it's going to make me crazy.

I try so hard not to think about Beaumont Court but sometimes it creeps in – that pitch-black darkness of the dorm at night – and I have to sleep with the lights on in every room just to know that if I open my eyes I'll see I'm not there. It was so strict there. Everything done to military-precision timing. Step out of line, turn up late – the punishments were harsh. Restraints in bed were the worst. The bastards! I only let them do that to me once. I just kept telling myself, 'Follow the rules, be good, wait for your chance.'

Nell really saved me then.

I was drowning. The letter she sent telling me she'd be outside waiting for me was a life jacket. All that day I could picture her sitting outside in her car and I knew I had to get out. My heart was racing the whole time but there were no chances. It got later and later and I started to worry that she'd leave. I cried with the fear of Nell driving away without me. One of the girls saw me crying and pushed me into the toilets before the staff could see. Tears were not acceptable behaviour. I told her everything, this girl. So much younger than me but tougher too. I didn't even know her name, but she told me she'd pull the fire alarm, and if we waited until 11 p.m. when the staff were half asleep, then there'd be loads of confusion. She was right. When we were outside, all of us crammed in the garden, she pulled me over to the wall and gave me a bunk-up.

I never said thank you. I always thought she'd reach out to me at some point or I'd see her face in the papers telling the story of how she helped Melanie Lange escape. But she never did.

I still have nightmares, dark vivid dreams of being back on that bed, unable to move, the staff screaming at me inside my head, and I wake in a cold feverish sweat that clings to me all day, no matter how many times I shower.

Nell was half frozen and half asleep when I reached her car. She screamed when she saw me and then she burst into tears, but I didn't cry until we were back at her place and she tucked me up in her bed like I was child.

I stayed there for a few days, paralysed with the knowledge that at any moment the door would burst open and the staff of Beaumont Court in their khaki polo shirts would drag me back. But it was Dad who came. I told him everything about that place, the abuse I saw, the time I was tied to a bed for ten hours, and when they untied me I had to wash the bedding and scrub the mattress because I'd wet myself.

Dad looked horrified and he apologized, of course. He told me he had no idea it was like that. Maybe I shouldn't have believed him. Maybe I shouldn't have forgiven him so easily, but I did. It was the story he told me about his sister, Janet. She hadn't fallen down the stairs like Zara and I had been told. She'd killed herself. That's why he'd reacted the way he had and put me in Beaumont Court. I was still upset, but I understood. He was my dad. He was trying to protect me.

Now I wonder if he knew the truth about that place all along. There was therapy there. Treatments to support me, but it was more about behaviour than mental health. Dad always liked rules and routine. I only have to look around me and see how my day runs like clockwork to know that.

I moved back home after Beaumont Court. Dad and I still argued. He said to me once, 'I will not tolerate you ignoring my wishes.'

I told him to go to hell.

I still remember what he said to me then. I didn't get what he meant at the time, but I do now. He said, 'Mellie, you live in my world. Anytime I like, I can take it away.'

That's what he's done. He's taken the world away from me. I am all alone. I am in a corner of hell.

Netflix Original Documentary:
Melanie Lange – The Ugly Truth

INTERVIEWS RECORDED 19–22 SEPTEMBER 2022
(220 DAYS SINCE MELANIE'S DISAPPEARANCE)

Lola
Nell phoned us in March and asked if we'd heard from Mel.

Jessie
And in April.

Lola
And May.

Nell
I called everyone I could think of. I called Sir Peter daily and Zara
too. They didn't answer. I must've called Finn twenty times before
he finally called me back. He said he was worried about Mel and
what did I think was going on? I told him I thought Sir Peter was
holding Mel somewhere against her will, and Finn said that he was
starting to think that too. We stayed in touch after that. The first
two members of the Save Melanie movement.

Seaview Clinic staff report

Date: 24 April 2022
Staff member initials: TH

Patient requested swimwear. Patient spending long periods of time at
the beach.
Request passed to SS.

Journal

Pages 28–29

Still April/Could be May

I made a stupid mistake when I was nineteen. I let everything get on top of me. I was really hungover, drinking and not thinking straight. I ended up in hospital having my stomach pumped.

If I really tried to kill myself again, then why didn't I go to hospital? Why didn't I have my stomach pumped? Instead I woke up here with a fuzzy head. Wine and Xanax are not a great combination.

I need to see my phone. Did I really call Dad that night? If I was sad or wanted help, I'd have called Nell. Plus, what pills would I have taken? It's not like I had a hundred painkillers kicking about. And I know I didn't leave the apartment to buy them.

Dad's lying!!!! That's what makes sense. I would not have tried to kill myself. I would never voluntarily leave my boys.

Here's what I think happened – Dad was waiting for a chance to bring me here. This house – my PRISON – this wasn't scrambled together in twelve hours. It was here and it was ready. I think he saw the story about me at the house and the police coming. I think he saw it as his chance.

How long had he been waiting to do this? Weeks? Months? Years? FUCK!!!! I feel like I strolled right into whatever plan he had for me – the spider and the fly – and there's no way out.

HELP!

Netflix Original Documentary:
Melanie Lange – The Ugly Truth

INTERVIEWS RECORDED 19–22 SEPTEMBER 2022
(220 DAYS SINCE MELANIE'S DISAPPEARANCE)

Narrator

In early April 2022, six weeks after Melanie's disappearance, her fans began to ask questions on social media. Where is Melanie Lange? Is she OK? Is she still alive? Melanie's fans wanted an update.

Lange Cosmetics, Lange Hotels and Melanie's family remained silent.

Nell

I wasn't the only one fired from Lange Cosmetics after Mel disappeared. Zara got rid of anyone she considered to be loyal to Mel. It wasn't all at once. She was crafty about it. Some were moved away from Lange Cosmetics and into Lange Hotels. Some found themselves head-hunted by rival brands with offers they couldn't turn down. There were a few redundancies but not so many that anyone but me noticed. As far as the business world was concerned, as far as the public knew – the press, Melanie's fans – it was business as usual.

Finn

By early April there were some rumblings on Twitter. Subscribers to Melanie's YouTube channel who wanted to know where Melanie was. There was a lot of speculation. I saw theories about electric shock therapy and psychiatric wards. I saw others saying she was in Barbados with a secret lover. More than a few suggested she'd had cosmetic surgery and it had all gone wrong.

Nell wanted to put her theories out there, but I was worried about backlash, and we still didn't know anything at that point. We didn't have any proof. The last contact with Mel was her posting a video telling the world she was taking some time out. I didn't want to draw attention to our concerns too soon in case we were wrong, and because I thought if we were torn apart in the press then it would make any future claims less credible.

There were times in those early days when, like Nell, I believed Sir Peter was hiding Melanie somewhere, but there were also times when memories would surface of how Mel would act sometimes, the days when she wouldn't leave the house and would spend hours in the bath, and I thought maybe Melanie was somewhere safe, getting help.

I suggested to Nell that she set up a few fake Twitter accounts. It became her full-time job. She made three accounts at first and began building up a following for them. It took about a month before she started using them to speculate about Melanie, and that's when we started using the Save Melanie hashtag.

Nell

Oh, Finn is taking credit for the Twitter idea, is he? What a surprise. Mel has a lot of fans obviously, and of those fans she has a core group who love her. And I mean love. They sell her products like they're magic beans. They follow her on every platform. They talk about her online. Two of them even have their own podcast where they talk about what Melanie is doing and her products, and of course what the tabloids and magazines are saying about her.

I got my Twitter accounts to start the rumour that Melanie was being held against her will by her dad. It didn't take long for her fans to latch on to that. The most popular account I created was @Mummyrulestheroost. That got fifty thousand followers over a couple of months.

By the start of May, we'd seen a few pieces in the tabloids but nothing like the front-page 'WHERE IS MELANIE?' headlines we were expecting. And even though I wanted to make more noise about it, I agreed with Finn that we needed proof. One way or another.

Seaview Clinic staff report

Date: 8 May 2022
Staff member initials: SS

Swimwear request denied.
Closer monitoring of patient during beach visits required.
Meeting held with patient's father. Treatment to continue.

Journal

Pages 30–31

Date??
Augustus (blond, tall)
Josh (monobrow)
Lena (tiny)
Gertrude (shoulders)
Dr Sam (bitch!)
Five people.

In the months that I've been here and with the exception of Dad's visit, these five people are the only people I've seen, and only one of them speaks to me. The others give their demands – get up, get dressed, eat, sleep, walk – but that's not talking, that's not communicating with me.

I don't know the real names of the guards. These are just the names I've given them.

Augustus is my favourite. He looks sad when I talk to him. He looks like he wants to reply. I don't know anything about him except that for six days out of seven he spends five hours watching me. I've made up a story about him. He's married to Lena, the tiny woman who cleans every morning except Sundays. Lena is from the Philippines and they hope to have children soon. They love watching cooking shows together. *MasterChef* is their favourite. Lena hopes to enter one day. She makes the best prawn noodle soup Augustus has ever tasted.

Gertrude and Josh are mother and son. They live together and eat microwave meals. Gertrude wishes her son would move out and get a life, but she belittles him constantly and has destroyed all of his confidence, so he'll never leave. She's a mean woman. I see it in the looks she gives me and the set of her shoulders. She looks like she would've enjoyed working at Beaumont Court. I'm glad she doesn't talk to me.

Augustus, Gertrude and Josh are the watchers, the guards. Lena does the cleaning. I think Gertrude cooks the meals. When Gertrude is on duty, she stands outside the door while I take a shower. I've heard her tell Josh to do the same. They can see the closed door just as easily as Augustus can from where he waits outside my bedroom.

I don't know how, or when, but if I can make it out of here, it will be under Augustus's watch.

Netflix Original Documentary:
Melanie Lange – The Ugly Truth

Nell

Despite Zara's efforts, I still have friends at Lange Cosmetic who tell me things.

I shouldn't have been surprised when I found out that Zara was making changes. Zara is good at keeping things ticking over, but she doesn't have Mel's vision or drive. Zara is focused on the bottom line. She's already dropped the more expensive ingredients from the products. She's thinking about saving costs and increasing revenue and not about what Lange Cosmetics and Baby Lange are all about. It's going to break Mel's heart when she finds out.

Towards the end of May I found out that Lange Cosmetics was gearing up to launch the new perfume Mel and I had been working on. It's called Ocean, and the original plan was to give half the proceeds of every bottle to a charity that removed plastic waste from the oceans. Under Zara's leadership that was cut to 10 per cent.

At first I couldn't believe they were going to launch the perfume without Mel. The first photos of every new product were always with her in them. Then I heard about a photo shoot taking place. Everything was kept really need-to-know, which was odd because normally the spec for the shoot was all we talked about for weeks. That's when I heard that Mel was going to be the model.

I couldn't believe it.

It was the first piece of evidence I had that Mel was fine. If she was so ill that she couldn't make phone calls or see her kids, then she would also have been too ill to pose for photographs, right?

I knew I had to do something. I had to get word to Mel and see if she was all right. I guess there was still this little voice in the back of my mind saying there was no way Sir Peter would imprison Mel. That maybe this was her choice.

But whatever was going on, I had to find out.

I got the name of an assistant who was going on the shoot. She was new at Lange so she didn't know Mel or me, but she'd become good friends with people I was close to. I contacted her on Facebook and explained my concerns. I made it clear that all I wanted was to make sure Mel was all right, and she agreed to give Mel a phone.

Seaview Clinic staff report

Date: 17 May 2022
Staff member initials: LV

Patient went into the sea fully clothed and began to swim away from the shore. It is unclear if this was an attempt to end her life or to flee the clinic.
Recommended restricting beach access to SS.

Journal

Pages 32–34

May???

I went in the sea today. I didn't mean to. Not at first.

I was at the beach reading a book and trying not to think about how the trees are no longer white with blossom but vibrant green, and how warm the sun feels on my face. The days are slipping away from me like sand through my fingers.

Augustus was with me today. He never comes on to the sand. He prefers to stay at the bottom of the steps, leaving me to walk to the far end of the cove and sit on the sand with my back leaning against the rocks. Maybe he's like Finn and hates the sand, or maybe he's trying to give me my space. Either way, he was a silent presence – a cloud in the sky threatening to block the sun.

I'm never alone but I'm so lonely. I'm going to stop talking to Dr Sam. I don't trust that woman. She asks stupid questions, pointless questions, like what do I miss the most in my life right now?

I want to scream at her, MY CHILDREN!!

At first my longing for the boys was so acute, so painful, that it drowned out every other feeling I had. But I miss Nell too – our chats, her amazing pep talks. I miss the office. My lovely workers who push themselves so hard because they believe in my products just as much as I do. I miss the energy of the teams and how even on my most exhausted days, when the boys were little and sleep was like gold, that energy was a hit of caffeine. I even miss London. I miss the traffic, the people, the signs of life.

I was thinking all this as I stared out to sea. It was mid-afternoon and I'd finished my book but I didn't want to go back to the house (PRISON!). I was watching the waves crash and roll, crash and roll to the shore, inching closer and closer to my bare feet. And then in the corner of my vision I see a flash of red, and when I look up there are two red kayaks coming around the edge of the cove, a hundred metres or so out to sea.

People!

Actual people!

I jump up. I wave. I scream too, but the cove is enclosed by cliffs and rocks and the sea breeze steals my voice. I'm too far back, too hidden by the rocks for them to see me. And before I can look back to see if Augustus is moving towards me, before I can stop and think, I'm running into the sea. God, it was cold. Icy cold and choppy. Straight away the current pulls at my legs, but all I can think about is swimming out to those kayaks.

Then they start to turn back. Between the bobbing waves I can see them swinging their paddles in the air and cutting through the water. They were leaving, but I couldn't let that happen.

I swim harder, kicking and kicking, but I'm going backwards not forwards, the tide dragging me back to the shore, and suddenly the rocks are looming over me and I can see a wave towering above me, ready to throw me against the rocks, and for the smallest of moments I wondered if maybe I should just let it.

Augustus caught me then, a strong arm pulling me back to the beach.

He helped me to the house and I stood in the shower until the water scorched my skin.

I wrote in my notebook for Dr Sam that I only wanted to talk to the kayakers, but that's not true. I wanted to escape, and for one moment when that wave shoved me towards the rocks, I didn't care what that escape looked like, just as long as I wasn't back here.

I can still taste the sea water at the back of my throat, but worse than that is the hope. A hope that is now a dead weight in the pit of my stomach.

Will I ever be free?

Netflix Original Documentary:
Melanie Lange – The Ugly Truth

INTERVIEWS RECORDED 19–22 SEPTEMBER 2022
(220 DAYS SINCE MELANIE'S DISAPPEARANCE)

Finn

Nell and I kept in close contact. She told me about the photo shoot. This was the end of May, when neither of us had seen or heard from Melanie for over three months. The boys had stopped asking about when they'd see Mummy again, but I put a photo wall up in each of their bedrooms with lots of pictures of her and them together, and I told them every day that their mummy loved them. It was pretty heart-breaking, to be honest.

But even though I knew something very dodgy was going on, I still couldn't believe that Sir Peter and Zara, and whoever else was or wasn't involved, would be so brazen as to lock Mel up and then cart her out for a photo shoot before putting her back again.

I've been wrong about a lot of things. I was wrong in how I treated Mel at points in our marriage. I was wrong to file for full custody. I was wrong to believe that Mel would disappear of her own free will and not say goodbye to the boys or tell me. And I was wrong about this too. Sir Peter would be exactly that brazen.

Seaview Clinic staff report

Date: 2 June 2022
Staff member initials: SS

Update call with patient's father. Visit scheduled.
Patient beach access restricted indefinitely.

Journal

Pages 34–36

6 June

Dad came to visit. No warning this time, no plates of chips and sandwiches. Just him, appearing in the door from the kitchen in the middle of the afternoon in his usual grey suit and white shirt.

He says, 'Mellie, it's so good to see you. You look so well.' Then he comes over and gives me this big hug like I've just come back from holiday. At first I can't even speak. I'm too stunned. Then it hits me like a punch in my face. This man is the reason I've been trapped in this place for months. I push him away and my heart starts racing, and the rage pushes up and I tell him I want to leave.

I say, 'You can't keep me locked up like this.'

And he agrees with me. He says, 'I know. You have every right to be angry with me, but I hope one day you'll look back at this time and this place and realize how much good it's done you. You'll see everything I've done is to keep you healthy, safe and above all, to keep you alive.'

I say, 'I'm not going to kill myself, Dad. I never was and you know it.'

He says, 'I don't want to go over everything that's happened. I don't want to destroy all of the good it's done you being here. You're so strong now, Mellie. I want you to have your life back.'

All the anger goes then and I collapse on to the sofa, and I cry and cry because I think he's letting me go and that I'll be free at last. I'll be able to hold my boys again. I should've known it wouldn't be that simple.

He says, 'We're launching Ocean next month and we would love you to do a photo shoot with the bottle. The same kind of thing you always do. What do you say?'

I nod. Anything to get out of here.

Then he says, 'Think of it as a test.'

I can feel the colour draining from my face as his words sink in. I ask him what he means and he explains that a very small crew are going to come to the house and set up on the beach. I'll be given clothes and there will be someone to do my make-up. I'll need to do

294

my hair myself because no one will be allowed in the house. He says, 'It'll take half a day, tops.'

I ask, 'And then you'll let me go?'

He says, 'If you can prove you're strong enough to cope with the photo shoot and behave in a way I think is appropriate, then yes, you will leave shortly afterwards.'

I sit there for a while, thinking. The rage returns, burning in my face. I want to say no. I want to scream at him that I'll do nothing he asks of me until I'm free. But I remember that he has all the cards and I have none.

When I don't say anything, he says, 'Mellie, if you don't feel strong enough to do the photo shoot, I completely understand. We have plenty of photos of you modelling other products. We can use one of them and superimpose the perfume.'

Straight away I see what he's saying. He's telling me I'm not really needed.

A threat.

I say, 'I'll do it.'

He smiles at that and gets up to leave. He says, 'They'll come next week. Tuesday.'

And I have to ask him what the date is. And he tells me before he unlocks the kitchen door and walks out. I sit on the sofa and listen to the click of the lock.

7 June

There is so much to process. Dad has said I can leave. I just need to get through this photo shoot.

Do I trust him?

Do I have a choice?

13 June

Tomorrow – photo shoot day – I'll have been here for exactly four months. Tomorrow I'm going home. The excitement is humming through me. I have to believe I'll be leaving.

Netflix Original Documentary:
Melanie Lange – The Ugly Truth
INTERVIEWS RECORDED 19–22 SEPTEMBER 2022
(220 DAYS SINCE MELANIE'S DISAPPEARANCE)

Nell

I spoke to the photo shoot assistant the night she got back. She told me she'd given Mel the phone and so it became a waiting game for me. I ask her how Mel is; she says she looks OK, but a bit skittish. Then I ask, 'Where did you go?' and she tells me that they all went in this minibus northeast out of London and drove to Bury St Edmunds. They pull over for a break and then the driver hands out these blindfolds. Can you believe that? She reckons they were on the road for another hour at least after that. All of them sat with these blindfolds on.

I stayed up all night waiting for a message to appear, and when it didn't arrive I seriously started to wonder if I had it all wrong.

Seaview Clinic staff report

Date: 14 June 2022
Staff member initials: SS

Staff requested to remain in main part of house. Therapy postponed for
visit.
Patient refused breakfast. Modify medication for evening meal.

Journal
Page 37

14 June
Photo shoot day! I'm panicking. I can't bear the thought of still being here another day, another minute. What if this is my only chance to tell someone what's really going on?

I'm going to write a note with the truth on it. I'll keep it tucked in my bra and I'll only use it if I have to.

Seaview Clinic staff report

Date: 14 June 2022
Staff member initials: SS

Patient agitated.
Recommend increased dose of sedative tonight.

Journal

Pages 38–39

15 June

It was a trick!! FUCK! I should never have trusted Dad!!!!

I'M SO ANGRY!!!!

The shoot was fine. I was nervous. I couldn't eat anything that morning.

Dad appears first and tells me he's proud of me. I play along. I even manage a thank you for helping me. BASTARD!!!!

He gives me the outfit to wear. It's beautiful. A white linen dress that will look perfect on the beach. I'm surprised how much I cared. Then the crew arrive at lunchtime and set up on the beach. I have my make-up done on the lawn and then I'm down on the sand.

Dad was right. It was a small crew but it felt unnerving having them all there on my beach. I've spent so much time alone.

But I got through it. I play my part, and then they all start to pack away and Dad is looking like he's leaving too. I go to him and whisper in his ear, 'Am I leaving now too?'

He gives a shake of his head. 'Soon,' is all he says, before kissing my cheek.

The panic whips through me and I think, I'm not leaving. They are leaving. My only contact with the world and they are leaving and I am not. It was the kayaks all over again. I pull out the note, and when I go to say thank you to the photographer I drop it inside his case. He watches me do it and then nods and closes the lid, and I feel this wave of dizzying relief wash over me. He'll give the note to someone. I'll be saved. I'll be free.

Then this girl appears and she's pushing this phone and charger into my hand and telling me Nell is worried about me. I almost cry at those words. I hide the phone in my pocket and that's when I see the photographer handing my note to Dad. He hadn't even read it.

Dad doesn't even look surprised or upset. That's when I knew he was never going to let me go. It was all a trick to get his photos. But now at least I have a phone hidden behind the toilet pipe in the bathroom.

Then the drugs kicked in and that wiped me out.

I've woken up groggy, but the urge to dial 999 and scream down the phone still burns through me. I stop myself though. My father has friends in high places and he's already shown that he's one step ahead of me. I can't make another stupid mistake.

Netflix Original Documentary:
Melanie Lange – The Ugly Truth

INTERVIEWS RECORDED 19–22 SEPTEMBER 2022
(220 DAYS SINCE MELANIE'S DISAPPEARANCE)

Nell

My phones beeps at seven the next morning. It's Mel. Getting that first text was like . . . I can't even describe it. It still gives me goosebumps. I've still got it here. It says: 'OMG Nell, thank you for the phone!!! Dad has got me hidden somewhere and I'm a prisoner! There are guards watching me all the time. I'm hiding in the bathroom with the shower on.'

Finn

Nell was at my door before the boys were even dressed for school, showing me this string of text messages between her and Mel. It knocked me for six, to be honest. After that I sent a few texts as well, reassured her the boys were fine and missing her, and apologizing for what I did.

Nell

Mel and I text back and forth for about five minutes that morning before she says she'd better go. I wanted to go straight to Sir Peter's house and have it out with him, but Mel told me not to. She said, 'If he can do this to his own daughter, what do you think he'll do to you?' We talked about going to the police, but Mel thought Sir Peter was too well connected, and with Mel's recent history in the press, it seemed unlikely anyone would take it seriously.

Finn

Nell and I realized pretty quick that however great it was to be in contact with Mel, there was very little we could do. If we showed the texts to anyone then Sir Peter would know about the phone, and that put Mel at risk of repercussions. She was going through hell already and we were very aware that we didn't want to make it worse. It was agonizing but we had to wait.

Nell

Mel was working on trying to find a way out from her end, and I suggested doing the videos as sort of a back-up. She'd done one for the boys already which I can't . . . I'm sorry. I still get emotional thinking about it. Phone calls were too risky because Mel needed to make sure the voices weren't overheard. It was better with her making videos and whispering, and even that she could only do every few days. Mel was reluctant. She was worried about the media storm, but even she saw that it might be her only hope.

Finn

The videos were a genius idea from Nell. Going to the press with just our claims and some text messages was never going to carry much weight. But having Mel talking into the camera, that was going to get people's attention. I really hoped we wouldn't have to use them.

Seaview Clinic staff report

Date: 15 June 2022
Staff member initials: SS

Sedative dose reduced.

Journal

Pages 40–42

16 June

I have a lifeline! A phone! There's no wifi access or 4G, but there is one bar of signal and it's enough to send texts.

I've been texting with Nell. Every time I get the phone from its hiding place my heart beats so fast it makes my head spin. I try to count how many minutes it's been so I know when I need to stop and actually get in the shower I'm pretending to have.

I wish I could call her (and the boys too!!!!), but it's too risky with the noise.

Even Finn has sent a few messages. I don't know how I feel about him right now. Not angry. Not even sad. I'm just relieved the boys are with him and that they're OK. I did a video for them. It was hard not to cry. I told them how much I missed them and loved them and thought about them always. I wanted to tell them I'd see them soon, but I didn't. I couldn't make that promise. It took ages to send. The signal kept dropping out.

Nell wants to go to the police. I could cry with relief that she believes me. That she and Finn are on my side. Others too. A whole group of fans. They're keeping me trending on Twitter with a hashtag. I don't want to tell Nell it's useless, but it is. If Dad was going to let me go, he would have done it by now. And there's no way he's going to bow to any amount of pressure from the police or my fans to let me go. He's got my video I did on YouTube in February. He's got photos from the shoot – tangible evidence that I'm alive and well. BASTARD!

We have to wait. We have to be careful. I have to find a way out of here.

17 June

I'm doing videos of what's happening to me. It was Nell's idea. A way to tell the world what's really going on. It's only as a back-up. I hate the idea of the tabloids seeing them. The stories they'll twist about me. More lies. But I might have to accept that it's my only way out. I have to be careful. The battery runs out fast on the phone and charging it is such a risk. I only do it when Augustus is watching me. I pretend to drop my pen and have this sneezing fit while I plug it in on the other side of the bed, hiding it under the mattress as best I can, all the while certain that one of them is going to walk around the room and see it.

29 June

Today Dr Sam asked, 'What are you hoping for, Melanie?'

I told her, 'I hope to die so I can escape this place.' It's not true but it got a reaction out of her. It was a stupid thing to say. I need to play along or I'll be drugged up to my eyeballs constantly.

3 July

Augustus is with me again today. I'm going to walk the grounds. There's a wooded area off to the left of the cliff. I've never been past the trees before. I don't even know where the edge of the property line is. All I can see is thick shrubs, impenetrable bushes. But maybe there's something.

INTERVIEWS RECORDED 19–22 SEPTEMBER 2022
(220 DAYS SINCE MELANIE'S DISAPPEARANCE)

Nell

When I received the first video, I burst into tears. It was a mix of emotions. I was so happy to see Mel's face and hear her voice, but then as she started speaking I couldn't believe what she was saying. It's still hard to process. Doing nothing was the hardest thing. The videos were back-up. Melanie was clear on that and I had to respect her wishes. I didn't want to do anything that could make life any harder for her.

Finn

Getting the phone to Mel, learning the truth, it made Nell and me feel hopeful. We thought we were nearly there. Realizing that nothing had actually changed was hard. Seeing the videos for the first time was even harder.

A part of me felt so certain that the second those videos were posted on Mel's YouTube channel for her fans to see, the second they were released to the media, Mel would be free. Mel knew differently.

Seaview Clinic staff report

Date: 3 July 2022
Staff member initials: SS

Patient ran into woodland and tried to climb a gate.
Garden access restricted.
Meeting held with patient's father. Treatment to continue.

Journal
Page 43

3 July

I almost escaped. I found a path through the trees and a gap in the hedges. I found the fences that border the property. They were too high to climb easily, but then I found a gate. It was locked but it was less than two metres high. I couldn't see over the top but I thought I could climb it. Augustus was two steps behind me and I just went for it. I threw myself at the fence. It was stupid. I should've planned it better, but Augustus was already getting agitated by the walk. I knew he'd report what we did. It was my only chance.

I got halfway up when Augustus's hands stopped me and pulled me down. He radioed it in and Josh was there in seconds. They took me back to the house together and locked the doors.

Netflix Original Documentary:
Melanie Lange – The Ugly Truth

INTERVIEWS RECORDED 19–22 SEPTEMBER 2022
(220 DAYS SINCE MELANIE'S DISAPPEARANCE)

Nell

You have to remember that this isn't the first time Sir Peter has imprisoned Melanie. That first spell in rehab when she was nineteen was exactly the same. He decided she needed to go away. He booked her in and she disappeared. The only difference now is that he realized he needed to create his own prison for her instead of relying on someone else's.

Mel understood Sir Peter's power more than anyone. She knew he wouldn't give up the moment the truth was out. And she was right. Just look at where we are. I posted those videos over a month ago and Mel is no closer to being free now than she was before.

[Crying]

Seaview Clinic staff report

Date: 29 July 2022
Staff member initials: LV

Patient found with mobile phone in bathroom. Phone removed. Patient
agitated.
Recommend increasing sedative dose.

Journal
Page 44

29 July

The phone is gone!

Augustus was outside my bedroom so I thought it was safe, but then Gertrude burst in as I was recording. I tried to fight her off and send it, but she snatched it away. I don't know if it sent!

I'm alone again. I hadn't realized how much having the phone and the contact with Nell and Finn, even doing the videos, made me feel connected to them, and now it's gone and I have nothing. I have no one.

The desire to smash and scream is with me again today. I can't stop crying.

That's it now.

I told Nell I would check in every third day. If she doesn't hear from me, she's going to post the videos I made on my YouTube channel.

I have been here nearly six months. I've seen Dad three times. I don't know if he's in the next room or a hundred miles away. I'm going to scream his name until they dose me up. I don't want to feel any more.

Netflix Original Documentary:
Melanie Lange – The Ugly Truth

INTERVIEWS RECORDED 19–22 SEPTEMBER 2022
(220 DAYS SINCE MELANIE'S DISAPPEARANCE)

Narrator

On the second of August this year, one hundred and sixty-nine days after Melanie disappeared, Nell Stevens posted Melanie's first video on her YouTube channel. Within hours it was national news and the Save Melanie campaign had exploded across social media.

Nell

Mel and I had an agreement that she would check in every three days. There was a staff member there who gave her more freedom and she would only use the phone if it was him on duty, so we didn't message every day.

The waiting nearly killed me. I wanted to be constantly in contact, but I had to let her contact me. That was the plan.

But by the second of August I knew I had to post the video. I mean, you saw that last one. It seemed pretty clear they'd discovered her phone. We – Finn and I – decided that the best way to do it was for me to record an opening and then post Mel's first video.

VIDEO FOOTAGE. SOURCE:
YOUTUBE, MELANIE LANGE CHANNEL

Date posted: 2 August 2022

I'm Nell Stevens. I'm Melanie's close friend and personal assistant. For the past six months I have been increasingly worried about Melanie's whereabouts. After posting her own video on this channel on the fourteenth of February, Melanie disappeared. This wasn't typical behaviour for Melanie and I knew she would never ever leave her sons the way that she did. On the fifteenth of June, after four months of no contact with Melanie, I discovered that she was being held against her will by her father, Sir Peter Lange. With secret contact, Melanie has been able to record videos detailing her imprisonment. I will be posting one or two of Melanie's videos each day.

Melanie wanted to find a way to free herself that didn't involve the media. These videos were her safety net should all else fail. She asked me to keep them safe and only publish them on her YouTube channel if contact between us stopped. And it has. I'm deeply concerned for her safety.

Finn

Nell told me she was doing an introduction video. I thought it was a good idea. She asked if I wanted to sit beside her and say something, which I did, but I didn't want the story to be about me and our marriage and the kids. I didn't want to dilute what needed to be said, which I knew Nell would do.

It was my idea to release the videos over several days. I thought it would help keep the media coverage of her imprisonment going for longer.

Nell

The papers went wild. My phone didn't stop ringing. There were TV requests too. I really thought . . . [crying] I thought it was happening, that Melanie would be set free. I heard Sir Peter was releasing a statement, and I called up Finn and we both thought we'd done it. I thought with all the evidence of the videos there was no way he could continue to pretend that Melanie was in a hospital somewhere recovering from a breakdown, but that's exactly what he did.

Seaview Clinic staff report

Date: 5 August 2022
Staff member initials: SS

Patient responding well to sedation.
Sedative dose reduced.

Journal

Pages 45–50

???

The days have gone.

Too fuzzy to write anything in this notebook or the one for Dr Sam.

What's the point? I'm going to die here.

August

Feeling better today. My head aches though. Right at the top like my brain is pushing into my skull. I'm trying to drink more water without anyone noticing. Sick of the drugs.

August

I thought Dad would come after the phone was taken but he didn't. No one has come. There has been no great rescue either. I wish I knew what was going on. Nell must have posted the videos by now. I always wondered what good they'd do. I did them for Nell mostly. It gave her hope. It gave us both hope, I think.

August

Something has changed. I can't believe I've only just noticed. The bloody drugs!

Dr Sam has stopped visiting. I only realized yesterday and thought it must be Sunday. Although I couldn't remember her visiting the day before either. I can't be sure but I think it's been four days since I saw her.

Gertrude is in charge now. There's a new glint in her eye, and she comes in to talk to the others sometimes. Last night she shouted at Augustus for staying outside the bathroom while I brushed my teeth. She opened the bathroom door and stood over me while I used the toilet.

I need to be extra careful with this notebook. I can't let them take this too. It's all I have. All that's keeping me sane. I've started pushing it further under the mattress when I'm not writing in it, and only swapping it with the other one when I'm sure it's safe.

August
I feel so sad today. So empty! SO ALONE! I don't know the date any more. I was thinking about how it's been weeks since I lost the phone and then I realized – Sebastian's seventh birthday!!!! It's the fifteenth of August. It could be today, tomorrow. It could have been yesterday. I don't know what party he wanted or what presents.

I've been shut up for so many months, but to miss his birthday, to miss six months of his life – there aren't the words to describe how much it hurts. I'm too sad to write any more.

August
I WANT TO BE FREE!!!

August
I wish I knew what was going on. Every morning I wake up and I feel hopeful. I picture an army of people marching towards me, ready to save me. I live for that hope, but the hours pass and nothing happens. The hope dies.

August
I've been thinking about Nell today. How she is always having to save me. I knew she wouldn't give up on me. She's the only person in my life right now who is on my side. We've been friends for so long that I think I've taken her for granted. I worry that I've ruined her life. It was because of me that she had to stop modelling. Her face was too famous, too connected to mine and all my shit. She should've hated me for that. Instead she gets a job and starts again until I beg her to help me with Lange Cosmetics. She's spent her

entire adult life by my side. I've shackled her to me and dragged her into all my shit so many times.

I feel bad for that.

She should have her own life.

Netflix Original Documentary:
Melanie Lange – The Ugly Truth

INTERVIEWS RECORDED 19–22 SEPTEMBER 2022
(220 DAYS SINCE MELANIE'S DISAPPEARANCE)

Narrator

Melanie Lange has still not been seen in public since the thirteenth of February this year. Despite growing pressure from the public, Melanie's father, Sir Peter Lange, has refused to comment any further on Melanie's wellbeing or whereabouts. As this documentary premieres on the seventh of October 2022, Melanie has not been freed.

Nell

What do I want to happen now? I want everyone who is sat watching this right now to get on social media, to call their MP, to come to one of the Save Melanie movement's regular marches. Every single person can make a difference. This is one of the biggest scandals this country has ever seen and no one with any authority is doing anything.

Finn

I really don't know what's going to happen. I hope this documentary will change something. What that is, I don't know. I don't think Sir Peter is going to change his mind. If he was going to bow to pressure to release Mel, he'd have done it by now.

Seaview Clinic staff report

Date: 18 August 2022
Staff member initials: TK

Patient attempted to escape through kitchen door while dinner was
being served.
Recommend restraints for twenty-four hours and during mealtimes.
Recommend increasing sedative dosage.
Meeting held with patient's father. Treatment to continue.

Journal

Page 51

???

I can't stay here any more.

No one is coming!

If I'm getting out of here, it's going to be up to me and me alone.

The doors and windows are locked. I can't escape through the gardens or from the beach. But every day, three times a day, the guard unlocks the door into the kitchen, disappears for less than a minute and returns with a plate of food.

I'm going to try and get past them. I have to hope that the rest of the house isn't locked. Why would it be? I'm the only prisoner. That much I'm certain of.

Seaview Clinic staff report

Date: 1 October 2022
Staff member initials: LV

Sedative dose reduced.

Journal

Pages 52–54

???

They've put me in restraints. Padded cuffs around my ankles with leather straps and a piece of leather connecting them. I can hobble but that's it. They're taken off once a day for a shower. Augustus takes them off at night if he's on duty. At least they've left my hands free so I can write this. It would tip me over the edge to have restraints on my wrists like that time at Beaumont Court. Bastards!!

All is lost. Nell said she'd do whatever it took to get me free and I know she would've done. We'd do anything for each other. But whatever she's done, it hasn't worked. Dad will have squashed whatever she tried.

There's no way I'll get away now.

???

How many days have passed? Weeks? All I do is sleep or lie on my bed and stare at the ceiling. FUCKING drugs!!

???

Too tired to write much today. The weather has turned. I sat on the sofa today and watched the wind batter the trees. It left a spray of leaves on the lawn. I can't bring myself to wonder what the day is or the month.

???

No one is coming

???

HELP

Seaview Clinic staff report

Date: 4 October 2022
Staff member initials: LV

Meeting held with patient's father. Treatment to continue.

Journal
Page 55

???

I have an idea! I thought I had no control here, but then I realized there is one thing – my food intake! I can stop eating. I can go on a hunger strike until Dad comes to see me.

I won't eat a thing. Not one thing.

Seaview Clinic staff report

Date: 5 October 2022
Staff member initials: LV

Patient refused to eat breakfast. Monitoring.
Call with patient's father.

Journal
Page 56

Hunger strike day 1

I've not eaten anything today. I'm shaking and sweating a little. Whatever drugs they're giving me, my body wants more. It makes me more determined not to eat. I don't even care how hungry I feel. It's nothing compared to the torture of being away from my boys all this time. Nothing compared to what they've put me through.

I keep waiting for them to come into my room and force-feed me. I won't swallow though. There's nothing more they can do to me.

Seaview Clinic staff report

Date: 6 October 2022
Staff member initials: LV

Patient has refused to eat any meals today.
Monitoring.

Journal

Page 57

Hunger strike day 2

Feel clear-headed for the first time in months.

Augustus pleaded with me to eat today. It's the first time he's properly spoken to me in all these months. He spoke fast, almost a whisper. I was so surprised to hear his voice that I burst into tears.

But I didn't eat.

As far as I can figure, there are three ways this is going to go:

1. They'll do nothing and I'll die.
2. They'll call an ambulance and I'll be free of here.
3. They'll call Dad and he'll visit and I'll kill him and I'll be free. I'll do it. I will! I have to!

Seaview Clinic staff report

Date: 7 October 2022
Staff member initials: TH

Patient has declared hunger strike until visit from father.
Patient has not eaten for two days.
Recommend monitoring.

Journal

Page 58

Hunger strike day 3
Too hungry to write much.
  I WILL NOT EAT!!

Seaview Clinic staff report

Date: 8 October 2022
Staff member initials: LV

Patient still refusing to eat.
Contacted father. Visit planned.

Journal

Pages 59–60

Hunger strike day 4

It's worked. Dad is coming to see me for lunch tomorrow. Augustus just told me.

I'm thinking about the ways I can kill him. I'll be given a knife with lunch. It won't be sharp, but if I stab it hard into his throat I think I can kill him.

I can't let him leave. I can't stay here any longer. One way or another I will not stay another night.

Hunger strike day 5

Someone is here. I'm lying on my bed. Can't exactly move around in these fucking restraints.

I can smell food – proper rich sauce and garlic. The pain in my stomach is crazy.

It's Dad. He's here. He's brought food.

I'm going to eat it. I'm going to get strength from it, and then I'm going to kill him.

PART IV

Norfolk Police Video Interview

9 October 2022

Interview between Melanie Lange and DI Paula Baker. Also present –
Lucy Winn (solicitor for the witness), and DS Douglas Wayne.

DI Paula Baker: Hi Melanie, my name is Detective Inspector Paula Baker. I'll try to make this as brief as possible. Before we start, I'd like to thank you for consenting to have your interview audio and visually recorded. It'll help us a great deal when we go over your statement, but I would like to reassure you that the recording is for our eyes only and will not be released to the general public. Are you still happy to consent?

Lucy Winn: You don't have to, Melanie.

Melanie Lange: It's fine. I don't care.

DI Paula Baker: Thank you. I also want to reassure you that while you were being examined by a doctor, four of the five staff members of Seaview Clinic have been arrested and are being held for questioning. Dr Sam, full name Dr Samantha Sloane, is believed to be at her Spanish residence. Spanish police are on their way and we expect her to be in police custody shortly.

Melanie Lange: Staff members? Was it actually a clinic? I always thought it was something my dad cooked up.

DI Paula Baker: I'm afraid you're right, and I apologize for suggesting that the place you were held was a legitimate facility. The property itself is owned by your father.

Melanie Lange: [Crying] I knew it.

DI Paula Baker: I'm very sorry. Thank you for telling us where to find your hidden diary. I've got it here and I've read it briefly. There is a lot to process, for us and for you. Right now, I'd like to talk about your father's visit today.

Lucy Winn: May I remind you, DI Baker, that my client has been through a horrific ordeal at the hands of her father, for many months of which the police were aware of her imprisonment and did nothing. So while she is very happy to cooperate, she does need rest.

DI Paula Baker: Of course, I understand. Melanie, do you need anything else to eat right now? Any water?

Melanie Lange: I'm fine. Thank you.

DI Paula Baker: Do you mind walking me through your day today, Melanie, from the moment you woke up? Everything you remember. Even the smallest details help us build a picture.

Melanie Lange: OK. I was woken up at 7 a.m. like always. That's the time I'm always shaken awake. This morning it was Josh on duty . . . I mean, I don't know any of their real names. They never spoke to me and they didn't have name tags. They always wore the same white polo shirts and black trousers. I made up names for them. Josh was the bigger of the two men. He has dark hair and thick, bushy eyebrows. He shook me awake and I got up. I had restraints on my ankles which made it hard to move, but he took them off so I could use the bathroom. I had a shower and washed my hair. Brushed my teeth. Sorry, is this too much information? I've not spoken to anyone properly for so long.

DI Paula Baker: It's perfect. In my line of work there is no such thing as too much information. You're doing really well.

Melanie Lange: I take clothes into the bathroom with me because it's the only place I have any privacy. Once I'm dressed, Josh – or whatever his name is – puts the restraints back on. I go into the living-room area and sit on the sofa. Josh gets my breakfast and puts it on the table but I don't eat it. I was doing a hunger strike, because . . . it was all I could do.

After a while I go back to my room and fall asleep for a bit, and then I write in my diary. It will be the last entry. I guess you've probably read what I was planning.

DI Paula Baker: I have.

Melanie Lange: A little while later – I don't know what time; about noon, I think – my dad came in.

He walks in with two big plates of spaghetti bolognese. I hadn't eaten for five days and the smell was amazing. I knew straight away that it was the recipe he used to make for us as kids.

I'm still in my ankle restraints and I'm pretty weak, so by the time I'm in the living room, he's got the doors open and is sitting outside. I go out to him and it feels so good to be outside in the cool air. I must've been inside at that point for maybe six weeks. I don't know. It was impossible to keep track of the days.

Dad smiles and says, 'Great to see you, Mellie,' like it's a normal family lunch. Like he's not locked me away for eight months, like I've not got fucking restraints around my ankles. Sorry! It's upsetting. I was angry with him. I still am.

There's nothing I can say to his greeting and there's no point telling him I want to leave because he knows that. I told him on his last visit and the one before that. Every request I made was ignored. Over the eight months I was in that house, he slowly stripped away the last of my freedoms and sent me half mad with the isolation some days.

He says, 'You need to eat,' and so I do.

There's only a fork and a spoon, which annoys me. He sees me looking at the cutlery and smiles again, like he knows what I'm planning. But I eat because somewhere inside me I know that it's the last day, the last chance I'll ever have to escape, and I need my strength.

Lucy Winn: Do you want to take a break, Melanie? It's OK if you do.

Melanie Lange: I'm fine, but thank you. So we sit down, and Dad does his usual thing of blindly ignoring the elephant in the room and starts talking about business. I eat as much as I can without feeling like I'm going to be sick, and then I push my plate away and he falls silent.

I say, 'What is this? What is your plan here? Am I going to be here until I die?'

Dad gets sad, and his face turns red and his eyes look watery and he says, 'Oh Mellie, I don't have a plan. For the first time in my life, I don't have a plan. All I know is that before I brought you here, things were so bad for you. You were so unstable and I was scared. I was just so scared, Mellie. I can't lose you. You're a parent now. You understand that I have to do everything I can to protect you.'

I ask him what he's scared of and he tells me he's scared I'm going to kill myself. He says, 'I know this place isn't right, but every time I think of you going back to the world, I think of how hard it is for you, how damaging you find it.' Then he says, 'You're my daughter. I have to do whatever I can to protect you.'

I think I stand up then. I try to pace and then I point at my restraints and ask him, 'How are these protecting me?'

He doesn't answer, but then he starts talking about his sister. She killed herself when she was a teenager. He'd told me the story before, years ago, and so I cut him off.

I say, 'I'm not your sister. I'm not going to kill myself.'

He says, 'But you tried. You called me that night in February and you told me you were going to do it.'

I say, 'Show me the proof, because I don't think I did, Dad. I think this is about business. About money. I think the reason I'm here is because you found out I was going to remove Lange Hotels as investors and start over on my own, and without Lange Cosmetics your hotels will go bust and you'll be ruined. You'll have nothing.'

He says, 'I know what you were planning. It's not why I'm doing this.'

There's sort of this moment when neither of us says anything, and then he stands up and comes towards me. I grab the fork from the table and I hold it out and tell him that one way or another I'm leaving.

He pleads with me. He says, 'Mellie, I don't care about money. I don't care about the business. Everything I've done has been to protect you. You're not cut out for fame. I've watched you struggle with it for more than half of your life. Do not try to tell me that every single negative tabloid jibe hasn't been like a bullet, because I've watched you. I've felt so helpless. This, this place, this is your sanctuary. No one can get to you here.'

I start crying then and I talk about Sebastian and William. I tell him he has no idea how much it's killed me to be away from them for so long. I say, 'Every day I've been here has been the worst kind of torture. I need to see my children. I don't care about the fame. I never have. I have never understood why people are so fascinated by me, but you're right – I didn't like the negative comments and for the last few years I found it hard to deal with. But this prison, however much I hate it, has given me perspective. You have to let me go now.'

He shakes his head and says, 'I can't. I'm sorry. You've no idea of the pressure I've been under. The whole world is watching now, Mellie. You have no idea how bright that spotlight is going to be if you walk out of that door.'

I'm starting to panic. I'd been thinking for a while that Dad's plan was to keep me locked away for ever, but hearing him say it was horrifying. He steps closer, but I scream at him to get back. He goes really red in the face, bright red, and he's sweating. I can see the droplets rolling down from his hairline, and then I start walking towards him. The fork is gripped so tight in my hand and I'm shaking with the effort of holding it up.

And then . . . it's like I'm not in my own body any more. Like I'm floating above myself watching. I feel this heat, this pent-up rage explode inside me. I step forwards and now he's moving back, knocking against the table. There's this second when we just stand and I'm staring into his eyes. They're so hard, so cold. I can see he's as determined to make me stay as I am to leave. This rush of energy hits me and I throw myself forwards, the fork stretched out ahead of me, and it lands in the fleshy part of his neck.

Dad stumbles back from me and then he moves his left hand up like he's going to grab at the wound, although there isn't much blood. But he sort of stops midway and then he just keels over on the ground. His eyes are still open but they're vacant and I know he's dead.

Then I turned and ran, or tried to in the restraints anyway. I went straight to the trees that border the garden. I'd seen a gate there and knew I could climb it. The whole time I'm moving I'm sure a hand is going to grab me and pull me back, but no one comes. I keep going and when I get to the gate, it's hard to get up because of the restraints and because I'm so weak from not eating, but I throw myself at the wood and I drag myself up. I don't care for a second that I can feel scratches and splinters digging into my skin. I just keep going.

I fall on the ground on the other side of the fence and there's nothing but cliffs and sea around me. I start crying. It feels so hopeless because surely someone is going to come and take me back. I picture Sebastian and William in my mind. I imagine I can hear them laughing, that if I just keep shuffling forwards they'll be there.

I don't know how long I walk for until I see the hikers. They rush over to me and thank God the woman recognizes me. She starts talking really fast about the documentary, and she starts crying and saying 'Save Melanie', and then I cry too. They call 999 and then an ambulance arrives, and that's it.

DI Paula Baker: Thank you, Melanie. I know it can't have been easy for you to go over it all again like that.

Melanie Lange: Is he dead?

DI Paula Baker: Your father? Yes. I'm sorry.

Melanie Lange: Don't be.

DI Paula Baker: There will be a full post-mortem but an early examination suggests it was cardiac arrest. I just have a couple of questions, if you don't mind.

Lucy Winn: Actually, I mind. My client has told you everything that happened today. She's visibly shaken and she needs rest. I suggest we delay any further questioning for a later date.

DI Paula Baker: That's no problem. If you'll excuse me one moment, I have some paperwork for Melanie to sign. It won't take long.

Lucy Winn: You did really well, Melanie.

Melanie Lange: Thank you. Is that it then? Can I go?

Lucy Winn: Yes. You're free now, Melanie. Finn and your children are waiting for you in reception. You can go home. You're free.

Melanie Lange: [Crying] Thank you. Thank you.

MELANIE LANGE FREE

OUR MELANIE HOME AT LAST

Twitter
10 October 2022

Nell Stevens @NellStevensOfficial
#SaveMelanie WE DID IT!!! She's free. Thank you to everyone who has supported this campaign.

> **Jessie W @Jessiebakescakes4U**
> OMG! I'm literally sobbing with joy
>
> **Connie Rose @Wannabeawritergirl**
> All those #HelpPeter supporters must be feeling pretty stupid now!
>
> **Kimberly F @Kimberly_T_Filch**
> They deserve a prison sentence!
>
> **Jane Godfellow @WorldofCats2002**
> I LOVE Melanie Lange! So happy she's home. I can't wait to see her get her life back.

Amy B @GirlAboutTownBlog
Melanie moving back in with Finn is the happy ever after to this story we all needed! #SaveMelanie

> **Tahlia J @TahliaJenkins55**
> That won't last!
>
> **Christy Gaus @RealMrsJones99**
> Good for them. She's been through so much.

Headlines from National Newspapers, 11 October 2022

MELANIE BACK WITH HER 'PRECIOUS BOYS'

#SAVEMELANIE MOVEMENT CELEBRATES

Headlines from National Newspapers, 17 October 2022

DOCTOR ARRESTED IN MELANIE LANGE CASE

SIR PETER THE MONSTER

Headlines from National Newspapers, 3 November 2022

MELANIE'S SISTER: MY DAD WAS TRYING TO HELP

MELANIE PRISON: WAS IT ALL ABOUT THE MONEY?

Twitter
3 November 2022

Kimberly F @Kimberly_T_Filch
Can't believe Zara Lange is still defending her dad! There is no excuse
#SaveMelanie

> **Dee S @DLSimpson**
> She's an ugly bitch who should watch her back!

> **Jane Godfellow @WorldofCats2002**
> Ha ha! Didn't Melanie look gorgeous in those photos playing in
> the park with her boys?! I wanna know her secret.

> **Tahlia J @TahliaJenkins55**
> She'll bring out a recipe book next month. My prison diet
> cookbook, LOLs

Jessie W @Jessiebakescakes4U
Melanie wasn't smiling though, was she? Thought she'd be happier!

Headline from National Newspaper, 30 November 2022

MELANIE DITCHES HOTELS INVESTMENT

Headlines from National Newspapers, 5 December 2022

ZARA FIRED FROM LANGE HOTELS

MELANIE LANGE SISTER QUESTIONED BY POLICE

Headline from National Newspaper, 24 December 2022

MELANIE LAUNCHES NEW MENTAL HEALTH CHARITY

Headlines from National Newspapers, 20 January 2023

MELANIE'S BACK! (AND LOOKS GORGEOUS)

PARTY TIME FOR MELANIE

Twitter
20 January 2023

Jane Godfellow @WorldofCats2002
Sooo happy to see Melanie Lange on a night out! She looked gorgeous!!
#MelanieLange

Dee S @DLSimpson
I love her so much. I practically bathe in her Ocean perfume.

Curtis Oliver @MelanieL_BiggestFan
She deserves to let her hair down.

Natty H @NataliaLH
I don't know why she always has to get so drunk though. Looked wasted in some of the photos. Blue is not her colour.

Meg Hillis @MegHillis88
Who was that man with #MelanieLange?

Curtis Oliver @MelanieL_BiggestFan
Poor Finn!!!

Tahlia J @TahliaJenkins55
Knew that wouldn't last.

B @BHallthe5s
SLUT!

Headlines from National Newspapers, 21 January 2023

MYSTERY MAN FOR MELANIE

MESSY MELANIE ON NIGHT OUT

Headlines from National Newspapers, 5 February 2023

MELANIE'S KID IN TEMPER TANTRUM

MELANIE PILES ON THE POUNDS

Headline from National Newspaper, 9 February 2023

MELANIE'S BOYS ARE BULLIES

Headline from National Newspaper, 10 February 2023

MAD MELANIE IN SCHOOL RUN FIGHT

Headline from National Newspaper, 13 February 2023

MELANIE BREAKDOWN PART II?

Twitter
13 February 2023

Kaitlyn M Davids @Mummyrulestheroost
Why are the papers turning on #MelanieLange? Breakdown Part II???
She didn't have a breakdown in the first place. She was imprisoned by
her father!!! Short memories!

> **Amy B @GirlAboutTownBlog**
> The British press are vile.

> **Tahlia J @TahliaJenkins55**
> No smoke without fire! Didn't you always use to say that
> @GirlAboutTownBlog?

> **Kimberly F @Kimberly_T_Filch**
> And her kids are going down the same road. Look like right
> monsters. That story about the poor little girl being bullied was
> awful.

> **Kaitlyn M Davids @Mummyrulestheroost**
> That wasn't bullying!! The girl was calling his mum names. He was
> sticking up for his mum.

Laura V @LauraLostHerPhone

It's the kids I feel sorry for! What chance have they got with #MadMelanie for a mum??

Extract from National Newspaper, 15 February 2023

MELANIE LANGE: FORMER MODEL FOUND DEAD IN LONDON HOME

The 35-year-old businesswoman at the centre of Netflix documentary *The Ugly Truth* has been found dead, less than five months after being released from the isolated property in which her father had been keeping her captive. Her father, business tycoon Sir Peter Lange (66), died on 9 October following a heart attack.

A spokesperson for Lange Cosmetics says: 'Melanie's sister, ex-husband and of course her children, Sebastian and William, are devastated by this news. They ask that you respect their privacy during this difficult time.'

Twitter
15 February 2023

Christy Gaus @RealMrsJones99

OMG just heard the news. Those poor boys! #SaveMelanie

Kaitlyn M Davids @Mummyrulestheroost

My heart is broken! The media would not leave Melanie alone!!! #SaveMelanie

Amy B @GirlAboutTownBlog

So tragic!!! Sending my condolences to the family! DM me if you wanna meet up and chat @Mummyrulestheroost

Connie Rose @Wannabeawritergirl

OMG Melanie was just getting her life back too!! #SaveMelanie

Tahlia J @TahliaJenkins55

Look at the photos of the last few weeks. She was clearly having another breakdown! Maybe #HelpPeter had it right all along!!

Becky J @Rebecca_Jackson89

Another angel in heaven tonight, ladies! You're free now, Melanie!! #SaveMelanie

Extract from National Newspaper, 21 March 2023

NETFLIX COMMISSIONS ONE-PART EXTENSION TO MELANIE LANGE STORY

Netflix are set to record a one-part special documentary to follow on from their award-winning documentary series: *Melanie Lange – The Ugly Truth*, which aired last year. Recording is due to take place in the coming months. Melanie's sister, Zara Lange, is rumoured to be taking part.

Netflix Original Documentary:
Melanie Lange – The Ugly Truth
What Happened Next

INTERVIEWS RECORDED 6 JUNE 2023
(112 DAYS AFTER MELANIE'S DEATH)

Narrator

On the ninth of October 2022, just days after the award-winning Netflix Original Documentary: *Melanie Lange – The Ugly Truth* aired to over one million viewers, Sir Peter Lange went to visit his daughter at a house on the Norfolk coast that he'd purchased, converted and staffed before locking Melanie away. While little is known about what happened between Melanie and her father that day, we do know that Sir Peter died following a fatal heart attack. And only after his death was Melanie able to escape her prison.

Following Melanie's return to freedom, it looked to those watching as though Melanie returned to normal life, her two sons, her friends, her business. But less than five months later, Melanie Lange was found dead in her apartment.

In this special one-part documentary, we now look at what happened to Melanie after her release from her father's imprisonment and what led to her sudden and unexpected death. And for the first time, we hear from Melanie's sister – Zara Lange.

Zara

I know what people think of me. They think I'm a heartless bitch. They think I was so jealous of my sister that I was working with our father to keep her in prison. Of course I was jealous of my little sister. She was everything I wasn't. She was beautiful and intelligent, and she had everyone in the palm of her hand. The whole world was jealous of her. Is it really any surprise that I was too?

[Pause]

351

There have been points in my life when I've hated Melanie, and I've done things I'm not proud of because of that hate. But I had nothing – not a single thing – to do with my sister's imprisonment. My only crime was trusting my father. He called me after Melanie's birthday last year and told me she'd had a breakdown and was very ill. He told me he was going to make sure she was safe and I should hold the fort with Lange Cosmetics for a few months. It was his idea to get rid of Nell, not mine. He thought she'd be too combative to work with, without Mel there.

I didn't have a reason to question him, and perhaps there's some truth in the fact that I was excited to take the lead on Melanie's business. Months later, when people started to question where Melanie was, I asked him outright if she was in a medical facility and he told me she was. I think, in his mind, that place he created was real.

I can see now that my hate was directed in the wrong place. It was my father who deserved that hate. He was the one who put Melanie so high on that pedestal, throwing me whatever scraps of affection he had left. Why did he do that? It's a question I'll never have the answer to. My guess? I've seen photos of my aunt – Dad's sister, who he never told me killed herself. I only found out through Melanie after his death. The resemblance to Melanie is pretty striking. My aunt didn't have the same slenderness as Melanie – she got that from our mother – but they had the same crystal-blue eyes. I think he saw so much of his sister in Melanie and the pain of his loss drove him to drastic lengths.

[Crying]

Now they're both gone . . . I'm alone. Completely. The grief and guilt I feel is unbearable. It's like a dark monster inside me, always there, prodding and nipping, reminding me every single day of what I've lost and what I never had, because I was too shallow, too jealous, to ever form a proper relationship with my sister. She knew I wasn't involved in what happened to her, but she still blamed me for not doing more to help her. I blame myself too.

My father's death, Melanie's – it's made me question everything. I had to move away, get out of London. I live in Cornwall now. I've found a community of people. We grow our own food, we care for each other. It's a life away from everything I've ever known.

[Pause]

I should have been a better sister. I see that now. And that knowledge will haunt me until the day I die.

Nell

I miss Melanie every single second. Nothing is the same without her. She has left an unimaginable void in my life.

Finn

I don't know what to say. I'm sorry. I just don't. It's still so raw. Melanie said it all.

VIDEO FOOTAGE. SOURCE:
YOUTUBE, MELANIE LANGE CHANNEL

Date posted: 14 February 2023

VIDEO TITLE: GOODBYE

I'm Melanie Lange. You all know that. You think you know everything about me. You think you have a right to talk about me and point out my flaws, my every mistake. You don't see me as being just like you. You don't even see me as a human being with thoughts and feelings and emotions. To you, I'm entertainment.

I used to believe that freedom was being able to go wherever I wanted. To see whoever I wanted, to talk, to laugh, to dance. I thought I was free after I escaped my father's prison, but I wasn't. I'll never be free in this life. And worse than that, so much worse, is that if I am not free, then neither are my boys, my wonderful

353

precious boys who mean the world to me. Who are kind and funny, and love Lego and dancing to Bon Jovi songs in the kitchen. They are my everything.

[Crying]

I will not give them this life.

[Crying]

I love them to the ends of the earth. They deserve better than this life, better than a mother who can't protect them.

[Crying]

Without me, they'll be free. I'll be free.

Nell

I still can't believe it happened. After all that time trapped in that house, all that time she was desperate to be free. She kept telling everyone she was OK, and we were all so happy to have her home that we didn't see she wasn't until it was too late.

Finn

Melanie was so happy at first. Being back with the boys and back to her life. She moved into the house. I stayed in the spare room. We didn't talk about us or our relationship. It wasn't about that. It was about her being with Sebastian and William, and just having people around her as well. But the time apart made me realize that I still loved Mel. I was giving her the time she needed to heal and then I hoped we might be able to start again.

Nell

The first thing Melanie did after settling in with her boys was to remove Lange Hotels as shareholders and set up new offices for Lange Cosmetics. It was exciting. It reminded me of those first months we worked together creating the business. Then she did something that really surprised me. She stepped back and put me in charge of the day-to-day. Mel said, 'I want to be at home with my boys. I love this business so much and I'll still be here for the overall strategy, but you love it too and I know I'm putting it in the safest of hands.'

That was about a month before she died. She took me and all the team out for a big night to celebrate. I remember seeing her dancing that night and thinking how happy she looked.

Finn

Everything was good. It was . . . she was happy. I swear she was happy. I suggested therapy but she laughed and said, 'Finn, I've had enough therapy to last me a lifetime. I'm home. I'm free. I have everything I need right here in this house.'

Then the British tabloids turned on her again.

[Crying]

I'm sorry. This is hard to talk about. It all happened so fast. One minute she was fine. The next, she wasn't.

When they started on the boys though, that's when I think Melanie went to a dark place. It was like she saw a life where our boys would be constantly picked at and ridiculed. She'd lived through it herself. She knew what it was like.

Narrator

Melanie's suicide on her thirty-fifth birthday – the fourteenth of February 2023 – shocked the nation. Melanie's family and her fans wanted answers. They wanted to know what would drive Melanie Lange to kill herself on her birthday – the exact day when, a year earlier, her father had imprisoned her. Those answers came a month later with the release of the coroner's report into Melanie's death.

Coroner Julie Freeman made the following statement: 'Ms Lange killed herself after a worsening of ongoing mental health issues and depression. There can be no doubt that this was not a cry for help. Ms Lange intended to take her own life and did so.

'Certain media outlets have been hounding Ms Lange for the

majority of her life. It is my ruling that intense, relentless and toxic scrutiny from the British media contributed to the deterioration of Ms Lange's mental health and her subsequent death. There is no doubt in my mind that the British media is to blame for Melanie Lange's death.'

This ruling added to mounting pressure on the government to launch a formal inquiry into the practices and integrity of the British media, but sources close to the Prime Minister believe no such inquiry will ever go ahead.

Finn

Who do I blame for Melanie's death? I blame myself, I guess. I was living with her. I missed the signs. It was . . . it was me that found her at her apartment. She was just . . .

[Crying]

Hanging there.

And I blame that monster of a father who imprisoned her. All those months she spent alone with only some nutty doctor talking to her for an hour a day. Melanie loved to be around people, she loved the buzz of life. She fed off it. Being alone like that broke something inside her. She couldn't cope with real life after those months locked away.

Of course, I blame the British media too. They may as well have tied the noose around her neck, them and her fucking messed-up, control-freak father.

Nell

I'm going to do everything I can to keep Mel's legacy alive. I've started the Melanie Lange Foundation to improve teenage mental health, and I'm pushing forward with her business exactly how she would've wanted. I know what the papers and all those Twitter trolls are saying about me. They think I'm trying to step into Melanie's shoes because I'm doing the morning shows on

TV, or because some photographer has a photo of me wearing something similar to what Mel once wore. Well, I don't give a damn what they think and I'm not going to let them . . . [crying] I'm not going to let them get to me. I won't let Melanie down again.

Who do I blame for Melanie's death? I blame myself. 100 per cent. I was . . .

[Pause]

I was so sure the Save Melanie campaign was the right thing. I was so single-minded and selfish. I wanted my best friend back. I tracked down that assistant going on the photo shoot. I gave her that phone. I pushed and I pushed, and I didn't stop for even a moment to wonder if I was doing the right thing.

I never stopped to think when it came to Melanie. And I don't just mean last year, but for our entire friendship. I ignored all the signs that Melanie was in real trouble. And there were so many signs. I didn't . . . I didn't know she'd gone to Beaumont Court because of a suicide attempt. And yet, I look back now and I wonder if somewhere in my mind, I knew. Like I knew she wasn't there for any kind of addiction. And I never asked her what the real reason behind her stay was.

I never pushed Melanie to talk to me. I never pulled her aside and truly tried to help her. I'll carry that guilt with me for the rest of my life.

I think now, maybe Sir Peter was right all along. She was alive when he was protecting her, and now she's gone.

VIDEO FOOTAGE. SOURCE:
YOUTUBE, MELANIE LANGE CHANNEL

Date posted: 6 August 2022

I'm Melanie Lange. Don't forget about me.

Narrator

The Ugly Truth started as an in-depth look into the life of Melanie Lange, her rise to fame, the troubled relationship with her father, Sir Peter Lange, her portrayal in the British media, and the effect thousands upon thousands of toxic stories had on Melanie over the course of nineteen years.

With both father and daughter now dead, Melanie's fans, her critics, the nation, the world, have been left with one question. A question we will end this one-part documentary with.

Whose side are you on?

#SaveMelanie

#HelpPeter

Credits

L. C. North would like to thank everyone who has worked on the publication of *The Ugly Truth*:

Editor: Imogen Nelson
Copy-editors: Claire Gatzen, Kate Samano, Katrina Whone
Proofreaders: Monica Byles, Hugh Davis, Barbara Thompson
Text design: Dan Prescott at Couper Street Type Co.
Cover design: Beci Kelly
Publicity: Hayley Barnes
Marketing: Holly Minter
Sales: Tom Chicken, Laura Garrod, Laura Ricchetti, Natasha Photiou, Louise Blakemore
Production: Phil Evans
Audiobook: Oli Grant
Agent: Tanera Simons
Agency: Darley Anderson Literary Agency
Beta readers: Zoe Lea, Laura Pearson, Nikki Smith and Kathryn Jones

About the Author

L. C. North studied Psychology at university before pursuing a career in Public Relations. Her first book-club thriller – *The Ugly Truth* – combines her love of psychology and her fascination with celebrities in the public eye.

L. C. North is currently working on her second novel, and when she's not writing she co-hosts the crime-thriller podcast *In Suspense*. She lives on the Suffolk borders with her family. You can follow her on Twitter @Lauren_C_North and Facebook @LaurenNorthAuthor.